Killer

Alex Gough is an author of Roman historical adventures. The Carbo Chronicles, including *Watchmen of Rome* and *Bandits of Rome*, was written as a result of a lifelong obsession with ancient Rome, and the culmination of a lot of research into the underclasses of the time. He has also written a collection of adventures following Carbo and other characters from *Watchmen of Rome*, where you can learn more about their rich lives.

For reviews of Roman fiction, and articles about Roman history go to www.romanfiction.com

Also by Alex Gough

Carbo and the Thief
Who All Die

Carbo of Rome

Watchmen of Rome
Bandits of Rome
Killer of Rome

The Imperial Assassin

Emperor's Sword
Emperor's Knife
Emperor's Axe
Emperor's Spear

KILLER
OF
ROME

ALEX GOUGH

🔟 CANELO

First published in the United Kingdom in 2021 by

Canelo
31 Helen Road
Oxford OX2 0DF
United Kingdom

A CIP catalogue record for this book is available from the British Library.

Print ISBN 978 1 80032 524 1
Ebook ISBN 978 1 80032 500 5

Look for more great books at www.canelo.co

Printed and bound in Great Britain by Clays Ltd, Elcograf S.p.A.

1

To my father for all his encouragement and love

Ian Gough 1940-2021

Chapter One

Subura in Rome, with its crowded buildings and stench of human activity, he could still never shake a feeling of discomfort when he was out in the wilderness, all fresh air and trees and not an insula or bathhouse in sight. He caught a root yet again, cursing as the pain from his toes shot up his leg. He had no idea why they were out here, patrolling into German territory. The various tribes of Germania were fairly quiet at the moment, and Brocchus couldn't see the point of stirring them up. The new *tribunus laticlavius*, however, temporarily in command while the legate was in Rome, seemed determined to make a mark. They always did, thought the veteran centurion with a sigh.

So here they were, his century turned into a vexillation, stumbling through Bructeri territory on a damp autumn afternoon, instead of back in their barracks in Castra Vetera. Not exactly lost, though not entirely sure where they were either. Cold, tired and generally miserable. Life as a Roman foot soldier, you couldn't beat it.

One of the new recruits stumbled on a tree stump and went sprawling, entrenching tool, saucepan, scutum and gladius all flying in different directions. The veterans

I

hooted with laughter as the recruit regained his feet, mud caking his face.

'Shut it,' growled Brocchus. 'In case you've forgotten, we are legionaries patrolling in enemy territory, not children playing games. Keep your wits about you. And you, Pullus, pick up your shit and try to stay on your feet.'

Pullus bent down to pick up his saucepan, and the first arrow to come from the trees sang through the space his head had occupied half a heartbeat before, and lodged in the throat of one of the laughing veterans. Brocchus' mouth dropped open, then he filled his lungs to yell a warning as a hail of arrows descended on them, close behind the first.

'Ambush!' he screamed. 'Close formation, shields up, they're both sides of us.'

The endless weeks and months of drilling saved the lives of most of them. A mere half a dozen had fallen before the shields clamped into place around the century, their own instant fortress, and then the majority of the arrows clattered harmlessly away. Brocchus peered out from between locked shields, catching glimpses of shirtless warriors darting between the trees, waving axes and swords. War cries echoed all around them, and Brocchus cursed his miserable luck.

The storm of arrows ceased, and the cries came nearer, together with the sounds of bodies crashing through the undergrowth.

'Here they come lads. Get ready to brace. And remember we are Romans. Let's show these fellators who they are fucking with.'

The wave of screaming Germans crashed into the shield wall, rocked back first one side, then the other as the pincer movement hit them. The legionaries at the front, braced by their colleagues behind, largely held firm. Nevertheless, some fell, knocked off-balance, or victim of a chance thrust through a gap in the defences. Wherever a shield dropped, sharp, heavy weapons struck, causing devastating injuries wherever they landed.

As soon as the initial impact had passed, Brocchus gave the order to advance. Huge axes and broadswords cleaved through Roman helmets, shields were dragged aside, limbs amputated, bodies decapitated as the berserk barbarians hacked at the soldiers. Roman discipline meant everything though, and their short stabbing swords thrusting between their shields into the unarmoured Germans soon took a savage toll.

In what seemed like years, but was only moments, the momentum of the German attack died down, the madness started to fade, and they began to back away. Brocchus waited until the Germans looked like they were about to break, picking his moment with precision.

'Right flank, hold fast, left flank, on me. Charge!'

Shields forward, the left flank of the century charged at the enemy, who hesitated then broke. Many escaped, less encumbered than the Romans, but the legionaries exacted a vicious revenge on any too slow, or too foolish to flee. The attack on the right flank faltered as the Germans saw their comrades running, and Brocchus' optio, Gratius, chose the moment to lead his own charge.

As quickly as the ambush had started, it was over. Brocchus had his *buccinator* sound the recall, and his men dutifully reformed. Brocchus inspected himself. An arrow had sliced across his ribs, but had not penetrated deeply, and his left arm was bruised from the impacts of axes and swords on his shield. He would hurt tomorrow, he knew, but he had got away lightly. Unlike many of his men.

Nearby, Pullus was sitting against a tree, clutching at a deep rent in his abdomen. Between his fingers, guts were bulging and blood was flowing freely. Pullus' eyes were wide, and as Brocchus bent down next to him, he stared at the centurion in pain and terror. Brocchus put an arm around him, and held him as the young recruit grew paler and paler. He seemed to want to speak, but couldn't get the words out. Brocchus for his part could think of nothing to say. He watched as the life faded from Pullus, and when he slumped and let the last sighing breath out, he gently laid him on the ground. With a grim shake of his head, he stood, and looked for his optio, who had been watching from a respectful distance.

'Gratius, report,' he said.

'Twelve dead, five who won't make it, six who will need to be stretchered. The rest can still walk.'

Eighty down to fifty-nine in the time it took to eat a meal. Time to head home. He turned to give the order, then noticed, through a gap in the trees, a whisp of smoke rising into the air. Gratius followed his gaze.

'A settlement?' suggested Gratius.

'Those bastards had to come from somewhere. They showed some co-ordination, but they didn't have the numbers to suggest anything more than a hastily organised ad hoc attack. They must have spotted us and raised what numbers they could at short notice from the local villages.'

Brocchus looked around him. The dead were already being arranged for a speedy burial, the dying being comforted by their friends, the wounded groaning or crying aloud, while the rest of the century, almost all nursing injuries of one sort or another, looked sullen and angry.

'Legionaries,' said Brocchus, raising his voice. 'We won. But many of them escaped, and they hurt us badly. We could march straight back to our barracks to lick our wounds. Or we could get some payback. It looks like there is a Bructeri village over there. Shall we take it? What do you say?'

There was a ragged chorus of shouts.

'Make them pay!'

'Let's get the *cunni*!'

Brocchus organised his men, a small, protesting detachment left behind to guard and tend the wounded, while the rest formed up to march. When they were ready, he led them forwards towards the smoke. The forest thinned and soon they reached a huge clearing. Within it were two dozen huts, simple thatch-roofed wattle and daub constructions. Between them ran women with babes in arms, old men and children, grabbing possessions and fleeing. A handful of German warriors remained, clustered together, looking defiant but resigned. The majority of the fearless warriors that had ambushed them earlier seemed to have fled, Brocchus realised with a wry smile.

At the sight of the century entering the village, women and children screamed and ran for the woods. The Bructeri men hefted their axes and swords and waited. Brocchus marched his men forwards at a steady walk, then, when they could clearly see the anxious eyes of the Germans, he gave the order to charge.

The Germans were barely able to swing their weapons before the impact of the front row of legionaries' shields bashed them to the ground. The second row despatched the fallen warriors with ease, and as simply as that, the village was theirs. The legionaries looked to Brocchus, a lust for murderous vengeance in their eyes. Brocchus looked around. A boy, no more than three or four, was sitting in the dirt, wailing loudly. His mother, already carrying a baby and with a toddler holding onto her leg, screamed desperately for him to run. An old lady stood in the doorway of her hut, leaning on a stick, and spat defiance when she caught his eye. Then Brocchus thought of Pullus, not much more than a child himself, spilling his blood and guts because of these cowardly barbarians.

He looked at his men. 'Do your worst.'

With a cheer, the men dropped their shields and scattered. Brocchus watched impassively as the butchery started. It wasn't nice, it wasn't pretty. It was life. His eyes were drawn to a small, innocuous looking hut on the far side of the clearing. His men hadn't entered it yet, looking for better pickings of women, gold and food in the larger, more impressive dwellings. Brocchus approached it, stepping over the twitching corpse of the young child, and kicking away some chickens. He peered in, but his eyes were adapted to the outdoor light, dim as it was, and he could see nothing. A movement from the edge of the clearing caught his attention. From the corner of his eye, he saw a woman, robed in white, but when he turned to look she was gone. Then he heard a noise from within, and he drew his gladius.

A figure lurched out and fell against him. A foul stench accompanied it, and Brocchus instinctively twisted and hurled the apparition to the ground. He looked down at a naked man, befouled in his own excrement, hair dirty and matted, beard long. He lifted his sword to end the creature, who raised his hands in supplication.

'Roman.' The voice came out in a croak, but it was clear. 'Mercy. I'm a Roman soldier.'

The legionaries ate and drank beer, a taste Brocchus himself had never acquired. He indulged them, but only to a point. They were still in enemy territory, and the last thing they needed was to be caught drunk by a larger enemy party. Soon he would gather them up and get them marching. He wanted to be a good distance from here before night fell. He threw the chicken leg he had been eating away, and walked over to where Gratius was sitting with the Roman he had found. Gratius and a couple of the others had helped clean him up, but he still looked a horror. He was lean, though not emaciated, and he was well muscled. His captors had obviously fed him, and put him to physical work. His wrists were chafed. They had found rope in the hut he had been in. He had clearly been bound, and managed to free himself.

Now he was cleaned up, the centurion could see that his body was covered in scars. Large straight wounds, burns, criss-cross incisions and bruises covered his torso and arms. His face was distorted, old breaks of his cheekbones and jaw and nose, Brocchus thought, and many of his teeth were broken stumps. He handed him a long cloak he had taken from one of the dead Germans – he couldn't bring himself to strip the corpse of one of his own men. The man took it gratefully and wrapped himself in it.

'What's your name, soldier?' asked Brocchus.

'C… Cicurinus, sir,' he replied. The words seemed hard to get out.

'How long have you been a captive?'

'Long… long time.'

'What legion were you? How were you captured? What battle was it?'

Cicurinus opened his mouth to reply, then caught sight of something in the forest. Brocchus turned to see what he was staring at, and saw the white-robed woman again. Her age was hard to determine, but she had long dark hair with a hint of white in it. She gazed at Cicurinus, and something seemed to pass between them. Then she looked at Brocchus, turned and was gone.

Cicurinus looked down at the ground, pulling his knees up under his chin and hugging his legs. He started to tremble violently.

'Gratius, get after that woman.'

Gratius looked up, confused. 'What woman, sir?'

Brocchus looked out into the forest, but there was no sign of her. He sighed. It would be foolish to send out a small detachment now. It surely didn't matter. Anyway, this place made his skin crawl. And he had heard stories about those German priestesses. The things they were capable of doing to a man. Maybe Cicurinus was a first-hand witness to that. It was time to leave.

'Legionaries, form up. Time to move.'

With some grumbling, the soldiers gathered up their equipment, their arms, and their newly acquired treasures and slaves. Discipline held, Brocchus was pleased to see. When they were all lined up, he gave the order to march out. As they left, he looked behind him. The village was a ruin, the fires set on the huts starting to die down, leaving smoking embers. Corpses littered the ground, and the soldiers had even nailed a village elder to a tree, where he hung, still just alive. Brocchus expected to catch another glimpse of the white-robed woman, but the forest was dark and quiet again. He squared his shoulders, faced to the front, and led his men away.

Cicurinus walked through the streets of Castra Vetera. It was his first night back within the borders of the Empire since he had been captured, all those years ago. The *tribunus laticlavius*, shocked at the state of the rescued legionary, had immediately released him from service with back pay and a pension. He would not want for the necessities of life.

Castra Vetera was a military town, newly built, and it had little in the way of amenities. As home to two legions though, the Vth Alaudae and the XXIst Rapax, a small industry had rapidly arisen to supply the needs of nearly ten thousand soldiers. Every spare space was taken up by sellers of hot food smothered in garum, taverns, barbers and brothels. Cicurinus stopped and purchased a pie.

He bit into it and winced. Broken teeth, a gift from Veleda the priestess, reacted to the heat of the filling and shot arrows through his jaw. He ignored the pain, as he had learned to do in captivity, chewed the tough meat and swallowed it down. A trip to a dentist would be necessary. He could suppress pain, but there was no need to embrace it for its own sake. Even if Veleda had taught him he should.

The priestess had been his constant companion throughout his long captivity. Hate and fear had transformed into adoration and need as their relationship had developed. She had broken him and reforged him. For every injury she had inflicted on his body, she had strengthened his soul. She had beaten him and kissed his forehead afterwards. She had set him to fight against the strongest warriors in the tribe and when they had left him bloodied and broken, she had tended his wounds. She had

9

set him to tasks of unimaginable endurance that had left his muscles and sinews weakened beyond what he imagined was the point of recovery, only to see them grow back stronger. And she had taught him the meaning of honour.

He missed her.

Two legionaries emerged from a tavern, supporting each other. One bent at the waist and vomited his last few drinks, while the other laughed uproariously. Around the corner, in a small alley, another drunk legionary was rutting against the wall, the prostitute whose legs were wrapped around him staring blankly at the opposite building. Two local men burst out of another tavern in a tangling of flailing limbs, hurled out by the owner to continue their fight on the street.

Cicurinus shook his head. This wasn't how he had envisaged his homecoming. Rome had been a city of marble, transformed from bricks by Augustus. His memories were filled with fine temples, grand bathhouses, noble senators declaiming in the forum, honest citizens smiling in the streets as they chatted and traded. Had the Empire changed, or had he?

He stopped and watched as the legionary finished with the prostitute, adjusted his clothing and stumbled away. The prostitute caught him watching and wandered over to him. She was young, acned, with long, tangled, greasy hair.

'One copper coin for me to suck you, two for you to fuck me,' she said, in a dull monotone. Cicurinus looked at her in horror and revulsion. An image came to his mind, the tall, beautiful, perfect Veleda. The priestess who had cared for him, tortured him, tended to him and abused him. What would she think of this town, this Empire? He could picture her contempt.

He turned and walked away. He had no idea what he was supposed to do now. Life was completely without purpose. He had enough money to subsist, so had no need to earn more. He had no goals, no friends. He squared his shoulders, suppressing the almost panicky feeling of dismay that threatened to overwhelm him, and entered a tavern.

It was crowded and noisy, and he shrank back from the press of flesh. It had been so long since he had been part of a crowd, and he shuddered at the proximity. He could smell people's breath, the rank odour from unwashed bodies, even feel the body heat from those closest to him. He swallowed and fought his way to the bar.

'What can I get you, sir?' asked the bartender.

'Water.' His voice was hoarse. He wondered if it always would be, now. He suspected that the amount of screaming he had done had led to some permanent damage. 'And some soup.'

He found a free seat at a table against a wall, and started to sip at the hot soup. It scalded the exposed pulp of his teeth, but he swallowed it down, savouring the warmth in his stomach. He swigged from the cup of water for which the barman had charged him an inflated price. It tasted both bitter and metallic.

From the corner of his eye, he noticed two legionaries on the next table looking at him. He looked down at his dish, then feeling that was impolite, he looked up again and raised his cup to them.

The legionaries looked away.

'What a mess,' said one, a man with an unusually clear complexion and broad shoulders, young and unscarred enough to be a new recruit.

'He was a legionary,' said the second, older, bearded and with a glaucomatous right eye.

'Then he should have more self-respect,' said the younger, not even trying to keep his comments from Cicurinus' hearing. 'He's a wreck. He should get to the bathhouse. And get some decent clothes.'

Cicurinus had indeed tried to bathe, but the attendants had turned him away with wrinkled noses, not willing to allow the filthy man to contaminate the water. He had instead found a fountain, and had stripped naked to wash the worst of the excrement and muck from himself. Too much was ingrained though, deep in the cracks and scars in his skin, and although he could not smell anything unpleasant himself, years of exposure having made him immune to his own odours, he could tell from the reactions of those who passed him that he still stank.

His clothing had been cast-offs donated by Brocchus, who had been in a hurry to get rid of him. Ripped and worn, the tunic was at least reasonably clean, and the *caligae* protected his damaged feet. Cicurinus returned to his soup, but he was unable to block out the conversation from the next table.

'He is the one they rescued from the Germans. The one who had been imprisoned all those years,' said the older legionary.

'I would rather have died than let myself get like that,' sniffed the younger one. 'Look at him. What would your hero Carbo say to one of his men if they came to him in that state?'

'He would have damned well had more sympathy than you. Don't forget, Carbo was captured himself.'

Carbo? Cicurinus looked up sharply, then just as quickly looked away.

'And he escaped. That's what this guy should have done. Escaped, and if he couldn't then he should have killed himself.'

Oh, he had tried. So many times he had tried to kill himself. Veleda wouldn't let him. And eventually she had taught him to love her, to love his ordeal. A wave of panic washed over him as he thought of life without her. With no one to look up to and respect. How could he cope?

'You don't know what you are talking about,' said the older legionary. 'Yes, Carbo was a hero, but he would never have treated a comrade with contempt. Anger, disappointment, yes. But he loved his men.'

'So why isn't your wonderful Carbo still serving the Empire?'

'He did his time in the legions. The Empire got their pound of flesh from him all right. Now he is back in Rome, relaxing and enjoying his retirement.'

'Sounds boring,' said the young man. 'Give me battle and glory over the easy life, any day.'

The older legionary shook his head. 'You know nothing.'

Cicurinus sipped his soup, and thought about Carbo.

Chapter Two

The two cockmasters held their champions up to the crowd that surrounded the cockpit, to a roar of approval. They flapped their wings as if accepting the acclaim but anxious to be getting to business. Carbo drank deeply from a cup of unwatered wine, and watched carefully. Though he wasn't at the front of the crowd, his height and bulk afforded him an excellent view, to the extent that those behind him cursed their luck. He drank again, and felt a thrill of anticipation at the upcoming contest.

'Where's your money?' asked the spectator beside him. Carbo turned to look at the young girl who had spoken.

'On Cicero,' he replied. 'The Median.'

'You mean, Melian?'

'If you like.' Melian was the suburan corruption of Median, ferocious cocks that came from the country of the Medes. When Carbo had been this girl's age, he would have probably used the common term himself. A full term of duty in the legions had afforded him better education and experience of the world, but he had no right to look down on anyone here, where he had been raised, and where he had now returned to live out his days. He looked over at the cock he had gambled on. It certainly looked full of itself, haughty and arrogant, living up to its name.

'You should have bet on Agrippa.'

Carbo sneered. 'That runt? Looks like it would barely make a small meal, let alone hold its own in a fight.'

'It's Tangrian. Fierce little shits. And they never give up. Good odds too.'

'There's a reason for the good odds. Bet on the favourite, bet heavily, and you will come out on top. That's my method.'

'Does it work?'

Carbo didn't reply. He fiddled with his betting token, and thought about his finances. Then he took another deep drink of his wine, letting the warmth flow through him.

'Fight's about to start,' he said.

The cockmasters held the birds close, thrusting them towards each other, annoying them and stoking their natural aggression to other males of their species. Each tried to peck the other when they came close, but the cockmasters held them far enough away to prevent contact. Both cocks had vicious spurs protruding sideways just above their feet, and Cicero's struggles opened a slash along the forearm of his handler, evoking cursing from the cockmaster and hilarity from the crowd.

The referee raised his voice and announced the bout to the crowd.

'Now the fight you have all been waiting for. Cicero the Melian at four to three against Agrippa the Tangrian, at three to one. Commence!'

The cockmasters placed their gamecocks down at opposite ends of the pit and let them go. Each cock danced forward, wings spread, neck feathers up, trying to look intimidating. Carbo wasn't sure if he was just humanising the bird, but Cicero did seem to have a contemptuous swagger as he approached the much smaller Agrippa. Cicero feinted, and Agrippa danced out of the way, sideways and up into the air with a desperate flap of his wings. The crowd jeered. Cicero lunged forward again, and again Agrippa dodged. But this time Cicero struck home, and a small plume of feathers flew into the air.

The birds parted and circled warily again, posturing and fluffing themselves out to the best of their abilities. Then Cicero dived at Agrippa, and the little bird went down beneath the heavier one. The speed of their strikes with their beaks and feet were impossible to follow for the crowd. All they could see were the two thrashing bodies with feathers erupting all around them. The crowd screeched. Carbo smiled at the young girl.

Cicero broke off first, leaving Agrippa lying on the floor. His beak was parted, and his chest heaving as he drew deep breaths. Cicero had bald patches across his back and was trailing one wing slightly, but his triumphant swagger was if anything even more exaggerated now. He circled Agrippa, as if toying with him. Then like a lightning bolt he threw himself at the Tangrian cock.

Agrippa leapt sideways, wings and feet giving him impetus, so Cicero's attack failed to strike home. Instantly, Agrippa was on Cicero's back, beak slashing into his neck, spurred feet digging into his flanks. Cicero flapped desperately, shook, rolled, trying to dislodge the smaller bird. It was to no avail. Agrippa fought with a breathtaking ferocity, strike after strike hitting home.

It was over in moments. Agrippa danced back, gasping for breath through wide beak, watching Cicero intently. Cicero didn't move. He lay on the sand of the cockpit, wings spread, neck stretched out, unmoving. One eye blinked. Carbo wondered if it was surprise or resignation.

Cicero's handler came back into the ring. He nudged his bird with a foot, shook his head when there was no reaction, then picked him up by one leg. Cicero dangled limply from his hand.

'Agrippa is the winner!' announced the referee, and Agrippa's cockmaster pumped his arm into the air, then jumped into the ring to pick up his champion. He gave him a hug and a kiss, and then held him up for the crowd. Half booed, half cheered. The bookmakers looked smug. Carbo looked at the betting token in his hand, and threw it on the ground in disgust.

'Pluto's fucking balls,' he swore.

'Not your day, Carbo?' came a Gallic-accented voice from behind him.

Carbo turned.

'Looks like it is yours, though, Olorix,' he said sourly.

'Well, we bookmakers rarely complain when a favourite loses. It helps make up for all the losses, trying to keep people like you entertained and rewarded.'

Olorix was a portly man, and Carbo regarded his fine robe and expensive looking gold bracelets and rings. Behind him, two bulky men stood close, scowling at Carbo as if daring him to try anything physical.

'I think you probably do well more often than not,' said Carbo.

'I sacrifice regularly to Fortuna. Maybe you should try that yourself. Anyway, can I tempt you to another wager today?'

Carbo put his hand on his purse. It was empty. He cursed. He would have to hope the tavern had done good business today. He supposed he would have to leave some money aside for stock purchase, and food for the slaves. That was a worry for another time. The same as his sorrow. This was not the time to face it. He drained his wine.

'Not today, Olorix.'

'Suit yourself. I'll be seeing you soon, I'm sure.'

Olorix turned and departed with a flounce, his two bodyguards in tow.

The young girl looked smugly at Carbo.

'What are you grinning at?' asked Carbo churlishly.

'A loser.'

Carbo clenched his fist, then relaxed it, letting his shoulders slump, the flash of anger passing in an instant. Not that he would hurt her. Whatever his state of mind, he hoped he would never fall that far.

'So how did you get to know so much about cock-fighting?'

'I keep my ear to the ground. I know lots of things.'

'Do you now?'

The girl nodded and tapped her nose.

'How old are you anyway?'

'Twenty-one,' she said. Carbo doubted she was a day over eighteen, but he let it pass.

'What's your name?'

'Camilla.'

'I'm Carbo.'

'I know. I told you, I know lots of things.'

Carbo regarded her steadily for a moment.

'So what else do you know?'

Camilla grinned conspiratorially.

'What's it worth?'

Carbo thought for a moment. 'Come back to the tavern with me and we can talk.'

The short walk through the Subura back to Carbo's tavern was passed largely without conversation between the two. Camilla seemed to be unwilling to divulge anything for free that she might be able to make money from, even if it was speculation about the weather. When they entered the tavern, Carbo was disappointed to find it quiet. Vatius sat in a corner as usual, Myia curled up by his feet keeping him company. A couple of off-duty legionaries from the urban cohorts diced in a corner. Marsia approached him.

'Welcome back, Master.'

He nodded to his slave.

'Have you had a good day?'

Carbo grunted. 'Get me a drink. Wine, unwatered. And one for this girl. What was your name again? Canina?'

'Camilla.'

Marsia looked at him with a sceptical eye. 'Where did you find this waif?'

'None of your business,' said Carbo. 'Where's that drink?'

'We met at a cockfight,' said Camilla, helpfully.

'I see,' said Marsia. 'And was Fortuna on your side today, Master?'

'I'm afraid your Master lost rather heavily. I suppose that's why I'm here, so he can get some tips in the future.'

'You do know, Master, that our takings are down? That our stock is low, and you owe money to the wine merchant and the baker?'

'I'm aware of all that, Marsia. If you did your job properly and made sure this place was busy, we wouldn't have any problems. We are due a payment from my farm in Campania, and I can always visit the argentarius and withdraw some savings if necessary.'

'You already did that, if you remember,' said Marsia tightly, her Germanic tones clipped short. 'Your savings went on a dogfight.'

Carbo grimaced and turned to Camilla. 'That dog was a dead cert.'

'And now it's just dead,' said Marsia.

'Get me my wine!' snapped Carbo.

Marsia put her hands on her hips and cocked her head on one side, then with an audible harumph, she turned and poured two cups of wine. Carbo took them grudgingly and went to sit at a table, nodding to Camilla to follow him. He looked over at Vatius, who was grinning broadly.

'Watch yourself, Carbo,' said Vatius. '"Once made equal to man, woman becomes his superior." Socrates told us that.'

'She is just a slave, and I only tolerate her nagging because I can't be bothered to discipline her. Sit, Camilla.'

Camilla sat and took a drink of her wine, then made a face.

'This tastes like cat piss.'

'Drunk a lot of cat piss in your time, have you, girl?' asked Vatius.

'I've drunk enough wine to know when it has been diluted to the consistency of Tiber water.'

'Oh, really,' said Vatius. 'Does it have turds and dead bodies in it, too?'

'Marsia,' yelled Carbo. 'Why have you served Camilla this muck?'

Marsia came over with an expression of mock innocence.

'I didn't think she looked old enough to drink strong wine.'

'I'm twenty-one,' said Camilla, forcefully.

'Really,' said Marsia. 'Then I must be ninety-three.'

'If you say so, old lady,' said Camilla tartly. Marsia made to reply but Carbo interrupted.

'Get her a proper drink, Marsia, before I have to instil some proper discipline.'

Marsia simply raised an eyebrow at him, then turned to fetch the wine.

'Now,' said Carbo, after taking a long drink from his cup. 'Tell me first, how do you know so much about the gambling dens?'

'My clients talk. A lot.'

'Your clients?' Carbo was surprised this young girl had a business. 'What's your profession?'

'Carbo, you are sweet. I'm a whore, of course.'

Carbo sat back.

'Oh, not so keen on my company now you know I earn my living on my back? Don't tell me you have never been with a whore.'

Not since he was a young man, he reflected. Not since his experiences at the hands of the German priestesses. There had only been one woman who had made him feel safe enough that he could be intimate with her. And she was gone.

Carbo took a deep slurp of his wine, closed his eyes while he waited for the drink to deaden his emotions, then opened them again.

'Are you a slave?' he asked.

'No, I am an independent businesswoman. Properly registered with the aediles and everything. Does it make a difference?'

Carbo shook his head uncertainly, feeling suddenly out of his depth.

Camilla slid her hand across the table and placed it over Carbo's.

'How about half price for the first one? I'm told I'm very talented.'

Carbo snatched his hand back like she had poured boiling water over it.

She raised her eyebrows in momentary surprise, then composed her features. Carbo glanced over to Marsia, who was glaring at him, mouth a thin line. He turned back to Camilla. 'You can help me? Inside information?'

'What's in it for me?' asked Camilla.

'You would escape a beating,' said Carbo.

'You really think that if you beat me, I would tell you the truth? I would advise you to back a three-legged donkey, and then you would never see me again.'

Carbo considered it. 'What's your suggestion then?'

'How much are you going to bet?'

'Let's say five denarii.'

'We only have six,' said Marsia, setting Camilla's new drink down.

'Then you had better earn some more,' said Carbo. 'Get back to work.'

Marsia flounced away.

'Fine,' said Camilla. 'You pay me one denarius up front. I give you a tip with odds of three to one. You bet four denarii, you come away with your four plus twelve more. You give me a third of your winnings, that's four denarii. You end up with twelve instead of your original five, and I end up with five.'

Carbo tried to follow the maths, but he was considerably slowed by the amount of wine he had drunk. It seemed to make sense though.

'You seem to do rather well out of the deal,' he said dubiously, 'Considering I am taking all the risks.'

'You don't know what risks I took to get the information,' countered Camilla.

Carbo considered, then nodded. 'Marsia, fetch me a denarius.'

Marsia did as she was told, tossing the coin onto the table contemptuously before heading back to the bar. Carbo looked after her for a moment, then shook his head and passed the coin to Camilla.

Camilla inspected it carefully, then slipped it into a small purse beneath her tunic.

'Very well.' She leaned in towards Carbo, her voice dropping, and Carbo leaned forward as well.

'There is a wrestling match in the basement of the Ass and Cart, you know, the tavern owned by Ulpius.'

'I know the one.'

'It's between a Greek called Echelaos, and a Syrian called Bacchides. The book is being run by Olorix. Bacchides is favourite, Echelaos is a three to one outsider. He is smaller and less experienced. But Olorix is going to nobble Bacchides with some sort of drugged wine before the match. It will be a walkover for Echelaos.'

'And how do I know you are telling me the truth?'

'Look at how much I have to gain. The down payment is small compared to the payoff if you win. Our interests are the same. Just as relevant, how do I know you will keep your end of the bargain?'

'You think me an oath breaker?' said Carbo loudly, fury flashing through him. The two cohort legionaries looked over at him curiously, briefly pausing in their dicing.

'No, no. I will accept your word,' said Camilla, soothingly. 'I apologise.'

Mollified, Carbo nodded. 'Then it is a deal. When is the match?'

'Tomorrow night. Just after sun-down. I will meet you there.' Camilla took a drink, then stood.

'Now I should go. Clients with valuable titbits of information don't just seek me out, you know.'

Camilla departed, and Vatius shook his head, tickling Myia between the ears.

'Well, she seemed trustworthy,' said Vatius.

'Mind your own business, philosopher,' said Carbo, and drained his drink.

–

Carbo diced with the legionaries, cursing his luck as he threw a one and two twos. He picked up the dice and inspected them, looking for evidence of weighting, but could see none. Fortuna really had turned her face from him today. Tomorrow would be different, though. He wouldn't need Fortuna, and he could get back to winning. That was all he needed, something to start the dice rolling in his favour. One good win, and it would all fall back into place. He tossed a sestertius into the pot in the centre of the table. The legionary opposite him rolled a four, a two and a three. A very beatable score. Carbo rolled again. Three ones! The worst possible throw.

The legionary laughed and scooped the money out of the pot. Carbo banged the table.

'You must be cheating!' he roared. The legionary exchanged a glance with his friend.

'Calm down,' he said. 'All's fair here.'

Carbo stood up abruptly, his stool crashing to the ground. 'Get out!' he yelled. 'I won't have cheats in my tavern.'

The legionaries stood. 'Don't worry, we're going. And we won't be back,' said the one he had been dicing with.

'And neither will our mates,' added the other.

They left, slamming the door behind them. Carbo looked around. Vatius was looking down, inspecting his wine seriously. Marsia regarded him with a steady stare, shaking her head slightly. The room started to spin a little, and he felt the sudden desperate urge to urinate.

He went out into the dark street, and leant one hand against the wall of his tavern, fumbling to take out his cock, and sighing in relief as a strong stream splashed against the wall. A hand clapped him on the back, and he tensed, looking round but unable to stop the flow.

'Keeping your customers happy, Carbo?' asked a familiar voice.

'Vespillo,' said Carbo. He finished off, wiped his damp hands on his tunic, and turned to face his friend. 'What do you want?'

'Nice greeting. Going to offer me a drink?'

'Yeah, I suppose. Come in.'

Marsia smiled broadly when she saw Vespillo, and brought over a cup of wine for him without prompting. Carbo looked at her in surprise. 'What about me?'

'Don't you think you have had enough, Master?'

Carbo gaped at her. 'I don't think that's for you to even consider, slave. Fetch me another drink.'

Marsia rolled her eyes at Vespillo, then went to do as she was told.

After she had returned, and then gone about her work, Vespillo said quietly, 'How are you doing, friend?'

Carbo grunted. 'I'm fine.'

'Good,' he said, sipping his drink. There was a pause. 'It's just it doesn't seem that way.'

'I'm fine,' said Carbo again.

'So the constant drinking? The gambling away of all your savings from twenty-five years in the legions? The scaring away your customers with your temper so your tavern is as quiet as a tomb?'

'Well, Vatius is nearly dead, so maybe that's appropriate.'

Vatius spoke up. 'I can hear you, you know. Not dead yet, nor deaf.'

Carbo ignored him. 'What do you want, Vespillo?'

'I'm worried about you.'

'Don't be.'

Vespillo shook his head, and beckoned Marsia over.

'Marsia, how does your Master seem to you?'

'Moody, prone to temper, frequently drunk, melancholy, acting rashly and irrationally...'

'Marsia!' gasped Carbo. 'Do you remember who you belong to?'

'I used to belong to a kind Master, strong and honourable. Now I seem to belong to a bad-tempered drunken gambler.'

'Would you like me to sell you to someone more to your liking?' asked Carbo, pointedly.

'No. I just want my old Master back.'

Carbo stared at her, noticed even through his drunken fog that her eyes were glistening. Without being dismissed, Marsia turned abruptly on her heels and walked away.

'She cares about you, Carbo,' said Vespillo quietly.

Carbo looked down, not trusting himself to speak.

'So do I,' continued Vespillo. 'So does Fabilla. She asks about you a lot. Wonders why you don't visit.'

'I... I can't.'

'You're grieving, it takes time. But don't ruin your life, your wealth, your health, your relationships, while you get over it.'

'Get over it? You think I can just get over it? Losing someone you love to violence. What in all Hades do you know about it, you fucking cunnus?'

Vespillo's voice was low and dangerous. 'You know what I know about it. You know that I've been there.'

Carbo slumped, looking down into his lap. 'Get the fuck out of my tavern, Vespillo. Just leave me alone.'

Vespillo hesitated, then sighed and left.

'Epictetus said, "Control your passions, lest they take vengeance on you,"' said Vatius.

'You can get out too,' said Carbo. 'We're closed.'

Vatius shrugged, finished his drink, gave Myia a pat, and left. Carbo sat where he was, staring at the table. Myia came over to him, gave him a nuzzle. Carbo stroked her absently, mind elsewhere. Marsia locked and barred the door, and tidied around him. When she had finished she asked, 'May I retire, Master?'

Carbo nodded, but remained where he was as she left, Myia trotting after her. He stayed there for some time, still, head foggy. He looked at his cup. It was empty, and he called for Marsia, before realising he had dismissed her. He considered fetching another one himself, but couldn't summon the energy.

His mind wandered to Sica, the girl he had rescued from the Sicilian mines. She was so bright and alive. Would she make him feel better if she was around? Or would the contrast with his own misery just make him feel even worse? He had heard she had set herself up in business. He guessed she was too busy to come and visit him. He put her from his thoughts.

One of the lamps on the wall guttered out, leaving only one still burning, the room now dim. Carbo remembered a time of captivity, of torture, isolation in a foreign land with a barbarian tribe. He pulled his knees up to his chest, wrapped his arms around them. He needed someone to put their arm around him. Someone who he had let get close to him, who had the power to soothe him. He needed Rufa.

He felt the panic coming back. The anxiety that used to overwhelm him, that Rufa was able to rid him of, had now returned worse than ever. His heart raced, his breathing became ragged. He stood, paced, feeling terror, that enemies were all around him; that he was in terrible danger.

He picked up his gladius from behind the bar, its familiar weight and solidity reassuring him a little. Then the last lamp guttered out, plunging the room into near darkness and a full-blown panic overtook him. He cried, desperate, little moans coming from the back of his throat, not knowing how to shake this overwhelming feeling. He pulled down the top of his tunic, ripping it open, and he drew his blade across his chest. He screamed.

Blood welled up, and the pain focused him. He felt the panic ease, his heart rate slow. He watched the blood soak into the tunic. He sat down against the bar, and closed his eyes.

The door leading to the kitchen opened. Lamplight shone through.

'Master. Master are you well? I heard a noise.'

Carbo quickly placed the gladius back in its home behind the bar and pulled his tunic up.

'Yes, I'm fine, thank you, Marsia.'

'Will you come to bed now?'

Carbo nodded, and got to his feet. The room suddenly spun dangerously, and he thought for a moment he would fall. Then a firm hand took his elbow, guided him out of the back of the tavern, and up the stairs.

Unresisting, Carbo allowed himself to be undressed. Marsia laid him in bed, then got in beside him. She knew better than to try to stimulate him sexually. Instead she lay behind him, arms around his chest. It wasn't like having Rufa there. But Vespillo was right, he knew Marsia cared about him, and it gave him some comfort.

Her fingers brushed against the incision on his chest, and he winced. She pulled her fingers away.

'Master, you are bleeding,' she said, concern in her voice.

'It's nothing, I cut myself on some glass.'

He lay on his side, staring blankly at the wall. The wine in his belly, the warm arms around him and the strange sensation of peace he had got when he cut himself, finally combined to numb him into sleep.

Chapter Three

Cicurinus walked down the Argiletum, the broad street leading to the Subura, wide-eyed. Castra Vetera had been overwhelming with its bustling populace, after his years in near isolation. It was nothing compared to Rome. He had grown up in the Subura, thought he had a clear memory of what it was like. He was wrong. He had forgotten the stench and noise of a million people. In captivity in various small settlements in German forests, he had become used to the fresh air, the quiet. Yes, the Germans were unwashed, as was he, but they lived in such wide open spaces that it was never overpowering, not like this. Though it was mid-winter, and the air was cold, the heat of all this humanity warmed the city. He felt like he could barely breathe.

A merchant to his left yelled out, causing Cicurinus to start, heart suddenly racing.

'Honeycakes, fresh baked, cheaper and tastier than Tubero's!'

Tubero's reply from the other side of the street made him spin round, body overreacting to this new threat.

'Didius' honeycakes taste like shit. Buy mine. They taste like nectar straight from Olympus!'

Cicurinus squared his shoulders and carried on walking. Passers-by crowded him, jostled him, and he had to fight down an urge to scream at them or strike out to keep them at a distance. He breathed slowly and deeply, the way he had learned to do in his isolation when panic threatened to conquer him. A degree of calm returned, and he carried on.

With more control of himself, he was able to observe this Rome that he had left so long ago. Were his memories true, or had Rome really changed this much? There were so many poor, beggars and cripples. So many foreigners with their outlandish clothing. So very many prostitutes. He looked at one of the women, a doris, standing naked in her doorway. She was beautiful, long black hair cascading over her chest, accentuating her full breasts. She looked at him, one hand on her hip, and smiled. He felt a stirring in his loins, and a surge of anger that she could affect him so easily. Veleda would be so disappointed in him.

He turned away in disgust and walked on. He was now fully in the Subura, the poorest, roughest part of Rome. The towering insulae leaned dangerously, cracks throughout the brickwork demonstrating how precarious their continued existence was. Every inch of street was crammed with traders and hawkers and beggars and prostitutes. Men thrust jewellery and perfumes into his face, whores reached out to touch him, grab at him. Anger and panic rose again, and he broke into a run, pushing his way through the crowds, curses and shouts of annoyance in his wake.

He saw a quiet looking tavern and burst in, panting. The bartender looked up from where he was wiping out an empty stew bowl, and regarded him curiously.

'Can I help you, sir?'

Cicurinus gulped down air, feeling like he was suffocating. The uncrowded room was unthreatening though, and after a moment he regained his composure. He sat, feeling a little light-headed, fingers tingling as they often did when he lost control of his breathing.

'Get me a beer,' growled Cicurinus.

'A what?' asked the bartender, looking confused.

Cicurinus cursed quietly. Another thing he had forgotten. During his time serving in the legions in Germany he had acquired a taste for the bitter drink, and had renewed his acquaintance with it after his rescue. In Rome though it was almost unheard of.

'Wine. Get me a cup of wine, well-watered.' Drunkenness was another vice he had forsworn. Veleda had taught him much.

'Yes, sir.' The bartender brought it over for him. 'Nasty sore throat you have there, sir. A lot of it about at this time of year.' The bartender sneezed, then wiped his nose on his sleeve. 'Think I might be coming down with something myself.'

Cicurinus ignored him, and when he realised this wouldn't be a two way conversation, the bartender shuffled back to his washing up. Cicurinus sipped his wine, wrinkling his nose. It was too sweet, but it was warm and quenched his thirst. He cradled it and looked around him. There were only two other customers in the tavern. One was a middle-aged, balding, pot-bellied man, at a table by the window. He was leaning against the wall as if he needed its support, even though he was seated. At the other side of the bar was a young man, maybe in his early twenties. He was well-dressed, clean, carefully barbered. He looked very out of place in this poor district. He appeared on edge, starting every time there was a noise from outside, and he kept his eye on the door. Cicurinus watched him with idle curiosity.

The bartender came back over.

'Would you like anything to eat, sir?'

Cicurinus considered. He realised he was hungry, and nodded. 'Soup and bread.'

'Yes, sir,' said the bartender turning away.

'And do you have a room?'

'To rent you mean? Yes, I have one free upstairs.' He named the price.

'I'll take it.' Cicurinus passed over the coins to pay for his food and drink and his lodgings. He looked over at the young man; he presumed him to be from a rich background from his dress, even though he seemed to have removed obvious ostentation like jewellery and expensive clothing. The man was getting increasingly edgy. Cicurinus' soup arrived, and he sipped it with the spoon that had been provided. His raw tooth protested, and he resolved again to visit the dentist.

The door opened, letting in some cold air. A young boy came in, seeming in his mid to late teens. He had a fair complexion, a feminine appearance, and was dressed in a well-made tunic, with a studded belt. Silver bracelets hung off each wrist, and a gold pendant hung round his neck. The nobleman, as Cicurinus presumed him to be, jumped up when he arrived, and embraced him, kissing both cheeks.

'Kyros! I was starting to think you wouldn't come.'

The young boy smiled. 'Quintus, how could I not?' he said in a light Greek accent.

'Sit, sit,' said Quintus, ushering Kyros to a chair at his table. 'Tell me how the show went last night.'

Kyros rolled his eyes.

'It was a disaster,' he moaned. 'Half the frogs were sick, so instead of croaking they just coughed and sneezed. In the scene with Aeschylus, he was late with the line

34

where he mocks Euripides, you know, "...lost his little flask of oil," every single time. And don't talk to me about Dionysius. Aristophanes would have been rolling in his grave.'

'And your Xanthius?'

Kyros tilted his head down and looked up at Quintus coquettishly. 'Modesty forbids...'

Quintus smiled, leaned in and kissed him on the cheek.

'I'm so sorry I couldn't make it,' said Quintus. 'My boorish father was hosting a dinner for some senator or other and insisted I attend. When I told him I was missing a play of wit and culture, he just laughed and said I was missing some young boy's arse.'

'Well, weren't you?'

'Very much,' said Quintus, smiling. He leaned in and kissed Kyros firmly on the lips.

Cicurinus turned away from the sight, stomach churning. He looked at his soup, and no longer felt hungry. What had happened to his Rome, the noble city that nurtured him? He needed to talk to someone, a man who understood the values of Rome and the virtues of the warrior. He called the bartender over.

'Do you know a man called Carbo?'

–

Carbo stood in the crowd packed into the basement of the Ass and Cart, sipping his third cup of unwatered wine. It had yet to calm his nerves. He seemed to have to drink more these days just to get to a point where his gut unclenched and his breathing was steady. He wasn't there yet, so he took another deep draught of wine. He looked across to where Olorix was sitting at a table, his body-guards behind him, taking in a steady stream of bets. The fight would start soon, and Olorix was lengthening the odds on the favourite, trying to encourage a last minute burst of flutters on the strapping Bacchides. Carbo had placed his bet already. The wager he had agreed with Camilla wasn't huge, partly because he didn't yet fully trust the girl, and partly because he didn't have that much ready cash to bet. He had cleared out the reserve behind the bar for this, much to Marsia's disgust.

Despite the fact that his bet was modest, Olorix had regarded him with surprise when he placed it.

'Not lost enough, recently, Carbo?' he had asked. 'I shouldn't stab myself in the foot, but if you want to change your bet to the favourite, I will let you. As it's you.' When Carbo had declined, Olorix regarded him steadily for a moment. Still, he took the bet and gave out the token with the amount and the odds scrawled on it.

Carbo was jostled from behind as someone tried to get a better view, and he pushed them back, causing mutters of protest all around him. No one thought it sensible to take the irritable, muscular Carbo to task over it, though. Carbo looked to Camilla, standing next to him. Camilla grinned and winked. It did nothing to calm the churning in Carbo's stomach.

A man appeared at Carbo's side.

'You have a bet on this fight?'

Carbo nodded, not looking around. 'Echelaos.'

An expression of mild disappointment flashed across the man's face, but Carbo was oblivious.

'Can I get you a drink?' asked the man.

Carbo looked around at the tall, well built, scarred man.

'That's kind, friend. Wine, unwatered. Will you have one yourself?'

The man seemed to consider, undergoing some internal conflict, then smiled and nodded.

'I will.' He pushed through the crowd to the bar, and returned quickly with the drinks. They clinked cups, and Carbo downed his in one long swig. The man hesitated, then did the same.

Ulpius, the tavern owner, was the referee, and he entered the roped-off circle in the centre of the basement room. Cheers and jeers rang out as he raised his voice to speak.

'Friends and fellow fight lovers. We have a special contest for you tonight.' He beckoned on the wrestlers, who pushed their way through the crowd, gathering some shoves and slaps as they went.

'To my right,' continued Ulpius, 'We have Bacchides the Syrian. Bacchides has won thirty bouts this year, and lost only four. He is tonight's favourite.'

The crowd roared their approval, fists waving in the air.

'To my left, we have Echelaos the Greek.' A few cheers sounded, but were rapidly drowned out by a chorus of boos. 'Echelaos has only been wrestling for three months, but has already won three of his first ten bouts.'

The record made Carbo's heart sink. He looked at the two wrestlers, appraising them with the eye of a professional fighter. Each was naked, allowing him to fully assess their physique. Bacchides was tall, well-muscled, and carried himself confidently. Echelaos was shorter, more wiry in stature, and looked around at the crowd with evident anxiety. Carbo narrowed his eyes, looking for signs of intoxication in the big Syrian. Bacchides looked focused, stable, at ease. Carbo looked at Camilla, doubt in his eyes. The girl had her eyes fixed on the ring now, excitement shining on her face.

Ulpius handed a cup of wine to each fighter. 'Drink, to the honour of Mercury, the god who first taught mortals to wrestle.' Each fighter took the cup and drained it, then cast it aside. Ulpius stepped back.

'Fight,' he commanded, and the two wrestlers closed and the crowd roared. Bacchides moved with grace and ease, while Echelaos appeared more uncertain. Bacchides reached out in an attempt to slide his arm around Echelaos' neck, but Echelaos ducked out of the way. Echelaos countered by charging his shoulder into Bacchides' chest, wrapping his arms around and gripping tightly. Bacchides was rocked back by the initial momentum, then steadied himself with a backward thrust leg. They struggled together as the crowd screamed.

Carbo himself was yelling incoherently, voice hoarse. 'Come on Echelaos. Kill the bastard!' Excitement coursed through him, and he felt alive at the vicarious enjoyment of the fight. Beside him, the man who had bought him the drink stared at the spectacle in fascination.

Echelaos was slowly pushed backwards, and Bacchides' superior height and weight began to force him down. Echelaos twisted, broke the grip, and the two fighters stepped back, panting. A few boos and cries to get on with it filled the room. Bacchides advanced again, and Echelaos met him. This time Bacchides got the grip he was looking for, arm around the back of Echelaos' neck. He twisted, forcing Echelaos sideways and down towards the straw-covered floor. Echelaos stamped down on Bacchides' foot, then punched him in the abdomen. Bacchides grunted, but didn't loosen his grip. The big Syrian extended a leg and wrapped it around one of Echelaos' legs, and with a sudden twist of his body, threw the Greek to the floor, following up so he landed heavily on the smaller man.

The air was driven out of the Greek's body with an audible whoosh, and the crowd went wild, while Carbo groaned. He looked over to Camilla, who betrayed no sign of anxiety. For a moment, Echelaos lay unmoving, and Bacchides took the opportunity to adjust his grip around the Greek's neck, squeezing tight. A couple of dozen heartbeats, and the Greek would be unconscious, the fight over.

Echelaos convulsed his body violently, bucking Bacchides up into the air. The Syrian kept a hold, but his grip loosened enough for Echelaos to get a hand between the Syrian's arm and his own neck. It was enough to get the blood and air flowing to his head again, literally giving him some breathing space. Bacchides reached to grab Echelaos' arm, but Echelaos managed to take hold of one of the Syrian's fingers, twisting it back viciously. Bacchides roared in pain, and this time Echelaos took advantage to wriggle out of the hold and spring to his feet. Bacchides stood as well, and immediately closed with Echelaos.

This time though, Carbo thought there was a slight unsteadiness in the bigger man's gait. As he lunged for Echelaos, the small Greek twisted his body, and with a grapple and a flick of his ankle, threw the Syrian to the floor. He leaped on top of him, working for an arm lock to force Bacchides into submission. Bacchides threw the Greek bodily off him, and again the two men got to their feet.

The man beside Carbo tried to talk to him.

'Interesting fighting technique. Not sure they would last long in the legions…'

Carbo cut him off with an angry gesture, all his attention fixed on the fight.

Bacchides was swaying now, and Echelaos could see it. Bacchides made a lunge for Echelaos, but the smaller man side stepped easily, taking the opportunity to swing an elbow into Bacchides' temple. The Syrian staggered but kept his footing. He turned again, clearly struggling, and threw himself at Echelaos. Echelaos pivoted and then put a foot out, tripping Bacchides so he fell heavily, face first onto the straw. Echelaos immediately pounced on him, gripping Bacchides' wrist and forcing it up behind his back. The Syrian cried out and struggled, slamming his free hand in frustration on the floor as he kicked his legs and bucked his body. Echelaos held on tight, the leverage he had keeping the larger man pinned down. The crowd was silent, holding its communal breath.

'Submit,' said Echelaos, clearly. Bacchides struggled harder, so Echelaos wrenched the trapped arm further up his back making Bacchides cry out.

'Submit,' repeated Echelaos, straining now with the force he was exerting. Bacchides' shoulder joint started to deform alarmingly.

'Never,' grunted Bacchides. Echelaos gave an upward jerk with his arm. There was a barely audible pop and then a high-pitched scream from Bacchides as his shoulder dislocated. All the fight left the big Syrian as he flopped weakly on the floor.

'I declare Echelaos the winner,' shouted Ulpius. The crowd erupted in boos and jeers, some directed at Ulpius, some at Echelaos, and some at the writhing Bacchides. Elation surged through Carbo and he punched the air, then turned to Camilla and hugged her. Carbo turned to the man beside him and hugged him too. The man hesitated, then hugged him back enthusiastically.

A medicus came over to tend Bacchides, and with the help of a couple of volunteers from the crowd, accompanied by shrieking from the injured man, he set about relocating the joint.

Carbo pushed his way through the crowd to where Olorix was sitting with a satisfied smile.

'Ah, Carbo. Luck was with you today.'

'And with you, Olorix. It seemed most of the crowd were expecting Bacchides to win.'

'He was the obvious favourite. He did look out of sorts today though, didn't he?'

Carbo glanced across to Camilla, who said nothing, then handed over his betting token. Olorix looked at it and snorted. 'Well, this will hardly bankrupt me, especially after a day like today.' Olorix counted out Carbo's winnings. 'Don't spend it all at once.'

Carbo took the coins, smiled and turned away, putting his arm around Camilla's waist, and around the shoulder of the man who had bought him the wine.

'Come on you two, let's celebrate.'

'Come back soon,' shouted Olorix after them. He watched them leave with narrow eyes.

—

Cicurinus wandered through the Subura, heading back to his lodgings, with a smile on his face for the first time in twenty years. He was slightly drunk, not enough to dull his senses, just enough to give him a warm feeling inside. He was glowing too, from the after-effects of his time in the brothel. It had been all too brief, and the girl had not been the prettiest, especially since she had succumbed to the plague of cold sores that was going around Rome this winter. He had been careful not to kiss her, but she had been enthusiastic, and the experience had been intense.

At the back of his mind he felt a small pang of guilt. What would Veleda think? Back in Rome for no time at all, and he was drinking, whoring and gambling. But it didn't matter. He had a new friend.

Carbo. The hero of the German legions. Captured like him, Carbo had gone through many of the same traumas, and had come out of it strong, self-assured and enjoying life. Carbo would be the star he would guide his new life by. He would be a mentor and friend, and Cicurinus would rebuild his life.

–

Carbo sat at a table near the bar, bowed over a cup of cheap wine. His head throbbed like a German was bashing it with an axe, and his stomach roiled. Another wave of nausea swept over him, and he thought he would have to run for the door to avoid Marsia's wrath for soiling her clean floor. He swallowed, and the nausea passed. He took a sip of the wine, swilling it round his mouth to try to wash away the dryness and the foul taste. He swallowed and waited for the feeling to wash over him, to ease the fine tremors in his hands. What had he been drinking last night? For that matter, what had he been eating? His breath smelled like he had been fermenting garum in his mouth.

The fact was he couldn't remember. He had been having more mornings like this than ever before, mornings that consisted of rising when the sun was already high in the sky, tottering down to the bar with a near fatal hangover, and then summoning Marsia for a glass of wine to try to restore some normality. Invariably his memory of the previous night was sketchy at best.

He remembered going out with Camilla, to toast their success. Someone else had been with them, a dim memory of a man, some hanger-on. Carbo couldn't remember having met him before, supposed that he was someone hoping to benefit from the largesse of a happy gambler. He had told Carbo his name, but Carbo had retained that fact for only a few heartbeats, referring to him just as 'my new friend' all night.

The early part of the night had consisted of some drinks in a nice tavern in the IIIrd district of Isis and Serapis. It had moved on from there to a not so nice tavern on the Viminal, where Carbo failed to tempt Camilla and this other fellow to match him drink for drink.

As they wandered, they had passed a brothel at the eastern end of the Subura, and Camilla had suggested the two men indulge. They had gone in together, and Carbo vaguely recalled enjoying the attentions of the prostitutes as they sidled up to him, stroked his broad chest and whispered compliments about how he made them feel, and what they wanted to do to him. He remembered as well, when he showed no inclination of taking them up on their offers, how he had got tossed out on to the street by a fat bodyguard, who he had challenged to a fight. Unfortunately, at that point he had lost the use of his legs, and so had the ignominy of sitting slumped against the brothel wall, waiting for his new friend, who emerged some time later looking like the cat who had got the cream.

Marsia swept the floor around Carbo, saying nothing, but her expression was disapproving. When the besom banged against his feet, he let out a low growl. Marsia shot him a glance, but carried on sweeping.

'How did I get home last night?' asked Carbo.

'A large man with terrible teeth and that silly girl Camilla carried you in. Woke me up to come and fetch you, and then between us we managed to get you up the stairs and into your bed.'

Carbo nodded, then wished he hadn't.

'Did I… bring any money home?'

'No,' said Marsia, and turned away.

Vatius strolled in and slammed the door behind him, causing shockwaves of pain to lance through Carbo. He groaned and clutched his head.

'Another hangover, Carbo?' asked Vatius cheerfully.

Carbo said nothing, but looked over at the elderly philosopher with a look of misery on his face.

'I've told you before. Fried canary and owl eggs. I used to swear by it back in my heavy drinking days.'

'Fine, fine. Marsia, go out and get me some.'

'Oh, just like that, I have to find you some fancy food to cure you from your own stupidity. Where from? With what money? And who will look after this place?'

'I will tend the tavern. Take some money from the float for the bar. And I don't know where, just go and find me some, before you have to arrange my funeral.'

Marsia tutted and retrieved some money from a lockbox behind the bar. 'You are lucky we had a good evening,' she said, as she headed for the door. 'Actually, it's not luck. It's because you weren't here.' She slammed the door behind her, causing Carbo to groan again.

'Remind me Carbo, is she your slave or your wife?' said Vatius with a grin.

'Very funny. Do you want a drink?'

'If you're up to it.'

Carbo struggled to his feet and poured Vatius a cup of wine. He set it down before his regular, and sat with him. Myia, who had been lying fast asleep in a corner, opened an eye, stretched, then wandered over to see if Vatius had something to eat. Vatius patted her, and dropped her a small piece of dried fish he had brought for her. She swallowed it whole, then looked at him expectantly for more. He laughed and showed her his empty hands, and her ears drooped. Then with an audible sigh, she curled herself up on the floor under their table.

'I won, yesterday,' said Carbo. 'Camilla was right.'

'Congratulations,' said Vatius. He took a deep sip of his wine. 'Ahhh. A remedy for the moroseness of old age, indeed.'

'Aristotle?' hazarded Carbo.

'Plato,' said Vatius. 'On the other hand, his mentor, Socrates, said that worthless people live only to eat and drink, people of worth drink and eat to live.' Vatius looked archly at Carbo, who held the gaze for a moment, before turning away and looking at the table.

'How are you, Carbo?' asked Vatius gently.

'Absolutely fantastic, by Mars' hairy arse. How do I look?'

'I mean how are you really. After… you know.'

Carbo looked around the tavern. It was empty, apart from Vatius, Myia and himself. Vatius regarded him sympathetically. Carbo felt something building inside him, like flood waters rising, about to burst the river banks. He wanted to tell Vatius everything. How the grief ate away at him every moment he let his guard down, how his terrors and episodes of panic were worse than ever, how he couldn't sleep, how every day he wondered if taking his own life was the solution. He wanted to tell Vatius that he could only make those feelings fade by drinking and gambling, to numb him and distract him and transport him to a place away from this Hadean city. He opened his mouth.

The door opened, and a large man came in. He looked around the tavern and his gaze fell on Carbo. He smiled a broken toothed smile, walked over to Carbo's table, and sat without invitation.

'Carbo,' he said with a smile. 'What a night, eh?'

Carbo looked at him with confusion, taking in the badly-healed breaks of nose and jaw, the scars, all much more visible in the daylight than they had been last night.

'Oh,' said Carbo, flatly. 'It's you.'

'Your new friend, as you kept calling me last night,' said the man.

'Right,' said Carbo.

'Aren't you going to introduce me?' asked Vatius.

'This is Vatius,' said Carbo.

'And your new friend?' asked Vatius.

Carbo struggled to recall but it was hopeless. He sighed. 'You will have to remind me.'

The man's face showed a flash of disappointment, but he recovered quickly.

'Cicurinus.' He offered his hand to Vatius who shook it respectfully.

'So what are we up to today?' asked Cicurinus brightly.

Carbo raised an eyebrow. 'I have no idea what the fuck you are up to. I am going to quietly die in the corner of my tavern.'

Cicurinus let out an uncertain laugh.

The door flew open, and three young men came in, laughing uproariously.

'And then I asked him if it was confusing in the sack, since his tits are bigger than hers.'

The other two men laughed at their fellow's joke, and dumped themselves down on stools at the back of the bar. Myia trotted over and settled under their table, waiting for any crumbs to fall. The first speaker looked around him, puzzled for a moment.

'Where's Marsia?' he called out to Carbo.

'She's out,' said Carbo, getting unsteadily to his feet. 'How can I help you?'

'Oh, you must be Carbo. I'm Porcius. Heard a lot about you when we were in here last night. You have a great slave in that Marsia you know.'

'Thank you. Would you like some drink? Food?'

The three men asked for some bread and nuts and three cups of wine. Carbo stumbled over to the bar to fetch their order.

'So that Marsia, she isn't available to your customers?'

'No,' said Carbo.

'Shame, great arse on her. I can see why you want to keep her to yourself. She is very sweet on you, you know. She clearly idolises you. Wish my slave had the same regard for me; no matter how much I beat her I can never raise a smile.'

Carbo set the food down in front of his customers, and then went to fetch their drinks. The room was still spinning slightly, but he navigated his way back across the room with the three cups in his hands, spilling only small drops. Then his foot landed on Myia's tail, where it was sticking out from under their table. With a yelp she leapt up, jolting the table just as Carbo was setting the cups down. One of them tipped over, spilling wine straight into

Porcius' lap. He jumped back, with a cry, knocking his stool over.

'You clumsy idiot,' said Porcius. 'That tunic was only cleaned the other week. It will cost a fortune to get those stains out.'

'I'm sorry,' said Carbo. 'The dog...'

'That's right, blame the dog. You're drunk, that's the problem. You know, when I came in here last night, all I heard about was Carbo the hero, who had defeated the local gang, and saved a slave child. All I see here is Carbo the drunk.'

Carbo balled his fists. 'Get out of my tavern, before I do something I regret.'

'Don't worry, we are going.' The three men stood, and headed for the door. As Porcius passed Carbo, he gave him a shove in the chest. Carbo tottered backwards, catching his heel on Myia, who had retreated behind him. With flailing arms, he fell onto his backside. The men laughed and opened the door, just as Marsia arrived, carrying a small basket with a fried canary and two large poached eggs.

Porcius scowled at her. 'I don't know where this Carbo you told me about last night is, but I would like to meet him one day.'

'Oh, sirs,' said Marsia hastily. 'Please don't leave. I'm sure there has been a misunderstanding.'

'Marsia,' roared Carbo, his authority slightly under-mined by the fact that he was sitting in the middle of the floor, legs splayed. 'Let them go. They aren't welcome here.'

Marsia gave Porcius an apologetic look and stepped aside, closing the door gently behind them. She looked down at Carbo, then across at Vatius, who shrugged. Then without another word, she took a plate, and started to prepare Carbo's late breakfast of fried canary and owl eggs.

Carbo looked at Cicurinus, who had been sitting quietly throughout this, face ashen.

'And you, whatever your name is. You can get out too. I don't know what your game is, or what you are after, but one night of drinking does not make you my new best friend. Piss off and don't come back.'

Carbo slumped into a chair and put his head in his hands.

Cicurinus stared at Carbo in shock. He stood, unsteadily, then left, glancing backwards as he went.

Chapter Four

Cicurinus sat on the floor of his small room, his elbows on his knees and his head in his hands, eyes squeezed shut. There was a sour taste in his mouth, and he didn't think it was last night's wine. His head throbbed, and it seemed for a brief moment like he was looking down on himself. He was back to his pre-capture body condition, good nourishment helping build up the muscles that had been tempered by the gruelling labour into which he had been forced. He was clean and presentable, but his scars still stood out livid on his skin, and there was a distant look in his eyes. The room spun for an instant, and he put his hands to the floor, feeling as if he would fall.

Memories came to him, the lash of the whip, the beatings and threats, the humiliation of the chores as he served his captor, his tormentress, his beloved Veleda. He missed her.

He felt a presence before him. There was a pleasant fragrance of woodland and wild flowers. A soft voice spoke.

'Why are you hiding?'

He jumped to his feet. A woman robed in white stood in his room, face serene. He looked at the door. She had closed it behind her, so quietly he hadn't heard.

'Veleda,' he gasped. 'Priestess. How did you...'

'Silence!' she commanded.

Cicurinus clamped his mouth shut.

Veleda walked around him, looking down at where he cowered. Her bare feet made no noise on the floorboards, but he felt the breeze from the swish of her robe as she circled him. She came to a stop in front of him, and her brow creased in apparent puzzlement.

'Why aren't you kneeling, Cicurinus?' she asked in genuine confusion.

Cicurinus scrambled into a kneeling position, and remained still with head bowed.

'After all our time together, you forget so quickly. How many times did I have to punish you, until your defiance dissipated, until you learned to give me appropriate deference?'

Flashes of whips, rods, knives, ropes, gags, blindfolds. Abruptly he was shivering, as if the room had become icy.

'I'm sorry, Priestess,' he mumbled.

'What else have you forgotten, Cicurinus?'

'Nothing, Priestess. I remember all your lessons.'

'Really? Where were you last night?'

'I...' His mind grasped for excuses, alibis, but when he looked into her eyes he realised she knew everything. She must have been watching him, maybe since he set foot in Rome. He bowed his head again, falling silent.

'Drinking. Gambling. Whoring.' Each spat word felt like a whip across his back. His fine shiver coarsened into a tremor afflicting his whole body.

'Oh, Cicurinus. I taught you to be pure, like a true warrior. Like the men of my tribe. Like the Romans once were, in their early years. Before greed and wine and immorality took their souls.'

'I can be better, Priestess.'

'I know this, child. You can restore Rome to the purity it once had. I believe this of you.'

Cicurinus nodded eagerly.

'Yes, Priestess, I can do it.'

'And maybe in cleansing Rome, you can restore your own honour and purity. You could be great, combining the best of both our peoples.'

Cicurinus stared up at her with terror and adoration, eyes wet. His mouth hung open, his chest was heaving, and he felt an overwhelming upwelling of emotions – purpose, pride, excitement, ecstasy.

'Most of Germania remains unconquered. The tribes of the lands east of the Rhine remain free and strong. But to keep strong, you need strong and worthy enemies. Your old senator, Corculum, argued against the destruction of Carthage, because he feared that the loss of the powerful enemy would lead to a decline in Roman discipline and morality. Yet they did it anyway, and look what Rome has become. The Cloaca Maxima runs beneath Rome, taking away the physical effluent, and yet the streets of the city and the hearts of the people are putrid. I fear for the spirits of my people if they do not have a strong enemy on which to whet their iron.'

'I understand, Priestess. I will seek out the infirm and immoral. It will be my duty and my goal to cleanse Rome, to make it strong again. I will set a sword to terrorise the evil and unworthy in the city. I will rid Rome of its foreigners and its sexual deviants and the beggars and scum who weaken it.'

Veleda smiled at him, and her gratification filled him with calm. She reached out a hand towards his head, and he closed his eyes.

'Do your duty, Cicurinus,' she said, her voice a whisper.

He felt her hand hovering above him. Then it was gone. After a while he opened his eyes, and found himself alone. Stiffly, he got to his feet, and sat on the edge of his bed. His eyes focused in the middle distance as the resolve hardened in his heart.

–

Cicurinus walked past the statue of Mercurius Sobrium, along the Clivus Suburanus, a fire burning inside him. It was getting late, and he had watched the Subura change over the last few hours. It felt darker in character as well as level of illumination. Groups of men stopped their conversations to watch him suspiciously as he passed. Very few people appeared to Cicurinus to be what he would think of as honest, upright citizens, and those that were, looked unhappy to be out. Cicurinus sensed an unpleasant taste in his mouth.

He passed a tavern with a sign of a cockerel on the door. It seemed quieter than most of the others nearby. He paused, tempted to enter, to find some peace. But his work would not be done that way. He looked around him. Who should he choose?

A portly, bald-headed man dressed in fine robes coloured with expensive-looking dyes caught his eye. His dark skin suggested he was of Eastern origin, maybe Egyptian or Syrian. His ostentatious jewellery looked very out of place in the district, and he obviously knew it, because he was glancing about him anxiously as he hurried along. Cicurinus wasn't the only one who had noticed him. Two large, thuggish looking men trailed him, ambling along nonchalantly, chatting to each other, but never letting the Eastern man get too far ahead. Cicurinus waited a few moments for all three to pass him, then followed along himself at a short distance.

The well-off Easterner glanced back, and spotted the two men following him. They looked away in an exaggerated, almost comedic attempt to pretend they hadn't noticed him. The Easterner sped up, and the thugs did likewise. Abruptly the Easterner turned a corner into a narrow lane, and the sound of running feet echoed back to Cicurinus. The thugs obviously heard it too, as they broke into a run themselves and chased off down the side lane. Cicurinus gave them a small head start, then broke into a loping trot, long legs eating up the ground easily.

He rounded the corner, and saw that it hadn't taken long for the thugs to catch up with the Easterner. They were a hundred feet down the alley, barely visible from that distance in the darkness. Cicurinus slowed to a walk and quietly approached. One of the thugs held the Easterner against a wall, gripping a fistful of his finery, forearm across his neck. The other, smaller one had a knife held close to the terrified man's eye.

'Take off your necklace,' growled the thug with the knife.

With trembling fingers, the Easterner did as he was told. 'Take it,' he whimpered.

'And the rings.' He pulled desperately at the gold rings on his fingers, but either fear had robbed him of his strength, or his podgy fingers had too good a hold on the rings, because they wouldn't loosen.

'Make sure he stays quiet,' said the thug with the knife. The other thrust his palm over the Easterner's mouth, who looked out with wide, flickering eyes. The knife-wielder gripped a ring-bearing index finger and clumsily hacked it off, while the Easterner struggled and screamed against the hand. The thug slipped the ring from the finger, cast the finger aside and looked at the piece of jewellery appraisingly.

'Not bad workmanship. Heavy too. Let's get the rest, kill him and get out of here.'

The Easterner shook his head and struggled desperately, but he was held tight. The smaller criminal took hold of the Easterner's hand again and gripped his knife, preparing to cut.

Cicurinus stepped behind the thug and took hold of the arm holding the knife, both his hands gripping his wrist. With one firm twist and thrust, he forced the knife into the assailant's stomach.

There was a moment's silence. The thug looked down at the knife protruding from his guts – blood welling around it rapidly – in disbelief. The larger thug didn't even notice immediately, so silent and quick had Cicurinus been. Then when he realised nothing was happening, he looked around, and saw the wound just as the man slumped to his knees.

The large thug threw the Easterner aside with a roar, and turned on Cicurinus. Powerful arms reached out to grapple him, but Cicurinus slipped underneath them. He reached down, taking hold of the knife, twisting it then pulling it out of the dying criminal. The blade was dark red, blood dripping off the tip, and he stared at it, mesmerised. The big thug swung a roundhouse punch at his head, but Cicurinus blocked it contemptuously with his forearm and thrust the knife into the man's heart. He fell without a sound.

Cicurinus stood for a moment, looking down at the two muggers, one dead, one gasping in pain as he slowly died.

'Thank the gods,' said the Easterner, in a strong accent. 'You saved me. How can I ever thank you?'

Cicurinus squatted on his haunches and withdrew the knife from the dead man's chest.

'You are Egyptian?' he asked the man as he turned the blade over in his hand.

'Yes, originally, but now I live near the Esquiline,' said the Egyptian, his words coming in a rush. He was holding the stump of his finger, but for now the pain didn't seem to have set in, maybe because of the shock and the emotion of his attack and rescue.

'You are well-dressed to be out on your own in the Subura at this time of night,' said Cicurinus, rising steadily to his feet.

'I know, it was so stupid. There was a woman I wanted to see, I trade with her husband, a potter, nice chap for a Roman, but he was away and… well, I'm sure you understand. It wouldn't have been discreet to have taken a bodyguard. But I stayed too long, got carried away, and it was dark before I realised. I don't suppose… you would escort me home? I would pay you well for the service, and of course reward you for saving my life.'

The knife slashed across the Egyptian's throat. He reached up to grip the gaping wound in his neck from which blood spouted, attempting vainly to staunch the flow. His wide, uncomprehending eyes fixed on Cicurinus. In just a few heart beats, he was lying dead on the floor with the others.

Cicurinus smiled. Two criminals, and a rich foreign merchant who was committing adultery with the wife of a hard-working Roman tradesman. That was a good start. He was sure Veleda would be pleased.

There was copious blood on the floor, and Cicurinus dipped his hand into the red liquid, scooping some up even as it started to congeal. He examined a nearby wall, then used the blood to paint letters on it.

'Hey!'

Cicurinus turned to see a figure at the end of the alley. A woman was standing there, clearly afraid to approach, but brave enough to try to warn him off. He studied the knife for a moment, running his finger along the blood-soaked edge. No, he had no reason to think this woman was one of his targets, and he wouldn't kill her simply because she was in the wrong place at the wrong time. He turned to walk away, and on the spur of the moment, and with a small smile, he affected a pronounced limp.

Chapter Five

Vespillo stood over the three bodies, shaking his head. Death was hardly unusual in the Subura at night, but three violent deaths in one place was not an everyday occurrence. The murders of two Suburan low-lifes and a rich merchant, who oddly still had some of his jewellery on him, was distinctly unusual. And to find daubed in large letters of blood on the wall of the street the words, 'ROME WILL BE CLEANSED' was completely outside his experience.

'Why did he write that, sir?' asked Plancus.

'Maybe he was embarrassed about the mess he has left,' muttered Taura. Vespillo shot his deputy a sideways glance. Taura had the good grace to look momentarily abashed. At the end of the alleyway, a small crowd of curious onlookers had gathered, held back by a couple of hefty watchmen.

Vespillo walked around the scene. He turned the merchant over with his foot. The body flopped onto its back, gloopy congealed blood slurping around the neck wound. Sightless eyes, wide open, stared up at Vespillo. He bent down, and picked up the merchant's hand, turning it over and frowning. One finger was missing, but there were chunky rings on two other fingers on that hand.

'Sir,' called Plancus. He was holding up the missing finger, bloodied, but with a clear indentation where a ring had been worn for a long period of time. He cast around him, then with a small cry of satisfaction, he retrieved the ring from a shallow puddle.

Vespillo looked from the dead thugs to the merchant, puzzled.

'It's obvious, sir,' said Taura. 'These two scumbags mugged the merchant. Then some other scumbags caught them in the act, and decided to take the spoils for themselves.'

'Except they didn't,' said Plancus. Taura shot him a filthy look. 'Sir, I mean, they left his jewellery behind.'

'Then maybe it was the merchant's bodyguards who managed to defeat the thugs, but were too late to save their master.'

'And then leave their master's body behind?'

'Maybe they were scared they would be punished for their failure. Maybe they ran.'

Vespillo looked doubtful. 'If they were slaves that would make them fugitives. If they were freedmen, suspicion would fall on them for the murder if they fled. Could these two men actually be the merchant's bodyguards? No.' He answered his own question. 'Look at their clothes, their condition. Bodyguards are stronger, fitter, better paid.'

'You may be right, sir,' said Taura. 'But what are the chances of ever finding out the truth?'

Vespillo sighed. 'Nevertheless, I should take this to the Urban Cohorts. Something isn't right here.'

'Do you think they will care, sir?'

'I doubt it, but I should try. Taura, get the men to work. Make this alley like this never happened.'

'Why should I care?' asked Pavo in surprise. Vespillo suppressed his irritation. They stood in the office of the Tribune of the second cohort of the Urban Cohorts. Vespillo noted the decor was a lot nicer than his office in the barracks of the IInd Firestation on the Esquiline.

'Because three men are dead?'

'Men die all the time. Were they important?'

'I suppose it depends on your perspective. To their families, I imagine they were, yes.'

Pavo made a sour face. 'And two of them were thieves, accosting this merchant?'

'It looks that way.'

'So, their mothers might be upset, but no one else will be. The merchant, what do you know about him?'

'Egyptian, spice trader. Lived in a nice house in the Trans Tiberim district. Handy for business I suppose.'

'Do we know what he was doing in the Subura?' asked Pavo.

'The part of Rome with the highest concentration of whorehouses, gambling dens and taverns? Not a clue.' Vespillo kept his face neutral. Pavo studied him with suspicion.

'I still don't understand why you have brought this to me.'

'Tribune Pavo, you must see that this is unusual. There must have been other people present, who need to be brought to justice. And the graffiti in blood? Tell me when you last saw that! If we joined our resources, asked around for witnesses, maybe we could find out what happened, find out if there is something going on here that we should be worrying about.'

'Listen, Tribune Vespillo. You and I are nominally of the same rank, although we both know that in practice, being a commander in the Urban Cohorts is more prestigious than the same position in the vigiles.'

Vespillo stiffened at this but said nothing. Pavo continued with his patronising tone. 'But we have different jobs. My job is to worry about the security of Rome. Make sure that the peace is kept, the slaves stay in their places, riots are put down and rioters punished. Your job is to put out fires, look tough, and bop bad people on the head that you catch in the act of doing their bad things. It isn't your job to worry about investigating and prosecuting crime, and it certainly isn't mine.'

'If not us, then who will?'

Pavo shrugged. 'I understand you were away in the legions a long time, but you have been in Rome long enough to know how justice works now, surely? If a victim of crime, or their relative, has evidence against a wrong-doer, they need to bring a private prosecution.'

Vespillo shook his head. 'Yes, of course. But this is different. I feel it in my guts.'

'Probably some bad garum you ate. If that's all, Vespillo? I have a report to write for the Prefect about the number of replacement caligae we require.'

Vespillo opened his mouth to speak, then realised the futility of it, and with as respectful a salute as he could muster, he left.

Carbo looked into the woman's face, trying to read what might be written in the heavily lined features, concealed beneath thick white lead make-up. The room was dim, lit by a single flickering oil lamp, and the air was thick with incense. He felt nauseous, though he didn't know whether that was from his perpetual hangover, from the dense atmosphere, or from his anxiety.

'Her name was Rufa?' The accent was Egyptian, matching the old woman's features.

'Yes,' he confirmed, trying to keep the tremor out of his voice. How many times had he attempted to pluck up the courage to do this? Look at him, brave hero of the legions, terrified to talk to an old lady.

He had got her name, Sitkamose, from a customer at the tavern, a veteran who swore blind she had helped him contact his dead son. He had paid her five denarii on entrance and told the seer that he wanted to contact Rufa, a woman he had known.

'You do understand that contacting those who have passed over the Styx is difficult, sometimes even dangerous. It is not like talking to someone in the room with you, or reading about them on a tablet.'

Carbo nodded his understanding.

She took hold of both of his wrists, thumbs at the points where his pulses throbbed rapidly. Her eyes were closed and her lips moved, muttering to herself in a foreign language, and he caught glimpses of yellow-brown teeth with large gummy gaps.

Suddenly her eyes flew open, red-veined whites surrounding wide pupils, and he took a startled breath.

'I can sense her.'

Carbo's heart hammered in his chest.

'You loved her very much,' said Sitkamose. Carbo swallowed, nodded again, not trusting himself to speak.

'She says she loves you too.'

Carbo gaped. 'You are talking to her?'

'Not exactly. But we communicate. She was taken from you too early.'

'Way too early,' he said, angrily.

'There was violence, I feel.'

'Yes,' said Carbo amazed. 'She was murdered.'

Sitkamose nodded. 'I thought as much. And you have had many thoughts of vengeance.'

'I've taken my vengeance,' he spat. 'Now I'm left with nothing.'

'She is talking to me. She is saying… she is saying Carbo, be calm. She is at peace. She knows you did everything you could. And she has to tell you… to tell you…'

The seer suddenly went rigid, head thrown back, fingernails digging painfully into Carbo's wrists. The oil lamp flickered out like it had been snuffed, though no hand had touched it. Carbo ignored the sudden darkness.

'Tell me what?' he hissed.

Sitkamose abruptly went limp. Her shoulders sagged and she let out a long breath, like a dying sigh.

'Tell me what?' demanded Carbo, voice rising in anger.

Sitkamose shook her head. 'She is gone. The connection is lost.'

'No. I need to know what she was going to say!'

'Remember, Carbo, she told you to be calm; that she is at peace. She will return, and she will tell you what you need to hear.' She stood and feeling her way, relit the oil lamp with a taper.

Carbo stared at her in frustration as the light returned. 'When can we try again?'

'Oh, not for a while. I am far too exhausted, and besides, she won't return today. We can attempt contact tomorrow, if you like. There will of course be another fee to pay.'

Carbo ground his teeth. The money was a problem, but he needed to know.

'Very well. Tomorrow. Thank you, Sitkamose.'

'You are welcome, Carbo of the legions. Go with the blessing of the gods.'

The dark liquid swirled in a miniature whirlpool as Carbo rotated the cup in small circles. He stared down into the wine, eyes unfocused, mind somewhere else. Was it real? He so wanted to believe. The drink called to him, but he resisted, at least for that instant. If Rufa was there, if she could speak to him, it meant one day they could be reunited. And if they were, what would she think of him now?

He hadn't taken a drink since visiting the seer. Maybe he didn't need to. When he had returned to the tavern, he had snapped his fingers for Marsia and demanded wine, but it was only habit. He looked up, and found Marsia regarding him with narrow eyes. She caught his gaze, held it defiantly for a moment, then returned to wiping tables.

Carbo looked back at the drink. The surface of the liquid showed fine waves, and he realised the cause was the tremor in his hand. He put the cup down and held his hand out straight, palm down. The tremor was grossly visible, and he pressed his hand onto the table. Drinking would eliminate the shake, he knew. It would be so easy. He took the cup in his hand, gripped it tight, lifted it from the table.

The door to the tavern opened. Carbo looked up, and saw Vespillo stride in. He put the cup down hastily.

'Marsia, water and one of those disgusting meat pies you make from the dead dogs you find in the gutter, and make it quick.'

Marsia glowered at him, but Carbo saw her smile as she turned to get his food and drink. Vespillo pulled up a stool and sat at Carbo's table.

'How are you doing, friend?'

Carbo clenched his fists and put them in his lap.

'I'm good, friend, you?'

Vespillo surveyed him suspiciously for a moment. 'Good to hear it. Me? Not so sure. Came across something strange this morning.'

'Oh? Tell me.'

Marsia brought the cup of water and the pie on a rough clay plate. Vespillo took a large bite, chewed and swallowed hungrily, despite his comments on the provenance of the meat.

'Three dead bodies.'

Carbo waited. Nothing strange so far. Dead bodies were a common sight on the streets of Rome. Elderly slaves thrown out to starve once they were no longer of use. Unwanted babies. Murder victims. The homeless and the sick, falling asleep for the last time at night, for the sun to rise over their cold corpses in the morning, waiting patiently to be cleared up and taken to the mass graves outside the city boundaries for those too poor to contribute to a funeral club.

'A merchant, and the two thugs that attacked him.'

Carbo's brow narrowed as he processed the information.

'The merchant killed some of the gang that robbed him before he died?'

Vespillo shook his head.

'The merchant wasn't robbed. He still had his jewellery with him, although the thugs that attacked him seemed to have made a good start of parting him from some of it. Quite literally.'

'The other dead weren't his bodyguards?'

'No way. You should have seen the state of them. An armpit plucker wouldn't have hired them, let alone a rich merchant. But there's more. A nearby wall was daubed with the blood of the victims to spell the words "Rome will be cleansed".'

'So some good may come of this,' snorted Marsia. 'Rome stinks. Rotting fish, shit on the streets, urine from the fullers, dead animals, dead horses...'

'No one asked you,' said Carbo. Marsia folded her arms truculently, but made no move to leave. Carbo sighed and looked back to Vespillo who gave him a small smile.

'So what are you saying?' asked Carbo. 'What do you think happened?'

'I really don't know. But it's troubling.'

'A little odd maybe. But really, who cares? Three more dead bodies in a city littered with them?'

'You sound like Pavo.'

'He wasn't interested either? Are you surprised?'

'Not surprised by him. I thought you might show more concern though. You fought for the people in this district.'

Carbo looked at his wine. It was calling harder to him now. He needed Rufa. He needed her right now, to hold him, to stroke his hair, to soothe the cramping anxiety in his belly, to slow his heart, to tell him everything would be all right.

'I suppose I should have known better. Fabilla keeps asking for you, you know. Severa looks after her well, cares for her. But she has lost her mother, and the man she had come to think of as her father won't see her.'

Carbo stared down, saying nothing, his full being concentrating on moving air in and out of his lungs. No matter how deep a breath he took it didn't seem to be enough. Every fibre of his body was screaming to run, or to fight. He didn't know whether to grab Vespillo and scream in his face, or overturn the table and flee out of the tavern.

He did neither. Instead he picked up the wine and drained the cup in one long swig. For a moment he held his breath, letting the strong drink seep into his core. Then he let out a shuddering sigh, and placed the cup back on the table with a trembling hand.

'That's your answer is it?' asked Vespillo, and the contemptuous look on his face made Carbo's heart sink. Vespillo stood, shaking his head. 'I don't have time for this. Please, Carbo. For all those who care about you. For Fabilla, for Marsia, for me. And yes, for Rufa too. Sort yourself out.'

He walked to the door and gripped the handle. 'And if either of you do hear anything from your customers…' He glanced around the empty tavern. 'Well, if you hear anything that might help, let me know.'

Carbo didn't reply or even look up. Marsia held the door for Vespillo as he left.

'Thank you, sir. I wish I knew what to do.'

Vespillo patted her arm, and looked back to Carbo, who stared into his cup, pretending not to hear them.

'So do I, Marsia. For now, all we can do is be ready to help him if he wants us to. Find me if you hear anything about these murders, won't you?'

'I will. Take care, sir.'

Marsia closed the door behind him and walked back to the bar.

'Marsia.'

She turned to look at Carbo hopefully.

'Bring me more wine.'

Cicurinus sat at a table in the street outside a sausage seller's stall, drinking water, and nibbling at a frugal meal. He wore a cloak over his tunic, the hood pulled up to ward off the chill late autumn wind, and to keep curious eyes from staring at his scars. Carbo's tavern was a couple of dozen yards down the street, and Cicurinus watched it through narrow eyes. He had watched Vatius arrive as usual early in the morning, and the philosopher had remained inside all day, except to come out into the street to urinate. In the afternoon he had seen a short, well-built man dressed as a member of the vigiles enter the tavern, and moving close to a half-shuttered window, he had been able to make out most of the conversation.

So Carbo didn't care about the killings? He wasn't sure how he felt about that. A condemnation of the murders from Carbo would confirm that the former hero was on the side of the foreigners and criminals. Praise would have gone some way to redeeming Carbo in Cicurinus' eyes. But apathy? Was Cicurinus' mission of so little importance to him? Well, he would make him pay attention. He would make him care.

The sky was clouded over, and night was falling fast. The sausage seller stood nearby, clearly uncertain whether he could ask the solemn stranger to move on so he could lock away his furniture until the morning. Cicurinus stood abruptly and stalked off down the street. The sausage seller moved quickly to clear up, before he changed his mind and came back.

Cicurinus was not going to change his mind. His path was set. Veleda had shown him the way. He would make Rome great again, worthy opponents of the mighty Germanic tribes. And he would make it happen, one contemptible wretch at a time.

The Subura's streets twisted and turned, came to dead ends unexpectedly, or just as suddenly opened into plazas and crossroads. Some buildings and alleys were familiar from his childhood, others he had known had collapsed or burnt down, and been rebuilt, so he had the unsettling feeling of being in a dreamworld, a place both familiar and alien. He came across the Eagle, an old bar for veterans that he had frequented as a youth, always desperate for tales of heroism and valour from the legions, and he smiled at the memories of how the old soldiers had indulged him, telling him stories he now knew were exaggerated and sanitised versions of reality. They had, however, induced a desperate longing in the naive boy he had been to join up and earn fame and honour for himself.

He looked up at the sign of the Eagle painted onto the wall high up. Faded and cracked now. Like much of Rome, uncared for, neglected. The front door opened, and a tough-looking, grizzled man emerged. Cicurinus greeted him like an old soldier, but the man looked down, seemingly embarrassed, pulled his cloak up and hurried away. Cicurinus frowned, aware that he was being distracted from his path, but curious as to what had become of the place. He pushed open the door and stepped inside.

He was immediately hit by an overwhelming scent of perfume. Although the aroma was qualitatively different from the stench of shit and decay on the streets, it was still powerful enough to make him gag. It was gloomy on the streets, but it was even darker inside, and for a moment, before his eyes adjusted, he could see next to nothing. A figure loomed before him out of the darkness, and as he blinked the features resolved into that of a woman.

She was young, maybe sixteen he guessed, and although the smile was welcoming, the resigned look in her eyes told him that she was no innocent. As he became accustomed to the dim light, he realised the bar room of the Eagle had been transformed. Soft couches were scattered throughout, most of which accommodated one or more women, all dressed, as was the one before him, in brightly coloured dresses, gaudy and made from cheap material, but cut to reveal thighs and cleavage to their best effect.

The woman reached out with one finger, and stroked it down his damaged face.

'Old soldier or old gladiator?' she asked, head tilted to one side.

'S… soldier.' Hades! She was attractive. Long dark hair, long eyelashes, lead-whitened cheeks, bosom demanding his gaze. He swallowed, tried to keep his eyes on hers.

'Does the old soldier need a massage? To ease those old wounds.'

'No, I didn't come here for…'

'Am I not pretty, soldier? Don't you want me? Wouldn't you like to take me upstairs?'

Cicurinus gaped. This girl was much more beautiful than the one he had paid for two nights before. As he looked down at her chest, he felt himself involuntarily start to harden.

'I... can't...'

'Are you worried about performance? Maybe it would help if there were two of us.'

The girl beckoned another girl over, dark of skin and hair, similar age, similarly beautiful.

'I'm Incerta,' said the first girl. 'And this is Veneria,' she said, indicating the second.

Veneria offered Cicurinus her hand, and when he didn't take it, she laid it on his shoulder, shifting her weight towards one leg so her hip stuck out provocatively.

'Just eight copper coins for both of us,' said Veneria, her accent Numidian. 'You won't get two more beautiful women for a better price in all of Rome.'

Cicurinus was about to turn and leave. Then the words of Veleda came back to him. *You can restore Rome to the purity it once had*. His jawline tightened, his eyes narrowed.

'Very well,' he said, voice husky.

Incerta looked at Veneria uncertainly, taken aback by the sudden change that had come over the shy veteran. Veneria hesitated. He had not done anything aggressive, or even impolite. Both girls were suddenly uneasy, but they had no reason to turn him down. Cicurinus fished in his purse for eight coins and gave them to Incerta. She tucked them away, then they both took a hand each, and led him out of the front door, and to the stairs on the outside of the building that led to the higher storeys. None of the girls or their clients paid them any attention as they left.

The wooden staircase creaked alarmingly under the weight of the three of them, though the two girls were slight. Some of the steps were splintered, and Cicurinus wondered if his foot might go straight through. They held though, as they ascended to the fourth floor, and Incerta led them through a tatty door made of planks roughly hammered together, into a small room containing just a single straw mattress on the floor.

The room offered no internal illumination, but a gibbous moon shining through a small window allowed him to make out the two feminine shapes. He closed the door behind him, and rested his back against it. The girls approached him hesitantly, but he gave no indication what he wanted. They looked at each other, then knelt before him. Incerta ran her hand up the inside of his thigh and Veneria reached around to stroke his buttocks. He was hard, but that was of no consequence – it was purely a physical reaction to the presence of these immoral women, and a clear demonstration of how they could corrupt a man.

He reached down, and with powerful hands, toughened by years of manual labour, he grabbed both women by the throat. They both clutched at his wrists, nails digging into his skin, clawing at him, trying to prise open his fingers. He lifted them up to their feet, watching with fascination as their faces turned red, then became tinged with blue. They made little noise, no air flowing through their windpipes, despite the heaving chests desperately trying to drag the wind into their lungs. Their feet kicked against the floorboards spasmodically, but they wore no shoes, and the tenants below this room would be well used to thumping and banging noises from above.

He walked them both backwards the short distance across the room until they were thrust up against the wall. He lifted, so they were suspended from his strong arms, legs flailing. Their eyes were wide with terror and incomprehension. He looked from one to the other, and a half-smile played across his lips. He remembered once skewering a rat on his dagger, and holding it in front of his face while it bled out, watching its death throes, and he felt the same fascination now that he had felt then.

Their struggles became weaker. Their hands dropped away, their legs stopped kicking. The terror left their eyes, which became unfocused; pupils dilated. For a while longer, their chests continued to spasm, the body refusing to give up even after the spirit had gone. Then they were still. He opened his fingers and let them fall in heaps to the floor, like discarded rag dolls.

He opened and closed his fists, working out the cramps that had started to appear. He looked down, and noticed that his erection had not subsided. If anything it had strengthened. He felt his anger grow, peak inside him. It was these whores' fault, making him feel like this. Their immorality was corrupting virtuous Roman men like himself. He let out an incoherent roar, grabbed the straw mattress – the only movable object in the room – and hurled it against the wall. It thudded softly, then toppled over with a muffled flop, doing nothing to quench the thirst of his rage.

He stared at the two bodies, still, pallid, limbs askew. The first one – what was her name? Incerta – had fallen with her dress around her waist, her sex on view in the moonlight, and his fury amplified. He kicked the corpse in the ribs, then again, harder, over and over. The body jerked with each blow, then flopped back into position, just like a sack of corn would. He turned to the other, Veneria, and started to kick her too. He heard cries of anger, and realised they were coming out if his mouth, in between the deep breaths his exertions required him to draw.

Eventually the fury burnt itself out. He put his hands on his knees, breathing heavily, regarding the corpses, which were now misshapen and oozing sticky blood, with contempt. He reached down and dipped his hand in the dark fluid. Using the sanguineous ink, he wrote on the wall. 'Destroy the immoral.'

He turned to leave, and started, his breath catching in his chest.

'Veleda. I didn't hear you come in.'

The priestess's face was stern. 'I'm not surprised, with all that noise you were making. It's as well that the tenants downstairs are used to noisy events in this room. Otherwise they may have come to investigate, or gone to look for the vigiles.'

Cicurinus bowed his head. 'I'm sorry, Priestess.' Then he looked up in confusion. 'How did you know I was here?'

Veleda shook her head, disappointed. 'You still doubt me, after all these years? I am always nearby, Cicurinus. I know your movements, your thoughts, your desires, your hopes and your fears. And all of those things belong to me.'

'Yes, Priestess.'

'Now close your eyes.'

He did as he was told. An age seemed to pass, and the room was silent, the only sounds coming through the little window from the streets way below. After a while, he thought he heard little noises from behind him, where the dead girls lay. Noises like little moans. Like fingernails running along the floorboards. Like the shuffling of legs.

He pictured the bodies reviving, standing, drawing new breaths.

He spun, opened his eyes wide, heart racing.

The dead girls lay where he had left them. He turned back. Veleda was gone.

Quietly, he opened the door, the creak as loud as a scream in his ears, now he was trying to be stealthy. He walked slowly down the staircase, paused at the bottom, looking left and right. The street was quiet, the nearest people too far away to be more than shapes in the gloom. He let out a breath he didn't realise he had been holding, and began to walk away from the Eagle.

The door flew open behind him, and he heard a man's voice, laughing and a little drunk, thanking a giggling girl for a wonderful evening.

'Hope you've had fun, too,' the man called to Cicurinus' back. Cicurinus lifted a hand in acknowledgement, then hunched his shoulders, and without turning, limped down the street.

Chapter Six

The sun was still well below the rooftops when Carbo pounded on Sitkamose's door. There was no sound of response from within, and he cursed and spat, thumping the wooden door hard enough to loosen a screw at the hinge.

'Sitkamose. Open up!' he called.

Now he heard sounds of life from within the small third floor apartment. He tapped his foot, anxiety and impatience warring inside him.

'Sitkamose!' he called again. His eyelids felt leaden, and his eyes felt like he had been staring into the wind unblinking. He had a nagging pain emanating from the centre of his forehead, and there was an uncomfortable sensation in the middle of his abdomen. He had drunk relatively lightly the previous night, at least by his current standards. Three or four cups of wine had been enough to take away the anxiety, and he had decided to take an early night, so he could return to Sitkamose as soon as possible, to find out what message the seer had for him.

Things hadn't worked out as planned. Although he had elected to go to bed at a sensible time, the customers in the bar had other ideas. His bedroom was above the main tavern, and as he lay awake, flat on his back, staring at the dark ceiling, lit only by the three-quarter moon, loud noises of revelry disturbed him, coming in through the window and with a bassier tone, up through the floorboards. Scraping chairs, slamming doors, singing, shouting, laughing, arguing, even the odd scream, kept him fully awake. His mind drifted to Rufa involuntarily, and the abrupt pain when he thought about her was like a physical blow. He tried instead to distract himself with other thoughts. He tried to think about sex, but that brought him back to Rufa, and besides, his libido was at such a low, the very concept bored him. He thought about his time in the legions, and this seemed to show some promise. As his mind recalled good times with comrades during leave in German and Gallic towns, replayed bar room brawls and drunken nights out, he felt himself start to drift, the scenes slowing, his mind becoming emptier as sleep approached.

And then a roar from downstairs, maybe in anger or jest, had jolted his thoughts even further back to that battle, the forest, the capture, the priestesses, the torture, and he was wide awake again and gasping for breath. He rose, throwing on his tunic, and stormed down into the bar.

'We're closed,' he had yelled at the customers. 'Get out, all of you!'

The customers knew better than to get on the wrong side of Carbo and left, though with poor grace. Marsia simply shook her head in despair, but Carbo ignored her and went back to bed.

Though it was quiet now, the anger was still coursing through him, and he stayed fully awake. When Marsia had finished tidying and locking up, she had come to his room. Wordlessly, she had undressed and settled down to sleep under a blanket on a mattress on the floor. She rarely attempted to share his bed any more, not even to hold him. Soon she was asleep, and Carbo listened to her light breaths, gritting his teeth at how even that light sound was enough to disturb him. Although the noise from his own bar had ceased, the sounds of carts, drunks, dogs and thieves still reverberated down the lanes of the Subura and through his window.

The night had gone on forever, the slow progress of the moon Carbo's only indication of time, and he had remained awake for almost all of it, sweating, gritting his teeth, fighting off waves of panic and resisting the urge with a titanic strength of will to go back to the bar and drink himself into oblivion. Some time before dawn, he had finally slipped into sleep, only to be woken what seemed like moments later by the sound of birds singing the dawn chorus, and the first merchants hitting the streets to set up their stalls. He had crawled out of his bed, dressed hastily, stepped over the stirring Marsia, and set off for the seer's house.

The door cracked open an inch.

'Who is it?' came a hoarse female voice.

'Carbo. You told me to return today.'

'Not at this time I didn't. Go away. We will make contact this afternoon.'

Carbo pushed the door open, not hard, but with enough force that an old lady would not be able to resist.

'No,' he said, voice firm. 'Now.'

Sitkamose looked even older without the benefit of her make up, and her hair looked like a bird's nest. She glared at him, and he glared back. Her eyes were steely, and Carbo wondered if he had the strength to win this battle of wills. He hoped she couldn't see how his legs were trembling.

Sitkamose dropped her gaze first.

'Very well. Now. But I told you already, there are no guarantees. Your friend, Rufa, she may not come when I call. If I am tired, or under stress, it may be harder for me to reach her.'

'If so, we try again another time.'

Sitkamose nodded wearily and beckoned him through. He sat, and she spent some time pottering around the room, lighting incense tapers and the single oil lamp, making sure the shutters were tightly closed against the light, and finally spending a few moments forcing a comb through her hair and applying the day's make up.

When, after a seemingly interminable length of time, she was finally ready, she joined Carbo and sat opposite him at the table. She looked at him expectantly, and Carbo frowned.

'The payment?'

'Oh of course.' He handed over the precious coins from the previous night's takings. She dropped them into her purse with a jingle. Then she took his hands and inhaled, then let her breath out slowly, five, six times.

'Is she there?' asked Carbo, eager, desperate.

A flicker of annoyance registered on Sitkamose's face, quickly replaced by a mask of serenity. Then she frowned, and gasped.

'What is it?' asked Carbo, alarmed.

'I see… violence. I see her kneeling, crying to you for help. But you can do nothing. Restrained, somehow. She needs you so much and despite your strength, you are impotent. Then there is a blade. And blood. So much blood.'

Carbo couldn't breathe. It felt like he was being strangled. He could draw no air through his constricted throat, as he was confronted by the image of the death of the only woman he had ever loved.

'Rufa. I'm sorry,' he gasped, tears flowing freely down his face.

'And now it is over. And although you can't see her, she is standing beside you. Even now, she has her hand on your shoulder. She is smiling.'

'S… smiling?'

'Yes, Carbo.' Sitkamose's face was beatific now. 'She is smiling. And she wants to tell you two things. She wants to tell you that it wasn't your fault. And she wants to tell you that she loves you, forever.'

Carbo let out a gasping sob, then another, then the dam broke and he collapsed forward onto the table, crying helplessly. Sitkamose put her hand on his shoulder and squeezed sympathetically.

When he finally regained some measure of control, he looked up at Sitkamose. She reached out with a cloth and gently dabbed his eyes dry.

'I'm sorry, I don't… it's just…'

She patted his hand sympathetically.

'Did she say any more?'

Sitkamose shook her head. 'She said everything she needed to.'

'So, if I come back, she won't have anything else to tell me?'

'Oh no, no,' said Sitkamose hastily. 'She would wish you to visit me regularly. I'm only sorry that I have to charge you each time. These sessions cost money – incense, offerings to the gods. And they take their toll on me, too…'

'The money isn't a problem. I'll return tomorrow.'

'Of course,' said Sitkamose. 'But maybe a little later tomorrow. The spirits of the departed aren't always so responsive in the early hours.'

'Last chance,' said the dentist, holding up the large cup of unwatered wine.

Cicurinus shook his head and gave a low growl.

'Suit yourself,' said the dentist. He was olive-skinned and spoke Greek with an oriental accent. Cicurinus was undecided whether he was an example of the foreigners who were polluting Rome. But Greeks weren't barbarians. They brought culture and learning and skills in medicine and arts. He hadn't seen Veleda since he had murdered the two prostitutes, which he was rather disappointed about, so he couldn't ask her advice. But the pain from his teeth was distracting him from his work.

The raw, broken stumps that he had been left with after all the years of abuse had become a feature of his life. It was not that you could ever get used to that sort of pain, but you could learn to accept it, even embrace it. Veleda had taught him that the pain was purifying, holy. And so he felt guilty that he was trying to do something about it.

But the pain had been intensifying, keeping him awake. When he tried to think, to plan, the incessant agony dragged his thoughts away. Besides, getting dental treatment would allow him to eat better, to become even stronger. He would need his strength for his mission.

'Open up then, let's have a look.' Cicurinus was lying on his back on a bench, in the open air, in front of the dentist's office. Two elderly ladies sat on stools on the opposite side of the road, watching and occasionally muttering comments to each other. Most people walked past with barely a glance in his direction.

He opened his mouth, and the dentist peered in. His eyes widened at the sight.

'Divine Apollo! What happened to you?'

'That is none of your business, dentist.'

'But... almost every tooth is broken. You have abscesses in the cavities. Your gums are rotten. What do you expect me to do?'

'Do whatever you have to. I was told you are the best.'

'I am, but... I will need to extract almost every tooth. It will take all day. And the pain, especially without wine, will be unbearable.'

Good, he thought. Purifying.

'You will be surprised at what I can bear. Begin.'

The dentist fingered his tools, scalpels of various shapes and sizes to slice the gums down to the roots, chunky iron forceps to wiggle and loosen the tooth before yanking it loose, picks for removing decayed flesh. He sighed, and picked up a sharp scalpel.

'Very well. Let's begin.'

-

Vespillo entered Carbo's tavern sheepishly, clearly not sure of his welcome. When Carbo leapt from his stool and grasped the older man's hand, then ushered him to a table, Vespillo's expression changed to surprise.

'Sit, sit, my friend. Marsia. Marsia! Food and wine.'

Vespillo regarded Carbo suspiciously.

'Are you well?'

'Really well,' said Carbo enthusiastically. 'Marsia, where's that wine?'

Marsia hurried over with a jug of wine and two cups, and poured a generous serving into both. Vespillo looked at her with raised eyebrows, but she simply shrugged and went back to the bar.

'You seem… bright, today,' said Vespillo.

'I feel it,' said Carbo. He took a small sip of his wine, savoured it before he swallowed. 'This is my first drink today.'

Vespillo nodded, clearly not as impressed as Carbo had hoped. The drink had been calling to him since he woke, but he had found the siren somehow easier to resist that day.

'What brings you here?' asked Carbo.

'Firstly, I wanted to apologise. I was harsh with you last time I was here.'

Carbo was waving away the apology before Vespillo had finished speaking.

'It doesn't matter. You were right. I wasn't myself. And it's not what Rufa would have wanted.'

Vespillo looked at his drink, but didn't touch it. 'Has something changed? Did you suddenly find a new religion? One of those eastern cults.'

'No, it's not that.' Carbo looked around, then leaned in closer, conspiratorially. 'I spoke to Rufa.'

Vespillo's eyes narrowed, and he looked suspiciously at the cup that Carbo was cradling.

'Carbo, my old friend…' he began.

'I know what you must be thinking. I'm not hearing voices in my head. I went to see someone. She can talk to people who are on the other side of the Styx.'

Vespillo sighed. 'Carbo, you aren't gullible, and you aren't naive. How much money did she take off you?'

'The money doesn't matter. She knew things. She told me about Rufa. And she told me Rufa's words. It was her, for sure. Rufa said it wasn't my fault.' He grasped Vespillo's hands in his own. 'Vespillo, do you understand? She doesn't blame me!'

Vespillo looked into his friends' eyes. 'If it makes you feel better...' He stopped himself.

Carbo laughed. 'You don't believe me, I know. But if you had been there, you would feel differently.'

Vespillo sat back. 'Fine, fine. So Rufa has told you everything is good. So you are going to change your ways now?'

'I know I have been behaving badly. But if I can talk to her regularly, I know she will keep me straight.'

'Regularly? You are going to keep seeing this woman?'

'Of course,' said Carbo earnestly. 'Vespillo, I have Rufa back.'

'And how much does this woman charge you?'

Carbo hesitated, then told him. Vespillo whistled. He looked across the room to Marsia, who was gently shaking her head. 'Carbo, you can't afford to keep paying her that!'

A frown of irritation crossed Carbo's face, the first negative emotion he had displayed to Vespillo that day. 'The money isn't important. I'll find it.'

Vespillo sighed. 'There were two more murders last night.'

Carbo raised his eyebrows but expressed no more interest than that.

'Couple of whores. Strangled and beaten. Not necessarily in that order. And the words, "destroy the immoral" daubed on the wall in their blood.'

'Strange,' said Carbo, tone flat. Then, with an effort at joining his friend's conversation, he said, 'Any witnesses?'

'Someone saw a big, well-built man with dark hair walking away from the brothel. Or, limping away, I should say.'

Carbo nodded, looking back into his wine. His thoughts drifted back to the message from Rufa, and he felt pain and hope in equal measures as her face floated in his mind.

Vespillo sat back, and pushed his drink away.

'I'm back on duty in a few hours, and I have barely slept today. I need to get home, or Severa will forget what I look like, and shack up with the local butcher. I'm sure he has his eye on her.'

'Well, thanks for the visit. However, brief.'

'Tomorrow,' said Vespillo, 'We will go to visit an old friend.'

'Who?'

'You'll see. I just think you will benefit from a chat with him.'

Carbo nodded non-committally, and rose when Vespillo stood, shaking his hand and bidding him goodbye. When his friend had left he turned to see Marsia regarding him, arms folded across her chest.

'What is it?' he said, tone harsh.

'We have no bread today.'

'Then get some.'

'We don't have any money.'

'What? Why not!' His voice rose.

'Well let me see,' said Marsia. 'Gambling. Drink. Mystic seers. No customers.' She counted the ideas off on her fingers.

'Stop! Go to the baker and ask for bread. Tell him Carbo asks it, and I will repay him, on my word.'

Marsia looked doubtful. 'You already owe the baker twelve denarii.'

'Just go. He won't refuse me.'

'And if he does? Will you threaten him?'

'Get out of here!'

Marsia strode out of the door and slammed it behind her. Carbo fingered his purse, which contained a few meagre coins. His mood had soured, but he had to admit that Marsia and Vespillo had a point. If he wanted to keep seeing Sitkamose, he would have to find some money soon, and the tavern wasn't bringing in nearly enough. He swirled the liquid in his cup around, and thought about Camilla, and her inside information. He finished his wine in one long draught, and left the tavern with a purposeful step.

–

It didn't take Carbo long to track Camilla down. After asking around at the Ass and Cart, he was directed to a brothel two streets away, with a few winks and 'give her one for me' comments. The bodyguard at the front door was a bulky Syrian slave who eyed Carbo suspiciously but let him enter. The madam who ran the place gave him a more friendly smile, and when he asked for Camilla, she told him to take a seat.

'She's with someone now, and this gentleman is next. Then it will be your turn.'

Carbo sat on a bench next to the client before him in the queue, a nervous looking youth, and waited. The madam offered him a drink, but he turned it down. The familiar anxiety was building inside him, inactivity, anticipation, unfamiliar environment all combining. He found himself gritting his teeth and clenching his fist and he took some deep breaths to try to relax.

The waiting area was small and had an overpowering stench of sweet perfume which couldn't completely mask the undertones of sweat and other fluids and the cheap make-up the prostitutes used to whiten their faces and rouge their cheeks. The walls were badly decorated with explicit images of various different practices that were on offer, and there was a price beneath each.

There were two cubicles separated from the waiting room by linen curtains, and from within both came the sounds of sex – the weird noises men made when in the throes of pleasure, and the encouragements and fake moans from the women. Eventually an animal grunt came from behind the left-hand curtain and moments later a portly, pox-scarred man came out, adjusting his tunic. In the cubicle, the prostitute was visible; a fat woman with face heavily whitened in lead, down which the kohl from her eyes had run in black streaks. She looked out into the room, and gave a leering smile that revealed brown teeth.

'Felicia is free,' said the madam.

'I'm waiting for Camilla,' said the youth in a high voice.

Carbo leaned close to him and whispered in his ear, in the conspiratorial tone of two men comparing notes. 'Take Felicia instead or I'll break your neck here and now.'

The youth swallowed, then stood. 'Actually, I'll go with Felicia.'

Felicia stretched out a hand, and when the youth was in reach, she grabbed him and pulled him inside. The curtain swung closed, and Carbo heard the youth give out a high-pitched cry that was suddenly cut off.

The other curtain opened, and a rough, dirty-looking man, maybe a dock worker or builder, came out with a satisfied grin written across his face. The curtain fell back behind him, concealing the occupant. He gave Carbo a wink, then said to the madam, 'She's fucking amazing, Priscilla.' Then to Carbo, 'Enjoy yourself mate.' And he was gone.

Carbo rose and walked to the cubicle. Priscilla coughed. 'Money first.' She pointed to the prices on the walls. Carbo ignored her, and pulled the curtain aside.

Camilla was seated on the edge of the bed – a stone platform built into the wall with a thin straw mattress on top. She was naked, and when she recognised Carbo, she attempted to cover herself with her arms. Carbo turned his back on her.

'Come on, Camilla,' he said over his shoulder. 'We're going.'

'I can't leave,' she said. 'I'm working.'

'Your shift's over.'

'If I walk out on them, they won't have me back. They will find someone else to fill this cubicle.'

'No they won't. You're young and popular. They might be annoyed, but they will want you back.'

'What's going on?' asked Priscilla irritably. 'Are you having her or what? I told you, cash up front.'

'Get your clothes on,' said Carbo. He heard Camilla dressing hastily.

'Antiochus,' called out Priscilla. 'Get in here.'

The Syrian slave swaggered in. He had a club on a strap hanging from his belt, and he untied it and slapped it into his hand, looking at Carbo with a theatrical menace.

Carbo took one swift step forward and head-butted Antiochus in the centre of his face. The slave crumpled, slumped backwards against the wall, head lolling as blood poured from his nose. Priscilla put both hands to her mouth and Camilla groaned. The noises of sex from the other cubicle stopped abruptly, and the curtain was flung back. Felicia was on top of the lad, and both stared wide-eyed at the scene.

Priscilla found her voice. 'Get out! Get out, both of you! And neither of you ever come back, or I will round up a group of thugs and have them beat you both to death!'

Camilla gave Carbo a shove, which did little to move his bulk. 'You idiot.' She turned to the madam. 'Priscilla, I'm sorry...'

'I don't need this kind of trouble. Find somewhere else to work.'

'Fine,' said Camilla. 'I was fed up with this shithole anyway. And you smell.'

She flounced out, and Carbo grinned and followed her.

Once they were outside, Camilla turned to Carbo and slapped him hard across the face.

'You had no right to do that.'

Carbo rubbed the stinging cheek slowly, looking down at her.

'That's how I earn money. How I eat! As well as pick up my tips on gambling. You know, the ones I share with you.'

'I'm sorry,' said Carbo. 'I should have been more patient.'

'Yes you should!' She turned away from him, spent a moment collecting herself, then turned back.

'What is it you want?'

'Your expertise.'

Camilla looked at him thoughtfully. 'Same deal as before?'

'Or something similar.'

She considered for a moment. 'Fine. There is a wrestling match. Proper rules, hold down for a count of three or a submission. Lots of money changing hands. The two contestants are quite evenly matched in size and experience, but one is generally thought to be the better fighter. I've heard that he has been bribed to throw the fight.'

'Good, I'm in.'

'Care to wager a bit more this time?'

Carbo hesitated. He could scrape together a few coins, a bit more than last time, but if he lost, it would really wipe him out. On the other hand, he really needed the money. And the thrill…

He felt a bit guilty, like Rufa would not approve. Now he had found her again, he shouldn't need the solace that gambling brought.

He would stop soon. This win might be enough. He could get the tavern back on track. Gradually pay off his debts. And he would talk to Rufa, and live out his retirement quietly.

One last win. Then he would stop.

Chapter Seven

Carbo didn't realise where Vespillo was taking him until he saw the signs painted on the outside wall of the house. Astrological symbols like a crab and a ram and a goat, and other mystic characters Carbo didn't recognise.

'Why have you brought me here?'

'I just thought it would be nice for us to check in.'

'He's a fraud.'

Vespillo didn't reply but knocked loudly on the door. A willowy slave answered the door with a radiant smile, but couldn't disguise a flicker of annoyance when she recognised Vespillo.

'My Master is resting now.'

'When has that ever stopped me seeing him, slave?' asked Vespillo with a friendly smile.

The slave gave a little show of reluctance, just for appearances, then let out a sigh, and stepped aside. Vespillo nodded his thanks and entered the vestibule. Carbo followed him through into the atrium, and took a seat on a marble bench.

Vespillo strode to the door leading to the interior of the apartment and let out a deep bellow.

'Kahotep! Wake up! You have visitors!'

There was a crash from somewhere inside, like the noise of someone falling out of bed, then a string of curses.

They waited, Vespillo's face showing a trace of amusement as they listened to the sounds of someone hurriedly getting dressed. When he finally emerged, it was without the make-up that Carbo had seen him wearing previously. He wore a blue, embroidered robe that appeared to be back to front, and his eyes held gloops of sleep in the corners. Carbo suspected his hair would have been a mess too, if it wasn't for the fact that he was completely bald.

Kahotep rubbed his face, and glared at Vespillo through his close-set eyes.

'Shit. It's you. Slave, why did you let them in?'

The girl shrugged helplessly.

'Your greetings are always so warm,' said Vespillo, smiling broadly. 'May we have a few moments of your time?'

'How much are you paying me?'

Vespillo looked over his shoulder. 'What's the state of your fire-fighting equipment? Do you have beaters and buckets of water at the ready? When was the last time you had an inspection?'

Kahotep let out an irritated grunt.

'Of course, there is no charge for the Tribune of our local vigiles,' he said, with a complete lack of grace. 'Come through.'

He showed them to two comfortable chairs on one side of a table in the tablinum and sat opposite them.

'So, Tribune Vespillo. To what do I owe this… pleasure?' The last word was forced out through clenched teeth. 'Is it about the murders?'

Vespillo's smile vanished. 'What do you know about the murders?' His voice was suddenly menacing.

Kahotep shrank back, spreading his hands before him. 'Only what everyone knows. That there is some crazy man killing randomly and leaving insane messages behind. A big man, with dark hair and a limp.' Kahotep gave a sidelong glance at Carbo, who frowned.

'If you know something you aren't telling me...' said Vespillo.

'I swear to Isis and Serapis I know no more than anyone else on the streets.'

'Make sure you come to me immediately if you hear anything. Understand?'

'Of course, Tribune. You know I would.'

'I know no such thing. Just remember how miserable I can make your life if I want to.'

'I never forget that. Well, it's been a lovely visit, so if that's all...' Kahotep started to rise, but Vespillo clamped his hand on Kahotep's forearm and forced him back down.

'Actually,' said Vespillo. 'That isn't why we came to visit.'

Kahotep's shoulders slumped. He flicked his fingers at his slave. 'Three cups of wine. Nothing too expensive.'

'Water for me,' said Vespillo. He looked at Carbo.

The greater part of Carbo craved the wine, but he took a deep breath and said, 'Water for me, too, please.'

Kahotep shrugged and waved the girl away. She hurried off and returned quickly with three cups and set them down before them. Carbo looked wistfully at Kahotep's wine, then took a sip of his water. It was flat and tasteless in his mouth, but he was more thirsty than he realised and he drained the cup quickly.

'So?' prompted Kahotep.

'You are aware my friend here suffered a tragic bereavement.'

'Yes, of course.' Kahotep looked at Carbo with genuine sympathy. 'I am so sorry. No one had a bad word for Rufa. A real loss.'

Carbo inclined his head, a lump growing in his throat that made it hard to speak or swallow.

'Yes,' said Vespillo. 'A wonderful woman, and truly loved by my friend. So imagine my feelings when Carbo told me he had been able to speak to her from across the Styx.' Vespillo's voice and expression were neutral, but Kahotep's eyes narrowed.

'He... what? How?'

'I thought you knew all about this sort of thing, wise one. Communing with the gods and the spirits of the departed.'

'Well, I dabble. It's not a precise art.'

'Carbo has been talking to a woman named Sitkamose.'

'That charlatan?' exclaimed Kahotep. 'She wouldn't know how to talk to the dead if they crossed the Styx to visit her personally for wine and honeycakes!'

'So you are saying she is lying to Carbo?'

Carbo felt a sudden unease at the back of his neck.

'Vespillo, what are you doing? Why are we here?' he said.

Kahotep looked from Carbo to Vespillo uncertainly.

'I... I wouldn't say she is lying. I mean...'

'Did you say you had three buckets or four?' asked Vespillo innocently, looking towards the peristylium. 'I really must arrange an inspection.'

Kahotep stared at Vespillo, then his shoulders slumped.

'She is conning you, Carbo. She just wants your money.'

Carbo froze. His skin became clammy and damp. His heart raced.

'No,' he said, his voice cracking. 'She can't be. It was her.'

'I know it seems real, Carbo. But listen to Kahotep. He knows what he is talking about.'

'But. It was her. I know it. Sitkamose knew too much about her to be lying.'

Vespillo looked to Kahotep who sighed. 'Sitkamose is good. Almost as good as me. When we say we are communing with the dead, we are actually reading your expressions, your words. We say vague things that could apply to anyone. We make guesses and when you respond positively we home in on those subjects. If we make a bad guess, we blame an evil spirit or that we can't hear the dead person properly. And we ask around to find out more. Did she know all about Rufa on your first or second visit?'

'The first visit was short,' said Carbo. 'She said she lost the connection and was too tired to try again.'

'And the next time she knew a lot more about Rufa?'

'Yes... but, how would she know that?'

'Carbo, you are notorious in the Subura. And what happened to Rufa is common knowledge, too. She wouldn't have to enquire too far before she had more than enough detail to convince you that she was speaking for her.'

Carbo shook his head. His hand trembled and he clenched it into a fist to hide it. He wished there was wine in front of him instead of water now.

'I don't believe it. It was her.'

Kahotep shrugged and sat back. 'Believe what you want. It makes no difference to me.'

Carbo looked at Vespillo. 'Why are you doing this to me?'

Vespillo put a hand on Carbo's shoulder. 'Maybe believing all this gives you some small comfort. But it doesn't help you, not really. You need to move on.'

'Move on? How can you say that?'

'I can say it because I know you can do it. I did, eventually, and you can too.'

Carbo shook his head. Anger and confusion warred inside him. He wouldn't accept Kahotep's words. He couldn't.

'Listen Carbo, maybe Kahotep is full of shit. It wouldn't be the first time.'

'Charming,' muttered Kahotep.

'I'm just saying, keep an open mind. Go and see her again. But test her. You aren't stupid. Ask her about something that only you and Rufa would know.'

Carbo stood abruptly. 'I'm not playing games, Vespillo.'

'Neither am I, friend.'

'I'm not so sure.' He turned his back and stalked angrily from the house.

–

When Vespillo caught up with him in his tavern, Carbo was staring into a full of cup of wine. Beside him was a plate of bread and olives, untouched. Marsia was fussing around, cleaning and tidying, and throwing him concerned glances.

Vespillo sat opposite him, but Carbo didn't look up. After a few moments of silence, Carbo said in a small voice, 'I'm too scared to go and see her.'

Vespillo gripped his wrist. 'I know. Do you want me to come with you?'

'I don't know. I'm embarrassed. Look at me. I'm shaking.'

'Carbo, after all we have been through together. After what I have seen you do. You believe I would think any less of you for this?'

Carbo shook his head.

'Thank you. I would appreciate the company.'

They walked together to Sitkamose's house, and when she answered the door to his knock, she gave him a broad, gap-toothed smile.

'Carbo, welcome back. I didn't think we had an appointment until tomorrow.'

'We don't but... can I talk to her? Are you available?'

'Yes, yes come in. And who is this?'

'Vespillo, Tribune of the vigiles,' said Vespillo politely.

'I see. I think you will find my fire-fighting arrangements are all in order. And there have been no crimes...'

'He is here with me,' said Carbo. 'He is a friend of mine.'

'Well, come in, come in. You are very welcome. Although there is a small extra charge for spectators.'

Vespillo looked around pointedly. 'I don't see a bucket of water or sand nearby.'

'But of course, a Tribune of the vigiles can observe for free,' said Sitkamose hastily, and Vespillo nodded a perfunctory thanks.

She ushered the two men into her chamber, and fussed around, lighting lamps and incense burners. When she was satisfied with the atmosphere, she sat across a small wooden table, and took Carbo's hands in her own.

'I have had little time to prepare today, I hope you understand. And the spirits are fickle. I don't know if she will come.'

'Try,' said Carbo, in a flat, firm voice.

Sitkamose gave Carbo a puzzled look. Then she closed her eyes, and began to mutter words that Carbo thought sounded Egyptian. He watched her face, saw her twitch and flinch, heard her raise her voice in what sounded like one side of an argument. Then she opened her eyes again and looked sorrowfully at Carbo.

'I'm sorry,' she said. 'I cannot reach her today. Maybe we could try next week. I will only charge you half price today...'

'No,' said Carbo. 'Try again. Try harder.'

Sitkamose glanced at Vespillo, alarm at Carbo's tone showing on her face. But she saw no support in the expression of the Tribune of the watch.

She tried again, muttering, arguing in her strange language. Then she became suddenly still. She stared straight into Carbo's eyes.

'I'm here, my love.'

A chill shot down Carbo's spine. Despite Vespillo's words, despite Kahotep's explanation, he *felt* her.

'Rufa. I... I miss you so much.'

'I know, Carbo.' The accent was Sitkamose's, but Carbo knew the words were coming from Rufa. 'Be strong. One day we will be reunited in the afterlife. We will be together again. Until then you must live your life.'

'It's so hard. I don't know if I can.'

'I know you better than anyone, my love. You are the strongest man I have ever known. You can do it. Be brave. For me. And take care of Fabilla.'

At this, Carbo's throat seemed to swell, making it hard to talk. He knew that he had neglected Rufa's daughter, her face a constant reminder of his loss. 'I will. I'm sorry I didn't do more for you when you were still... when you were with me.'

'You gave me yourself. That is all I ever wanted.'

'Do you still have the gift I bought you, just before you... before you left?'

'Of course.'

Vespillo squeezed Carbo's knee. Carbo looked at him questioningly. Then he knew what his friend wanted him to do.

It felt like a betrayal. To doubt her seemed like doubting her loyalty, her honesty, her love.

'You still wear that necklace? In the underworld?'

Sitkamose put a hand to her neck. 'Of course, my love. I never take it off. It reminds me of you.'

Carbo felt like a bucket of ice cold water had been dumped on his head. He struggled for breath for a moment. His last gift to her had been copper earrings. She had taken an age to choose them. It had exasperated and amused him. She had been killed not long after.

Vespillo watched his friend struggle, and put a gentle hand on his arm. Carbo shrugged it off, then leapt to his feet. With a roar, he slammed both fists into the table, splitting it into two.

The seer started to scream hysterically. Carbo clutched at his hair, trying to relieve the intense pressure building inside his skull. He spun and punched a wall, his fist penetrating right through the flimsy partition. He pulled it back and looked at the blood on his knuckles with a strange sense of detachment.

He turned to look at Sitkamose, who was cowering away from him.

'Carbo,' said Vespillo, his voice soft and low. 'You have your proof now. We can bring a prosecution. We can let it be known she is a fake, so she can't work any more. Let's go.'

Carbo regarded Vespillo for a long moment.

Then he threw himself at Sitkamose.

The old mystic was surprisingly nimble. She shrieked and ducked, and Carbo's arms grasped the space where she had been a moment before. He spun, braced himself to leap on her. Sitkamose backed against the wall, wide-eyed, face blanched.

Vespillo hurled himself through the air. He hit Carbo in the side of his chest with his shoulder, knocking the bigger man off balance. Carbo gripped his friend's arms, tried to prise them off.

'Run!' gasped Vespillo. 'I can't hold him long.'

Carbo roared in frustration and used his clenched fist to club Vespillo around the side of his temple. Vespillo's head snapped back, but he hung on tight.

'Run!' Vespillo cried again.

Sitkamose pulled her dress up around her knees and fled out of the house. Carbo lunged for her, breaking free of Vespillo's bear hug. But Vespillo stretched out and grabbed his ankle, and Carbo fell forwards, He lashed out backwards with his free foot, catching Vespillo in the nose, and blood flowed freely down into the Tribune's beard. Still the smaller, older man held on.

It was just long enough. Carbo kicked back again, the blow landing on Vespillo's shoulder and breaking the grip. Carbo jumped up, but the old lady was gone. He spun and stared furiously at Vespillo, balling his hands into tight fists, breathing heavily through flared nostrils.

Vespillo struggled to his feet, and wiped the blood pouring from his nose with the back of his hand.

'What are you waiting for, friend? You need someone to take it all out on? I'm right here. I won't even fight back. Just put me up against the wall and pound me until you feel better.'

Carbo glared at him, but made no move.

'But you won't feel better, will you? Rufa will still be dead, and you will still be a violent, drunk gambler, who people used to admire.'

The brutal words were like knives, twisting in his guts. He stared, open-mouthed.

'Vespillo,' Carbo said, his voice even. 'Go fuck yourself.'

He turned his back on his best friend, and walked away.

-

Carbo stalked into his tavern, slamming the door behind him. The few customers present looked up from their drinks in consternation. Most were regulars, and knew that Carbo in this sort of mood was not to be messed with.

For a moment he stood just inside the threshold, fists clenched, staring at the ground, breathing hard. Marsia hurried over to him, a cup of unwatered wine in her outstretched hand. He batted it away and she let out a little cry as the liquid sprayed across her and the cup cracked on the floor, the sodden straw carpeting the ground not sufficient to cushion its fall.

Shocked silence fell over the tavern. Carbo looked around him now for the first time. He saw Vatius, two legionaries from the Urban Cohorts, that odd veteran that he had met when gambling that time – he thought he had told him where to go already – and a couple he hadn't seen before. A young wealthy man, probably noble, and an even younger actor type.

'Everybody get out,' he said. His voice was low, but those who knew him understood the threat it held. Marsia retreated to the back of the bar. The legionaries hurried to finish their drinks. Vatius gave Myia a little fuss behind her ears and slowly stood with an exaggerated groan as he got his aching old joints moving. The odd veteran looked resentful, but he shuffled his stool back, preparing to leave.

Unfortunately, the nobleman did not know Carbo's reputation. He got to his feet slowly, drawing himself up to his full height, which was a good foot shorter than Carbo, adjusted his fine tunic and strode purposefully over to him. To Carbo's amazement, the rich young man prodded him in the chest and looked up at him with an expression of outrage and indignation.

'Now look here, you ruffian. Who do you think you are?'

'I'm Carbo,' said Carbo, surprised, presuming that would be enough.

'Well, listen here, Carbo. I think you can tell I am a man of importance. Of substance. And I will not take any nonsense from the likes of you. If I want to take a drink in this grotty establishment with my friend, I will do so. And I will stay for as long as I wish.'

Carbo's meaty hand shot out and grabbed the presumptuous nobleman by the neck. He thrust him back against the wall, and the back of his head thumped painfully against the brickwork. Carbo squeezed, slowly, relentlessly increasing the pressure. The nobleman tried to loosen the fingers with both hands, as his face turned red, then purple, then blue. His wide, panicked eyes began to roll upwards. Carbo squeezed harder.

'Master, please no. Think what they will do to you if he dies.'

Carbo looked at Marsia. At first her words seemed meaningless. Then rationality began to return. This man was important. Punishment would be certain and cruel.

He let go, and the nobleman slumped to the ground. His little catamite rushed over to him, stroked his hair as the choked man gasped air through his bruised windpipe.

Slowly, unsteadily, with assistance from his companion, the nobleman regained his feet.

'Get out,' said Carbo. 'And if I ever see you again, I will kill you.'

The nobleman fled, his lover chasing after him. The other customers filed out too, the legionaries looking shame-faced that they hadn't intervened, but clearly not foolhardy enough to risk a confrontation with an angry Carbo. Last to leave was the tall, scarred, muscular, but somehow broken veteran. He gave Carbo an odd look, then nodded to Marsia and left, closing the door behind him.

Marsia put a hand on Carbo's arm, but he shrugged her away, and slumped down on a stool.

'Get me another cup of wine.'

–

Carbo stared at the deep-fried canary on the plate before him, and tried to hold in the contents of his stomach. He couldn't remember much of the previous night, but he had flashes of memory involving Camilla, betting heavily on some dicing games, drinking, and possibly some fighting. His cheekbone throbbed and he reached up to touch it gingerly, wincing as his fingers made contact. He had definitely taken a punch there.

Marsia served a couple of customers, keeping delib-erately out of Carbo's way, looking away when he tried to catch her eye. She was obviously disappointed in him, but despite that she had gone out early to buy him his favourite hangover cure, and had it ready for him when he rose from his bed in the late morning.

He took a nibble from the breast meat. It was fatty, with a taste somewhere between duck and chicken. He nearly retched, but swallowed hard, and then ate some more. His stomach calmed infinitesimally.

The door opened and someone walked in. Carbo didn't look up until they came and sat next to him.

'You look like shit,' said Olorix.

'I feel worse,' said Carbo.

Olorix's expression was grave. 'You lost a lot of money last night, Carbo.'

Had he? Mercury's bollocks.

'A *lot* of money. You owe me big.'

Carbo took a sip of the water that Marsia had provided him, grimaced at its tastelessness and lack of warming afterglow.

'It will be fine,' said Carbo. 'I'll sort something out.'

'It's not that simple,' said Olorix. 'I have expenses. Pork nipple scratchings and nightingale tongue pasties don't grow on trees. And besides, if I let one person off payment, I will look weak. Others will try to take advantage.'

Carbo sat back and looked at him steadily. 'So? What am I supposed to do? I don't have the cash.'

'That isn't my problem now, is it? Where does one get cash in this city if one doesn't have any? Labouring at the docks? You should pay off your debt in a few years. Unfortunately I'm not that patient.' Olorix looked over to Marsia and signalled for a drink. 'Robbery? Extortion? You could even sell your body for sexual services. I'm sure there is some rich noblewoman who would love to bed a rugged veteran like yourself. Or rich noble*man*.'

Carbo gripped the edge of the table and half-rose, his posture full of menace. Olorix appeared unperturbed. He held up his hand, palm forward. 'Please, Carbo. With the sum you owe me, I could have you carted off into slavery. You're getting on a bit, and don't have the manners to be a house slave, but I think you could put a decent shift in at the mines.'

Carbo shuddered and sat down heavily.

'Oh, I forgot. You have been there already. I take it you don't relish the prospect of going back. In that case. Get. Me. My. Money.' Each word was like the crack of a whip as Olorix's tone sharpened.

Marsia approached the table with a cup of wine. As she placed it down, Olorix put an arm around her waist and pulled her close. He squeezed her backside, and she slapped his hand and stepped back, glaring.

'You know what, I would take this one. Full and final settlement. She wouldn't fetch the amount you owe me if you sold her on the open market. But I like her spirit. I would enjoy breaking it.'

Marsia looked at Carbo in alarm, and the mere fact that she thought he would agree made his heart sink. He looked down. 'You can have the farm,' he said quietly.

'I didn't hear that,' said Olorix, cupping his hand theatrically to his ear.

'I said you can have the farm,' said Carbo miserably.

'The olive farm in Campania? The one where you fought off those bandits so heroically? Back when you were still a real man?'

Carbo nodded. 'I'm sure that will cover it.'

'Master,' said Marsia tentatively. 'We need the income from the farm to keep the tavern afloat.'

'Then you will just have to work harder to make sure this place actually turns a profit. Go and fetch the deeds.' Carbo snapped. Marsia's eyes filled with tears, but she simply walked away. Olorix sat back and folded his arms, watching Carbo with a smug expression. Carbo swirled his cup of water, and suddenly craved a large cup of unwatered wine, despite the sickness and headache from the previous night's overindulgence.

Marsia returned with a scroll sealed with a wax stamp and handed it over to Olorix. Olorix broke the seal and scrutinised the contents. He nodded, then he stood and offered his hand to Carbo. Carbo looked at it, but made no move to take it.

'It's nothing personal, Carbo. The gods weren't with you last night. Maybe your luck will change. But if Fortuna does turn her face from you once more, just remember, I always recover what I'm owed.'

He left the tavern whistling tunelessly.

Carbo wasn't sure how long he remained sitting there, staring down without seeing. Rufa was gone. To have that connection dangled in front of him, then snatched away was agonisingly cruel. He hated Vespillo for doing that to him, whatever his motivation. He never wanted to see him again, nor that child of Rufa's whose every mannerism, facial feature, laugh, reminded him of her.

And now he had lost the farm, and he knew Marsia was right. Maybe if he could restrain his spending, his gambling and drinking, there would be enough left at the end of the day to keep the tavern from going under. But how was he supposed to stop those things, when they were all that stopped him from throwing himself into the Tiber with bricks tied around his neck?

The chair opposite him creaked as it slid back across the floor and someone sat down. For a moment he didn't look up. Then he felt a light hand hold his.

'Carbo.'

He sighed, then looked into Camilla's face.

'What do you want?'

'I thought you might need someone to talk to.'

'Why would you think that?'

'Olorix is bragging that he has stripped the tunic off the back of the great Carbo. He took your farm?'

Carbo clenched his jaw, then let out the breath he hadn't realised he had been holding and nodded.

'I'm sorry if it's my fault.' Her voice was small, and Carbo thought she sounded genuinely apologetic. He looked at her in surprise. 'Your fault?'

'I should have stopped you. You were betting too much, on all the wrong things. I tried to stop you, tried to tell you what to back, but you weren't listening to me. Your mood last night...'

Carbo watched her expression as she struggled for words.

'I hope I didn't frighten you,' said Carbo eventually.

Camilla looked surprised. 'Frighten me? No. Of course not. You were always courteous with me, even when you were losing and angry. Unlike with that rich fellow.'

Carbo rubbed his hand over his face. 'What did I do?'

'He deserved it. He kept making advances on you, even when you made it clear you weren't interested.'

'What happened?'

'He took offence at your refusal and set his muscle on you.'

'Oh. I'm guessing it ended badly.'

'You pummelled the bodyguard into the ground, then choked the man until he nearly passed out.'

'I didn't kill him?' Carbo asked, a sudden chill coming over him.

'No, no. But you did loudly tell him you would break his neck if you ever saw him again. You should have seen him run.' Camilla giggled but Carbo didn't join in. Advances from a man or a woman were equally unwelcome to him, and he felt justified in firmly rebuffing them. Especially when they wouldn't take no for an answer. But he was losing control too often. Briefly he wondered what he should do about it. Then he remembered what a state his life was in, grief mingling with the threat of financial ruin, and he found he could summon no motivation to change his behaviour even slightly.

'Why are you here?'

Camilla put her hand on his. 'I want to help.'

'Why?'

She didn't answer directly, but said, 'We can get your farm back.'

'Go on.'

'There's a horse race…'

Carbo put up a hand. 'Stop. I don't want to hear any more.'

'But Carbo…'

'You think the way out of bankruptcy due to gambling is more gambling.'

'Please, let me finish.'

'I need a drink.' He flicked his fingers at Marsia. She brought him some strong wine, making no comment and avoiding eye contact, though he couldn't help but notice the contemptuous glare she gave Camilla. He drank deeply, waited for the warmth to begin to spread from his centre, then nodded. 'Fine. Go on.'

'There's a race in the Circus tomorrow. The usual teams, three quadriga chariots each. The odds between the Blues and Greens are about the same.'

'So how do I make any money?'

'You are going to bet on the Whites.'

'The Whites? They never win.'

'Exactly. The odds are huge. You will quadruple your money.'

'You're missing the point, Camilla. The Whites never win.'

'Not in a fair race.'

Carbo sat back. 'I see.'

'This is big, Carbo. They have been working on this for months. They have people in the Blue, Green and Red camps.'

'Who are "they"?'

'You don't need to know that. All you need to know is that all the teams apart from White are going to suffer mysterious misfortunes. Drivers coming down sick. Horses badly shod. Axles falling apart. There is some big money going into this.'

'Won't the bookies get suspicious if too much money is bet on the hopeless underdogs?'

'These people aren't stupid. The bets are going to come from multiple sources, and will be spread out among all the bookies. Those guys are going to take a real hit, believe me. Including Olorix. He knows nothing about this.'

'Fine, you've convinced me. More or less. But you're forgetting one thing. I have no money. I can't put down a sestertius as a stake, let alone anything big enough to recoup my losses.'

Camilla looked around her meaningfully.

'The tavern? Camilla. It's all I have.'

'Word is, you won't have even this for much longer.' Camilla gripped his hands in both of hers and looked earnestly into his eyes. 'Come on, Carbo. You can get your life back on track. One big win, and you can start to move on. What have you got to lose?'

Carbo noticed Marsia was staring at him, her mouth open, expression dismayed. For a reason he couldn't quite put his finger on, her reaction irritated him.

'Tomorrow afternoon? White?'

Camilla nodded.

'Then I guess I need to go and see Olorix.'

Chapter Eight

Cicurinus watched the couple from a discreet distance, hidden by a thick tree trunk and the overcast night sky. They were in one of the gardens on the Pincian Hill, just north of the Quirinal. Technically the gardens were owned by some senator or other, but their gates were left open and were rarely patrolled by the owner's guards, and so they had become a popular location for lovers. The man Cicurinus was watching was called Quintus Servilius Ahala, Cicurinus had found out. It hadn't taken much asking, he was notorious. A rich man getting his kicks in the slums of the Subura, finding rough lovers that the higher echelons of society could not provide.

At that moment, Quintus was sitting on a marbled bench beneath an ornamental willow tree, whose branches, with few leaves left, dangled down over him, like a lover bending over to kiss his upturned face. His actual lover, a young boy who had probably not long ago cast aside his childhood tunic and bulla, was kneeling with his face buried between Quintus' legs, head bobbing up and down.

The act made Cicurinus nauseous and furious in equal measures. That Quintus was at least the one receiving fellatio instead of giving it should have mitigated the perversion – to be the submissive partner was even worse – but Cicurinus had no doubt this degenerate would be bending over and baring his arse to his young lover before long.

Cicurinus had argued with Veleda that night. She had chastised him for being too passive, too inactive. The implication of sexual passivity had hung in the air between them, shaming him.

In truth he had done little to advance his mission recently. The pain of his dental treatment had been so excruciating he had taken to bed for a whole day, despite Veleda's excoriating admonishments at his weakness. But he had refused the poppy juice and willow bark that the dentist had offered him, and felt more virtuous for his avoidance of the medicines. Pain was a part of his life, and it purified. When he had emerged from his bed, the swelling and throbbing from his gums had reduced enough for him to wear the wooden dentures the dentist had provided him with, at least for short periods at a time. He had been able to chew hard food for the first time in many years. He wasn't sure how that made him feel. Was meat a luxury? But it was a man's meal, and it gave him strength. Strength for his task of cleansing Rome.

And Quintus was just the sort of man that Rome needed to be cleansed of. Not only that, Carbo had assaulted and threatened him the previous evening. It was too perfect.

He fingered the blade concealed in a fold of his tunic. The edge was wickedly sharp. It should be, he had spent hours honing it. When was the perfect time? Quintus was emitting audible moans now as the boy moved faster. The moment was approaching. He stepped from the shadows. The boy's face was hidden in the folds of his lover's tunic, and Quintus' eyes were closed in ecstasy. Cicurinus drew the blade and approached silently.

A high-pitched giggle split the air. Cicurinus whirled around to see a group of youths approaching along the path between the trees. At the front a girl dressed in an overly revealing stola was bent double with laughter while a young man in a finely decorated tunic and ostentatious jewellery held her upright. Behind them were half a dozen others, men with arms around girls, smiling, laughing, singing, and weaving drunkenly towards them.

Quintus heard the group's approach as well, and shoved the boy between his legs hard, so he tumbled onto his backside in hurt confusion. Then Quintus saw Cicurinus and his gaze dropped to the knife in Cicurinus' hand. His eyes widened and he looked back at Cicurinus' face, squinting through the gloom to make out his features.

'Carbo?' asked Quintus. 'Is that you? Please. I didn't know you would be here. I didn't mean to offend you last night. I'm sorry. I'll never come near you again. I'll never even go to the Subura any more.'

The group of revellers were nearly on him. He hesitated. Veleda would be so disappointed. But he couldn't kill so openly. The young men of the group wouldn't stand by and let him murder someone before their eyes, especially when they were in the company of a group of girls they wanted to impress. Maybe he could overpower them, but it would be a risk. And if he failed, he was caught, or killed, his mission would be over before it had really got started.

He turned his back on Quintus, and on the approaching party, his mind in turmoil. He walked away, just remembering to affect a limp as he went.

–

The blood thumped in Cicurinus' ears. There was a pressure inside his head that he couldn't relieve, even when he pounded his temples with his fists. He gripped his knife hilt till his knuckles turned white.

The frustration of being so close to the kill, to that feeling of release and pride that it brought him, and then having it snatched away at the last moment, felt unbearable.

'Sestertius for a war veteran, Master?'

Cicurinus looked down. He had nearly tripped over the bundle of rags at his feet in his self-absorption, hadn't realised it was a person. Now he could see that it was a man, sitting against the wall of a shuttered shop. He wore a tattered tunic and a dirty cloak. His face was covered by a matted grey beard, and his hair was long and unkempt. His right leg ended at a stump above the knee. Beside him was a wooden crutch. He smelled of urine.

He could almost feel Veleda's powerful disapproval. He knew what she would say, if she was with him right now. Maybe she was. Maybe she was nearby, watching him, testing him. He looked around, but saw only the dark, empty street, the towering insulae on either side increasing the gloom as the moon tried to break through the cloudy sky.

When the derelict saw that Cicurinus had stopped, he held up a cracked clay dish and wiggled it hopefully. Cicurinus regarded him wordlessly for a long moment.

'Just a copper as?' said the old veteran, a slight tremor in his voice now. It was common for drunken revellers to give Rome's destitute a good kicking for a bit of wholesome fun, and the veteran would no doubt have received a few beatings in his time begging. But still he persisted, maybe driven by a hunger suggested by his emaciated frame.

'Please, sir. I was with the great Germanicus when he beat that Arminius bastard.'

Cicurinus stiffened. This broken human had taken part in the battles that revenged Rome on the victor of the battle of Teutoberg forest? That didn't seem right. Someone as weak as this had helped defeat the best of the Germans?

The conflict inherent in Cicurinus' position came to the fore. Was he doing this for Rome or Germania? Was cleansing Rome of its weak, making it more powerful and honourable, really helping his beloved Veleda and her people? His hand loosened on his knife hilt.

The beggar, taking Cicurinus' hesitation as a sign for hope, wiggled his empty dish again. 'You're a veteran too, aren't you, sir? I can tell. Did you fight the barbarians too? Spare a coin for one who didn't make it out whole, sir.'

That this could have been him, if fate had been slightly different, had not occurred to him. If a sword thrust that had missed his leg, that he maybe hadn't even noticed in the heat of battle, had instead been nudged by Fortuna two inches to the side so it penetrated his calf muscles, then maybe it would have been him lying in the street, leg amputated to stop the gangrene spreading, begging for coin to provide the bare minimum sustenance to stay alive. His hand moved towards his purse.

'Kill him.'

Veleda's whispered words were so close he could hear the breath caress his ear. How had she got so close without him realising? He froze, not turning, not speaking.

'He is your mission. Do not give in to pity, to mercy. Cleaning the streets of Rome of filth like this glorifies all nations.'

His breath came slow and even. His doubts melted away like the ice under the spring sun. He felt a serene calm descend on him. He watched the beggar's eyes with a sense of detachment as he clamped his hands around his neck, watched the panic flare and fade, ignoring the hands that clutched him feebly, the one leg that kicked, until all was still.

He stepped back and let the body slump to the ground, head lolling. The odour of urine was more powerful now, joined with the acrid stench of voided bowels. It gave an emphasis to his desire for purification. He looked around for Veleda, for guidance, approval, but she had disappeared, as silently as she had come.

He looked at the corpse, sitting in a puddle of its own excrement. He scooped some faeces onto his fingers, wrinkled his nose, tried not to gag. But no one would know why this wretch had died, if he did not tell them. Using the filth like paint, his fingers like a brush, he began to write on the wall.

—

'He wrote, "Rome will be purified of such as these," on the wall in the dead man's own shit!' said Vespillo, exasperated.

'Well, this killer is clearly insane,' said Pavo calmly, taking a nut from a small bowl on his desk and picking at the shell.

'Exactly!' said Vespillo.

'But I still don't understand why you have brought this to me. We discussed this before. This is what I like to call, "your problem".'

'You're a tribune of the Urban Cohorts. It's your job to keep the peace!'

'A murder or two does not disturb the peace.' He popped the nut into his mouth and crunched it loudly.

'That's easy for you to say. People are getting scared now. Everywhere I go, people are accosting me, asking me what I'm going to do about the killer. What am I supposed to tell them?'

'Everywhere you go?' said Pavo, rubbing his chin. 'And where is that exactly? The palaces of the palatine? The wealthy residences on the Esquiline?'

'You know where I patrol.'

'The slums, Vespillo. The criminals and the poor. No one that matters. Look at the people that are being killed, for Jupiter's sake. Prostitutes and beggars and thieves. The people I talk to believe this madman is doing Rome a favour.'

'The people you talk to? The Senators and Equestrians?'

Pavo nodded. 'People from those echelons of society, yes. And to my boss. Lucius Calpurnius Piso. You may have heard of him? Urban Prefect?'

Vespillo grimaced at the weak sarcasm.

'Look,' said Pavo, 'until this madman kills someone of importance, there is no appetite to do anything about him.'

'And when the poor of Rome erupt in riots because they fear for their safety? What then?'

'Well, then we crush them with my Cohorts. As you say, Vespillo, it is my job to keep the peace.'

'You know in my job, we prefer to prevent fires from starting, rather than fighting them when they have already burned down half the city.'

'Well, your track record there isn't exactly pristine now, is it?'

Vespillo glowered. It was hardly his fault a group of cultist arsonists had tried to destroy Rome, and without the valour of his vigiles, they may have succeeded.

'I'll look for this killer with or without your help, Pavo. But don't say I haven't warned you. There is more to follow.'

'Then we will cross that bridge when we come to it. Now if that's all, Vespillo.'

Vespillo didn't bother to bid him good day.

–

Carbo sat impatiently through the pre-race entertainment. The religious ceremony to open the afternoon's activities was endured by the crowd respectfully, not least because the Praetorians were out in force. Sejanus, the de facto ruler of Rome with Tiberius withdrawn to self-imposed exile in Capri, had decided to honour this relatively small half-day programme with his attendance, so everyone was supposed to be on best behaviour. But the first event, a foot race of two laps by half a dozen naked compet-itors was greeted with disinterest, and the small troupe of amateurish acrobats and tumblers that followed had the crowd booing and throwing soft fruit.

The execution of three criminals – Carbo couldn't quite hear what their offences were when they were read out, banditry he thought but he didn't really care – caught the crowd's interest briefly. But their method of dispatch, tied to posts and then savaged by large dogs, smacked of cheapness. No mock gladiatorial displays, no tigers or elephants. This was no *ludi romani* or one of the other lavish spectacles funded by the emperor. Probably it was paid for by a minor official trying to work his way up the *cursus honorum*, though Carbo was too far back in the crowd to hear the announcement of who was footing the bill. Sejanus must have had a quiet day to have bothered to attend at all.

But none of that mattered to Carbo. He wasn't here for entertainment. This was business. It was all or nothing today. Win big, or lose everything. Yet despite that, the sense of excitement in the pit of his stomach was like the hit from a draught of strong, expensive wine.

The chariots drove out onto the track, and at last the crowd went wild, whoops, shouts, jeers and cheers echoing around the vast stadium. Each team, Blue, Green, Red and White, sported three quadriga chariots, led by four horses in one row, their reins bunched in the fist of one charioteer per chariot. The Blue and Green chariots were the most ornate, brightly painted with their team colour inlaid with gold and silver. The charioteers' leather costumes, also dyed in their teams' colours, looked brand new. Their horses' tack was polished to a mirror-like shine, and the horses were well-trained, disciplined, finely muscled athletes.

By contrast, the Reds and Whites had an air of neglect. The chariots showed signs of damage from previous races, botched repairs not disguised by a thin veneer of paint. The horses were a combination of older beasts, past their best, and youngsters showing a lack of discipline, shifting restlessly in their yokes. These two teams felt like they were just there to make up the numbers, and while their charioteers may have hoped for a miracle win that could make their careers and have them snapped up by one of the big teams, the bookmakers didn't share their optimism. The odds on the White chariot that Carbo had bet the tavern on winning the race were twelve to one.

Olorix had taken his bet with surprise and delight. He had written Carbo a chit, confirming an agreed value of the tavern and all its contents at a price generous enough that Carbo could have no argument. Even so, he had hesitated. But Camilla, who now sat on his right, had encouraged him. She had told him to be brave and bold, and he would recover all that he had lost. Grateful for her support he had placed the bet, and they had walked together to the Circus, Camilla chattering inconsequentially, Carbo in brooding silence.

Now, as the horses lined up, one to each of the twelve starting gates, Carbo felt the familiar thrill, the tension in his guts. But this was no mere recreational flutter, something to numb the pain and take him away from himself for a brief moment. This was existential. All or nothing. It felt like the starting gate was his Rubicon, and the White team were his soldiers, lined up against Pompey and the forces of the Republic.

The Circus track was half a mile long, rounded at one end like the letter V when handwritten in the cursive style. Down the centre ran a decorated barrier called the spine, dotted with obelisks, statues of the most important gods, and pine trees. At either end of the track were conical turning posts, and large bronze dolphin-shaped lap counters were placed up high so they were clearly visible to the crowd. At the end of each of the seven laps, one would tip forward so all knew how long the race had to run.

An expectant hush descended on the crowd, so that Carbo could clearly hear the whinnying from the more excitable of the horses.

A trumpet blared.

The statues of men's heads and torsos that acted as gates sprung into the air. The horses lunged out of the stalls, the slack in the yokes was taken up and the chariots jerked into motion.

The dice were cast.

The crowd erupted into a cacophony of noise – cheers, boos, encouragement, threats. Some prayed loudly to Fortuna for success of their favourites, others chanted curses, begging the demons of the underworld to rise and destroy the chariots of their rivals.

On the track, the first half of the first lap was messy. Charioteers whipped their horses, then flicked their whips at each other. They guided their horses with four reins bunched in one hand, while keeping their balance and lashing out to the front and sides. No single chariot made significant progress in that initial dash for the first corner, though the lead Blue and Green quadrigas were ahead of those from the other two factions when they reached the turning post at the end of the spine.

This was when it got really chaotic.

With little to separate the teams, they all tried to corner together. Their positions in the starting gates had been chosen by drawing of lots, so it was luck that a Red chariot had the inside line, and theoretical shortest distance around the bend. But that was less of an advantage than it was to, for example, a runner on the inside lane of a curved track. The bend was impossibly tight for the horses, so they had to swing out to get a sufficiently large turning circle. And the teams outside them boxed them in preventing this.

The Blue chariot next to the Red on the inside track, which had pulled slightly ahead, swerved sharply inwards. Though the Red tried to respond, his horses leaning against their neighbours as they galloped, the Red charioteer whipping desperately at the Blue, it was hopeless. The more powerful, faster Blue quadriga drove the hapless Red into the turning post.

The inside horse went down, its cries as its front legs snapped like dry twigs lost in the noise. The weight of the recumbent equine dragged the rest of its companions inwards, and they too lost their footing. The chariot flipped, and the charioteer was thrown clear, landing with great fortune in the safe area within the central spine. He rolled and got to his feet, remarkably unharmed. He stared at the wreckage he had just cleared, then raised one hand to the crowd and walked away, cheers and boos following him.

'What a shipwreck!' exclaimed Camilla, eyes wide with delight. 'How did he get away with that?'

Carbo was more thoughtful. Even if the race was fixed, it could still all go wrong. A bad move by the White driver he had backed, a dirty move by another team, and his money, his tavern, could be gone like so much smoke in the wind.

Not every charioteer was as fortunate as the Red. The Blue quadriga that had been drawn in the outside gate had gone wide, hoping to avoid the melee that inevitably occurred at the first turn. But the Green on its inside saw the tactic and swung wide too, forcing his chariot outwards and into the Blues' horses. The chariots ran wheel to wheel, and the Blue charioteer drew the knife they all carried to cut themselves free in the event they got tangled in the reins during a crash. He slashed at the Green charioteer, opened a gash along the Blue's shoulder. The Green charioteer recoiled in pain, but yanked the reins left as he did so.

The outer wheel of the Blue chariot touched the perimeter wall and shattered into a thousand splinters. The chariot lurched to the side, tipped, and the charioteer disappeared under the wreckage. The horses stumbled, regained their footing, and ran on, dragging the broken chariot behind them. The crushed body of the Blue charioteer lay on the track unmoving, until the attendant slaves were able to safely rush over and drag him back to the spine, leaving a thick trail of blood in the sand.

All the other chariots made the first turn safely, and as they charged down the back straight, a lead began to open up between the more powerful, better funded Blue and Green teams and their poorer relatives, the Reds and Whites. Carbo noticed nervously that the White team he had backed – driven by a ridiculously young charioteer and led by a motley collection of a chestnut, a bay, a grey and a black horse that Carbo thought looked ready for the butcher – was second to last, only a Red team further back.

He glanced across at Camilla nervously. She grasped his knee.

'Don't worry, Carbo. They haven't planned anything for the first lap. It's important that there is nothing obvious that might allow the bookmakers to cry foul and invalidate the bets.'

Carbo nodded, a nagging doubt rising inside him. But as the race progressed, hope began to rise.

On the second lap, the leader, a Blue quadriga, had a sudden catastrophic failure. As it cornered tightly, the shaft attaching the chariot to the horses split in two. The chariot flew off at a tangent into the perimeter while the horses continued forward. The charioteer had wrapped the reins around his wrist and was yanked out of the chariot. The horses galloped on regardless of the charioteer's screams as he was dragged at high speed round the track. Eventually he managed to retrieve his knife from his belt and slash at the reins. He came free, rolling end over end until he came to a halt on the sand, sitting on his backside like a bemused toddler who had taken an unexpected tumble.

The second placed chariot, a Green, swerved to avoid him, but the next, another Blue, had sight of the track blocked by the Green and had no time to take evasive action. The Blue charioteer disappeared under the hooves and wheels of his team mate's quadriga, and when the chariot had passed his body was twitching feebly, hand stretched out towards the spine. Three more chariots passed over him before the track slaves were able to retrieve the corpse, by which time it resembled more bone and offal than a human. The slaves hurried back to safety with the pieces bundled in their arms, dripping gore down their tunics.

Over the next two laps, three more chariots, two Greens and a Red, withdrew with mechanical failure – snapped reins, a broken axle and loss of the pin that held the shaft of the chariot to the yoke. All managed to guide their chariots to safety and avoid the grisly deaths that had fallen their two competitors.

When Carbo's White chariot collided accidentally with another White along the home straight, Carbo thought his heart stopped. But it was the other team that went spinning out of control. The charioteer walked away from that crash but his horses were not so lucky, and they lay by the perimeter, a pathetically crying group of obstacles, attempting to rise on shattered limbs, forced to wait until the race was over so they could be mercifully dispatched.

With three laps to go, the last remaining Blue pulled off the track when one of his horses went suddenly lame. The Blue fans in the crowd yelled and hurled coins, stones and fruit onto the track in their anger. The Greens laughed and mocked their misfortune. The Praetorians loosened their swords in their scabbards, but in the absence of a threat to Sejanus, they kept their position.

On the next lap the last Green chariot inexplicably slowed, the horses tiring, breathing hard, until coming to a complete stop, heads down, snorting steam out of flared nostrils. No amount of whipping, shouting or pleading by the charioteer could exhort them to race again, and the best he could do was persuade them to walk slowly off the track.

As they entered the last lap, only three chariots remained; two Whites, one of which was Carbo's, and one Red. Carbo's White chariot was a horse's length in front of the other. The Red was half a lap back, its horses clearly winded. Camilla turned to Carbo, smiling broadly. 'I told you.' He nodded acknowledgement, but he would not believe he had won until it was over. Still, he allowed himself some hope, and his mind drifted to what he could do with the money. Repurchase the farm. Refurbish and restock the tavern. Buy a new slave to help Marsia. And then put his feet up, drink and gamble, in moderation of course, and begin to get his life back.

The final catastrophe happened so quickly, Carbo almost missed it, and he was only able to piece it together by replaying it in his mind over and over, after the event.

The White that Carbo had not backed had the inside lane as they took the final turn, but was clearly behind, and the inside advantage was not going to be enough to make up the distance. He couldn't work out if it was a tactic by the lagging White charioteer, or deliberate sabotage. If it was a tactic, it was a stupid one, costing the White faction a rare and heroic victory.

The trailing White charioteer yanked his reins to the left so his horses veered into the chariot Carbo had backed. The chariot flipped upside down, and the wooden edge landed heavily across its driver's middle, crushing his backbone and innards. The up-ended chariot acted like a brake, and the horses, no longer being whipped, slowed and stopped.

The other White chariot fared little better. The horses lost their footing, and tumbled over in a mess of broken legs and necks. The White charioteer, obviously prepared for disaster, leapt nimbly clear, and quickly made it to the safety of the spine.

The remaining chariot, the slow, lowly Red, rumbled past the wreckage, giving it a wide berth, and crossed the finish line with the speed and grace of a general in a triumph.

The crowd erupted, the delighted cheers of the few Red supporters drowned out by the fury of the fans of the other factions. Carbo stared in disbelief, not willing to accept what had happened. He turned to Camilla.

She was gone.

Chapter Nine

Carbo's feet took him automatically home, while his mind reeled in disbelief. It wasn't until he actually arrived at his tavern that he realised where he was. He reached out a hand, then pulled it back like the handle had been heated in a blacksmith's fire. He stared at the closed door, completely unable to force himself to open it. His legs trembled and a cold sweat broke out on his forehead.

The door flew open, and he had to stifle a cry of alarm. Two legionaries of the Urban Cohorts, mildly inebriated and laughing, emerged. They glanced at Carbo as they left, then did a double take as they realised who it was.

'Sorry mate,' muttered one, not meeting his eyes. The other one clapped him sympathetically on the shoulder and then they both moved on, continuing their banter, Carbo's misery instantly forgotten.

Standing a short way inside the tavern was Marsia. Her eyes were wet. Her expression combined the empathy of someone comforting the bereaved, with the fear of a newly orphaned child.

Carbo swallowed and stepped into the tavern. He glanced around. There were a few drinkers present, but a hush descended as they noticed Carbo enter. He looked around at his customers. A couple of vigiles he counted as acquaintances bordering on friends. A few local traders and craftsmen. Vatius, stroking Myia who was nestled into his lap. That odd veteran that had latched himself onto Carbo previously, before Carbo had sent him packing, sitting at a table on his own, wine and food untouched before him.

'Marsia…' He prepared himself for her anger, his well-deserved tongue-lashing for his stupidity, for ignoring her.

Instead she stepped forward and threw her arms around him.

'Master, I'm so sorry,' she said, voice thick with emotion.

The compassion was so genuine it took him completely by surprise. He had been prepared for anger, not kindness. It was too much.

He buried his face in her shoulder and sobbed uncontrollably, not caring that he was the centre of attention, that all his customers were watching with embarrassment this unmanly, un-Roman display.

Marsia ushered him away to the back room, away from the staring eyes, and sat him down on a stool. She fetched him a cup of strong, unwatered wine and encouraged him to take a deep drink.

When he had regained enough control to speak, he said in a small voice, as if a naughty child talking to his mother, 'I've lost it all, Marsia. First Rufa. Then my friends. Then the farm and all my money. And now the tavern. It was the last thing.'

Marsia knelt before him and put her head on his knee. 'You still have me, Master,' she said in a whisper. He put a hand on her head, stroking her hair, staring at the wall, eyes unfocused.

A call came from the tavern, 'Carbo, Marsia.'

'It's Vatius,' said Marsia. 'He probably wants a top-up.' She stood and adjusted her tunic, wiped the sleeve over her eyes, then disappeared off to serve the elderly philosopher. She returned a brief moment later. Her face was white, and her hands shook even though she had them clasped tightly in front of her.

Carbo slowly stood and followed her into the tavern.

Olorix stood in the centre of the room, grinning broadly. His hands were resting on his large belly, as if he was holding in an uproarious laugh. Behind him were half a dozen bodyguards, armed with swords despite Rome's laws prohibiting this. This was not a group that Carbo could fight, even if he was in peak condition, and the right frame of mind.

Olorix spread his arms wide. 'Carbo, Carbo, Carbo. What misfortune. I mean, not entirely unexpected. You did bet everything on the no-hoper. But it was brave, and it's tragic it didn't pay off for you.'

Carbo said nothing. What could he say?

'I have to confess, I have had my eye on this place for a while. I have a few businesses that supplement my bookmaking income, but this one has potential you know, despite the way you have run it down. Great location, and with a bit of imagination it could double up as a den for gambling. Turn the upper floors into cubicles for the girls to work in. Cock fights and boxing matches in the street outside. So many possibilities.'

Carbo's guts clenched. He felt all eyes on him, Olorix, his guards, his customers, Marsia. All waiting for a reaction. Waiting to see the old Carbo roar into life, thrash these interlopers within an inch of their lives, then throw them out on their backsides.

'Give me a few moments to gather my things,' he said.

A sigh went around the onlookers, a soft sound of disappointment.

'Technically,' said Olorix, 'All the contents of the tavern belong to me, too.'

Carbo hesitated. 'But I'm not an unreasonable man. Go and fetch some clothes and any personal items.'

With head bowed he went out of the back of the tavern. Marsia helped him put a few things in a bag, but in fact he had little in possessions, fewer that meant anything to him. When he had pulled the drawstring, he took his sword down from its place behind the bar, and strapped it around his waist.

'The sword isn't a personal item,' said Olorix.

'It's the most personal item I possess,' said Carbo, summoning a modicum of defiance.

Olorix shrugged. 'So be it. I have plenty.' He gestured to his guards.

Carbo couldn't bear to drag it out farther. Without even a last look around, he headed for the door, Marsia on his heels.

As Marsia passed Olorix, the fat bookmaker grabbed her wrist and pulled her back.

'Where do you think you are going?'

Marsia gasped.

Carbo stopped, the door open, and looked back.

'What are you doing, Olorix?' he said, his voice low, uncertain.

Olorix kept a tight grip on Marsia. He smiled, revealing two perfect rows of ivory dentures.

'The tavern, and all its contents, Carbo. Those were the terms of the bet.'

'That means the stores, the tables and chairs. Not the people.'

'Just the property, is that how you interpreted our bet?' asked Olorix, his grin broadening.

'Yes,' said Carbo firmly.

'No,' whispered Marsia and Carbo realised he had stepped straight into Olorix's trap.

'You are all witnesses,' Olorix said in a loud voice to all those in the tavern, the customers as well as his lackeys. 'Carbo has acknowledged that all property within this tavern is forfeit to me by the terms of our wager.' He turned to Carbo. 'Now tell me. I understand you have no legal training, but what is the status of slaves in law?'

Carbo stared in disbelief. 'Don't do this.'

'Property, is the answer. Isn't that right?'

'I free her,' said Carbo desperately. 'Right now, she becomes a freedwoman.'

Olorix shook his head sadly. 'You have no power to do that, Carbo. From the moment your chariot lost the race, she became mine.'

He spun Marsia to face him. 'She has spirit,' he continued. 'And is attractive, in a certain way. I think she can earn some money for me on her back, or on her knees. There is always a market for German slaves. Especially among those men who wish to prove their masculinity against the barbarians. You know the type. Wannabe legionaries who think it's brave to beat up a woman. It's risky for me, because the merchandise gets damaged, but charging premium prices can overcome that.'

Marsia was shaking violently from head to toe, trying in vain to stifle choking sobs.

'Or maybe I will keep her for my own private use. I really can't decide.'

'Let me buy her off you.'

Olorix let out a scoffing laugh. 'With what, exactly? You don't have a copper coin to your name.'

'I'll get it. I'll borrow, or find some work.'

'No, Carbo. I don't believe you are good for it. And even if I did, I wouldn't sell her to you. Can't you see how good it is for my standing around here. Not only do I now possess the great Carbo's tavern. I also own his prized slave. Maybe I will keep her chained to my bed. Or set her up with a mattress here and make her free for all to use. That would be good for business. And the people of the Subura will know who has true power around here.'

'Marsia,' said Carbo reaching out a hand. 'Come to me.'

Olorix pulled her behind him, and two of his guards took her arm. She struggled violently, and one of them cuffed her around the side of her head with an open palm.

She gazed at Carbo with terror in her streaming eyes.

'Master,' she said. 'Please.'

Carbo put his hand on the hilt of his sword. Two other guards stepped forward menacingly, weapons drawn. Carbo looked at them, then at Olorix, then at Marsia. Then his shoulders slumped. He turned his back and left the tavern that used to belong to him. Marsia's cries echoed after him as he walked away.

—

It had been the most joyous thing he had witnessed since he had returned to Rome. Cicurinus replayed the scene over and over in his mind as he walked slowly back to his lodgings, a broad smile lodged firmly on his face. The great Carbo, the hero the legionaries had talked about in Germany, the champion of the downtrodden in the Subura, who had cast him aside like a used rag. That Carbo had been completely humiliated by a fat, foreign bookmaker. Olorix had taken everything of material value from him. He was even going to break that uppity whore as well. It was all good.

But it wasn't enough. Cicurinus wanted revenge for himself. And though Olorix had taken Carbo's property, and humbled him, the man still had his reputation. He had heard the talk in the tavern afterwards, when Olorix had left, taking Marsia with him and leaving a nervous looking slave behind to run the place.

The vigiles had muttered to each other about the injustice of it all, how the man had saved the city, working alongside them, and this was his reward. One of the craftsmen had said loudly that it was a damn shame how far someone so honourable had fallen, but he was sure that he had it in him to rise back up again. The old philosopher, who was holding that runty dog protectively in his arms, said something about Euripides, and whom the gods wanted to destroy, and how gambling was a form of madness.

It just made Cicurinus more sure of his course. Yes, his mission of purification was the priority. But in doing so, he could destroy Carbo, so he would never rise again.

–

He still had friends. At some level, deep inside him, he knew that. But he felt totally alone. How could he ask for help when he couldn't bear to see anyone? What would Vespillo say to him right now? What would he be thinking? Even if he threw his arms around him and told him everything was going to be fine, and we all make mistakes, Carbo knew what would be in his head. How did you let it come to this? What became of you?

He limped through the dark streets, head down. His leg ached worse than ever. It was raining, the late autumn precipitation feeling like a thousand pinpricks on his skin. He wandered down the main street through the Subura, the night-time wheeled traffic splashing mud and effluent over his lower legs.

He considered just laying down in front of an ox cart. The driver wouldn't see him in the dark. The dumb beasts wouldn't stop for him. The wheels, pressed down by their heavy load, would crush his body. Would it be quick? He didn't really care. Would it be certain? He was less sure.

He turned off the main thoroughfare and ambled down a side street. The people out in the streets of the Subura that late were hurrying to be home, were homeless, or were loitering with intent. The homeless and those on their way home gave Carbo's bulky figure a wide berth. Those with more mischief in mind watched him with interest, but the sword at his belt suggested no easy mark, and they left him alone.

He came across a run-down tavern that he had never visited before. The door was shut, the tables and stools that would have lined the street in the day time were stowed safely away inside. He pounded on the door. There was no response. He thumped again, hard, and yelled loudly. 'Open up!'

He heard movement from inside. The sound of a wooden bar being lifted. The door opened a crack.

'What do you want? It's the middle of the night!'

'I need a bed.'

'We're closed.'

The door began to shut again. Carbo leaned his shoulder against it and pushed. Despite the man inside desperately trying to prevent him, he eased the door wide open and stepped inside.

The tavern-keeper was a slim, bald man with a sparse beard and large, red birthmark across his forehead. He took in Carbo's size and his sword, and stepped back, hands held forward in a gesture of peace.

'Please, I have little.'

'I need a bed,' repeated Carbo.

'Uh… of course.'

'Show me my room.'

The tavern-keeper hurriedly led him through to a small room at the back. 'You can sleep here, sir.'

Carbo entered and looked around. The room was about six foot in width and length, just enough space for a stone bed that protruded from the wall, with a rough straw mattress atop it.

'It's one sestertius for the night,' said the tavern-keeper, lighting a small oil lamp.

Carbo turned and with one hand on the man's chest, pushed him gently out of the room. He closed the door on him, and stared at the flickering flame from the lamp for a moment. Then he propped his sword in the corner, sat on the bed and put his face in his hands.

He didn't cry. He was too numb for that. His situation was beyond his comprehension. He couldn't understand how he had arrived here. It seemed unreal. Many times he had had nightmares, of being in battle, of his torture in Germania, of his time as a slave in the mines, and yet he had always known even in the depths of sleep that they weren't real, that he would awake.

This was real.

And he could envisage no way back.

He reached out and picked up his sword. Ran his thumb along the edge. Still keen enough to draw blood.

There was a way out. It was a path trodden by honourable Romans through history. Like Brutus, when all was lost.

He held the sword by the blade and placed the hilt in the join where the stone bed met the floor. He placed his finger on the tip, felt the sharpness indent the pad. He stood before it and pressed the end of the sword into his belly, the blade angled up through his liver into his chest.

He stayed in that position for a long moment. Was he doing this right? Was this what he wanted? What happened next? Would someone take care of his funeral, so he could cross the Styx to Hades? Or would his wrongdoings destine him for Tartarus and eternal torment? Or would he be thrown into the Tiber, no rites to ensure his onward passage, so he was doomed to walk the earth as one of the lemures?

Or was there nothing at all, as some people said? Just oblivion? It was hard to imagine not existing at all, but at the same time it sounded like an end to pain. And that was what he wanted, more than anything else.

He clenched his jaw. Took deep breaths. Prepared himself for the brief agony, to be followed by the ending. He clenched his fists. Shut his eyes.

Rufa was before him. Looming out of the darkness behind his closed lids. She didn't say anything but her expression was one of supreme sorrow.

'Please,' he whispered. 'Don't stop me. Let me do this.'

Still she said nothing. Remained still. But a tear welled in the corner of one eye, rolled down her face.

'I want to be with you.'

Now she shook her head, a small movement, but a clear refusal.

Carbo roared in frustration. He stepped back, kicked the sword so it clattered across the room. Then he grabbed the hilt, ripped off his tunic, and drew the edge in a swift slide across his chest.

The pain was delayed by just a moment. It hit him at the same time the blood began to flow in rivulets down his skin, over his belly. He cast the sword aside, and threw himself onto the bed, on his back. He gazed at the ceiling, focusing on the throbbing, the stinging, as his blood soaked the mattress.

Chapter Ten

It was simple enough to find out where Quintus lived. Just a few queries in the right places, a simple lie that he had to make a delivery to the house of the wealthy Equestrian's son. Now, late at night, he waited in the shadows of a small public garden by the Equestrian's sumptuous domus, high on the Viminal hill. The moon had broken through the cloud, bathing the well-to-do area of the city in a beautiful pale light.

Maybe it wouldn't be tonight. If not, he would return another night. And another. He had time. Nothing but time. He caressed the hilt of his sword, the feel of the ridges against his palm soothing him.

The moon moved slowly across the sky as the hours slipped by. From time to time he imagined he saw Veleda, white-robed, standing under a tree and watching him steadily, or walking past in the distance, glancing sideways at him from under the folds of her palla. But each time when he looked harder, he realised it was just a trick of his mind – a statue, an ordinary passer-by. Still, it wouldn't surprise him if she was lurking nearby. She always seemed to know what he was doing. He would do his best for her.

A figure came out of the house. It paused for a brief, argumentative conversation with the night porter stationed just inside the door in the vestibule. Then it scurried out into the city.

Cicurinus followed at a discreet distance behind. The hooded figure glanced around him frequently, looking like a mouse who had bravely come out to nibble at crumbs on the kitchen floor, while keeping an eye out for the cat. But Cicurinus kept far enough away that he was either not seen, or not considered a threat.

The man moved quickly through the city, skirting round anyone who looked like trouble, until he came to an insula in the northern part of the Subura. A rickety wooden staircase clung to the side of the building, and the man quickly ascended, two steps at a time, until he got to the top floor. He knocked three times, and looked around nervously while he waited. Although he had been in no doubt, Cicurinus now clearly saw the features of Quintus Servilius Ahala. Then the door opened and he ducked inside.

Cicurinus slowly climbed the staircase. Each step creaked with his weight, the noise loud in his ears. When he reached the top he paused. He closed his eyes, and took in a deep breath through his nose, then slowly exhaled. One more breath, in and out. He was ready.

He kicked the door hard. The latch snapped, some of the shoddily nailed-together planks splintered apart, and the door flew backwards with a mighty crash. He stepped into the tiny, dark apartment.

Quintus and his lover – Kyros, Cicurinus had heard him called, – had wasted no time. Kyros was sitting on the side of his bed, fully naked, legs open. Quintus was kneeling between them, holding his stiff cock in one hand, looking up into his lover's eyes. They both stared at him, a frozen tableaux of fear and guilt.

He drew his sword in one smooth motion.

'What do you want with us?' gasped Quintus in a voice that shook in terror.

'You know why I'm here. Your perversions bring shame on the city and its people. One in your position, son of a nobleman. On his knees like a submissive whore. You make me sick.'

'We aren't hurting anyone.' Quintus' tone was shrill.

'You are injuring the dignity and majesty of Rome itself. How will our Empire stay great, and be a worthy opponent to the noble barbarians, if it is home to such as the pair of you?'

Quintus shuffled round, still on his knees, so he was facing Cicurinus. He put his hands together. 'Please, don't do this.'

Cicurinus lifted his sword.

'Carbo, no!' screamed Quintus. Cicurinus smiled broadly. Shadows concealed his scars, and Quintus had taken his bulk and dark hair to be Carbo, once more. The walls of these apartments were as thin as parchment. Carbo's name would have echoed around the entire building for all the residents to hear. This is why the gods had stayed his hand two nights prior, sent those youths to stop him killing Quintus and his lover at that moment. Because now he could escape easily, but there would still be witnesses, and Carbo would be condemned.

He thrust his sword forward, one smooth stab. It penetrated between the ribs, straight into Quintus' heart. The young nobleman stared down at the weapon protruding from his chest in disbelief. Then he toppled backwards, blood fountaining out of the rent in his torso.

Kyros shuffled backwards on the bed, letting out a high-pitched, girlish scream that went on and on. Cicurinus advanced on him, and the scream changed into a series of panting howls of despair. The naked boy held his hands before his face in a futile warding gesture.

Cicurinus stabbed him in the groin. The sword penetrated up through his genitals and into his guts. The boy's scream turned inhuman, the dying howl of a wild animal. Cicurinus withdrew his blade and for a moment regarded with satisfaction the mess he had made of the boy's lower body. Then he pulled his arm back, and thrust the blade straight through the boy's open mouth, so the tip burst out of the back of his head.

The boy instantly went silent, body stiff, and his eyes rolled up into his head. Cicurinus let him slip off his sword and onto his back.

Then he dipped his sword in the copious blood, which was already starting to drip through the floorboards into the apartment below, and using the tip of the sword as his stylus, and the wall as his tablet, he began to write.

—

'This has gone too far!' said Pavo, knuckles on his desk like a gorilla, his face so close to Vespillo's that he could feel the breath and the spittle, smell the onions from his last meal. He wasn't in the mood for this. He had been up all night directing the vigiles fighting a fire in a warehouse by the Tiber. It had been a big one with the potential to spread further. It took until dawn to get it under control, and the sun was poking over the horizon by the time he got home, to find a messenger summoning him to a meeting with Pavo. He hadn't had time to change or wash, and his tunic, hair and beard still smelled of smoke, and his eyes stung like they had grit in them.

'There is no need to shout. I can hear perfectly well.'

'I'm not shouting!' shouted Pavo.

'May I ask why it has gone too far now?' Vespillo asked innocently. 'What bridge was crossed that was one too many?'

'Don't try to be smart, Vespillo. It doesn't suit you. You know exactly why.'

'Because this time someone who matters is dead.'

'Because this time, Someone-who-matters' son is dead, and Someone-who-matters is ready to start throwing bodies to the beasts until the killer is caught.'

'Getting your balls twisted now, are you? Maybe if you had listened to me sooner...'

Pavo slumped into his chair, the anger dissipating to be replaced by despair.

'I'm in trouble, Vespillo. I don't need shit from you, too.'

Vespillo frowned. 'Trouble?'

'Lucius Calpurnius Piso.'

'What has the Urban Prefect got against you?'

Pavo sighed. 'I was at his domus on the Palatine, at a party. I had had one too many. For some reason we were talking about Caesar. Julius Caesar. I made some joke about wishing I had a wife like Calpurnia, who would let me screw as many other women as Caesar had.'

'And?'

'Calpurnia was his older sister.'

'Calpurnia? I feel like I should have known that. But... she is part of history. How old is Piso, anyway?'

Pavo shrugged. 'In his seventies? There was quite an age gap between him and his sister. But clearly there is still a lot of filial loyalty there. I was given a stern dressing-down and a lecture on the morality and faithfulness of his sister, who was clearly a paragon of traditional Roman womanhood. Not to mention an admonishment of my slur on the divine Caesar, grandfather by adoption of our own dear Emperor. All in front of a crowd of nobles and other people who matter.'

'Oops,' said Vespillo, knowing he should be more sympathetic, but still smarting from Pavo's neglect of the previous murders.

'So I've not been in Piso's good books for a while, and he'll jump at any excuse to drum me out of the Cohort. On the other hand, he is getting it in the ear from this dead boy's father, Titus Servilius Ahala.'

'The name rings a bell, but I don't really move in those circles.'

'He made a fortune in cheese and honey when he was financial procurator of Raetia, and now he performs some sort of judicial role in the law courts. He is an equestrian, but he is rich enough for senatorial rank, and is hoping to get promoted by getting in with Sejanus. He is not a man to mess with.'

Vespillo whistled. This killer had really stirred the hornets' nest. There was no way the authorities would turn a deaf ear now.

'So what do you want from me?'

Piso's tone became more pleading, ingratiating. 'Look, my friend. Investigating murders in the grubby parts of the city isn't really my thing. It's much more up your street. And you have been looking into this already. All I'm asking is you continue to do your job. Find out who is behind this, and let's get them nailed to a cross, before I'm out of a job.'

'Before he kills again, you mean.'

'Gods yes,' said Pavo. 'Just imagine if he killed someone else important.'

Vespillo let the man's bigotry pass. It was just ingrained in Roman culture, to look down on those below you in the social strata. But Vespillo lived and worked among those who were deemed unimportant by the elites, and to him they mattered.

'I intended to do so anyway.'

'Good man,' said Pavo, and the relaxation in his shoulders told of his relief, like the burden had been removed from him and given to someone else. 'Of course, I'll give you any assistance in my power.'

'I appreciate that,' said Vespillo, wondering what use Pavo could possibly be. But maybe at some point he would want to use the Urban Cohorts for some muscle. And it wouldn't hurt to have Pavo owe him a favour in the future. 'I'll do what I can.'

Pavo reached for a jug of wine on his desk and poured some of the thick red liquid into a delicately decorated glass. He offered it to Vespillo. 'Join me for a drink.'

'Thank you, but not at this time of the morning. I'm going to head over to the insula where the murders took place and see what I can find out.'

'Suit yourself,' said Pavo, and tipping his head back, he poured the wine into his mouth.

–

Vespillo looked around the blood-spattered room. It was dingy and small. The mid-morning light, filtered through an overcast sky threatening rain, provided enough illumination to see by, while tingeing everything a gloomy grey.

The bodies had been removed before he arrived, of course. The corpse of the son of a prominent equestrian could not be allowed to lay where it was where any riff-raff, such as himself, could lay eyes on it. So too, the body of the actor boy who had been found with him. The shame of the company the young nobleman had kept at the time of his death would remain theoretically confidential, albeit widely discussed by all levels of society. The semblance of secrecy though would be enough to maintain the father's dignity.

He had been told about the wounds on the bodies, observed by the first vigiles on the scene, before the rich young man had been returned to his family, and the young actor hauled off to be thrown into a mass grave outside the city walls. He had never seen what anyone could call a gentle murder. Even for bloodless deaths like strangulation, the violence showed in the bruises around the neck, the bulging, staring, bloodshot eyes. But these killings seemed particularly vicious and violent, as if the point had not just been the deaths themselves, but the manner of the deaths. The now-familiar words daubed in blood on the walls emphasised the point.

Rome will be cleansed.

Vespillo replayed the scene as best he could in his mind. He examined the spot where the nobleman's son, Quintus, had been found. A large sticky pool of congealed blood marked the location, just in front of the bed. And on the bed itself, more blood soaked into the mattress, and the spray of arterial blood up the walls, consistent with the reported stab wound to the groin.

'Do we know who the boy was yet?' Vespillo asked the watchman standing guard. The man shook his head. 'Has anyone talked to the neighbours?' The man looked at his commander in surprise.

'I was just told to stand guard.'

Vespillo suppressed a wave of annoyance. Of course the fireman–nightwatchman wouldn't have thought it was his job to go investigating the crime. Why would it be?

'Stay here, I'm going to see what I can find out.'

He exited the small apartment and walked down the external staircase to the floor below. The door to this apartment looked in slightly better shape than the one to the murder scene, which was expected – lower floors attracted higher rents, not least because you were more likely to escape alive in the event of a fire – but the difference was marginal. He knocked loudly.

For a while he thought no one was in. Then he heard a shuffling noise, and the door opened a few inches.

'What is it?' croaked an elderly man, face lined and weathered, his bald pate greasy and scabby, with fluid running down his cheek from one rheumy eye.

'I'm Tribune Vespillo of the vigiles. Can I talk to you for a moment?'

'Eh? You're who?'

Vespillo raised his voice.

'I'm Vespillo. From the vigiles.'

'What do you want? Is there a fire?'

'I want to ask you about last night. Did you hear anything?'

'Did I what? Speak up lad.'

'I said,' said Vespillo, nearly shouting, 'Did you hear anything unusual last night?'

'No, no, no. Quiet as a mouse sneaking past a cat.'

'Two people were killed upstairs. You didn't hear anything?'

The old man looked shocked. 'No, not a thing. It must have been some sort of demon, to kill two people so quiet, like.'

Vespillo sighed. 'Did you know the boy who lived in the flat above you?'

'Kyros? Is he one of the dead 'uns?'

'I'm afraid so.'

The old man's face dropped. 'He was a good lad. Actor type. And… well, you know what other job actors do. He took plenty of men up there. Different one most nights. All sorts they were – working men, soldiers. One man was a regular though, a noble sort.'

'He's dead too.'

'Ah. Poor Kyros. He used to go to the market for me. I don't manage these stairs as well as I used to.'

'I'm going to find out who did it,' said Vespillo with more confidence than he felt.

'You're what?'

'I'm going to find out who did it!' shouted Vespillo. A couple of passers-by at ground level looked up curiously at the man shouting on the stairs above them.

'Good for you. Kyros didn't deserve that.'

Vespillo loudly thanked the man for his help, and descended another floor. The young mother, with a crying babe in her arms and a toddler clutching her leg and staring up at Vespillo unblinking, was also little use. She thought maybe she had heard something, but then the baby had started to wail, and she had thought nothing more of it.

The other occupants of the insula were of no help. Even trying the apartment on the other side of the building which shared a dividing wall with Kyros' apartment was pointless, since it was currently vacant. He trudged back down to ground level, dog tired, sleep a distant memory. He looked up at Kyros' apartment, and saw how the insula leaned outwards into the street, a deliberate design to maximise the living space without increasing the footprint on the ground. But due to shoddy workmanship, the gap between the top floor of this insula and the one on the other side of the street was a bare few feet apart, near enough to easily toss a ball from the window of one apartment to the other.

Groaning inwardly at the prospect of another tall, rickety staircase to climb, he trudged up to the top floor of the insula across the road and hammered firmly on the door. Almost straight away it flew open, and Vespillo found himself confronted by a red-faced, plump woman.

'What do you want?'

'I'm Tribune Vespillo…' he began.

'Oh, the vigiles. I was wondering when you would show up. Took your time.'

'I…'

'I suppose you're here about the murders.'

'I'm… what?'

'Doesn't surprise me one bit, what with all the goings-on in that apartment. You can see everything from here you know. He doesn't even close the shutters half the time. And I've got a daughter. It ain't right.'

Vespillo felt he was losing control of the conversation. 'You saw what happened?'

'Not saw, no. He was more discrete when he had someone posh with him. But I heard plenty. All their little chit-chat, and their filthy noises. And then their screams. Frightened us to death, me and my daughter. "Where are the vigiles?" I said to her. "We could all be murdered in our beds and all they care about is putting out fires."'

Vespillo bridled at the unfairness. Two of his men had been badly injured the previous night, stopping the fire spreading to residential areas, where it would have killed many, especially those at the top of insulae, like this woman. But he held his tongue.

'Did you hear anything apart from screams?'

'Oh yes. I heard that nobleman begging for his life. I mean, dirty immoral man yes, but he didn't deserve to die like that.'

'What did he say exactly?'

'He said something like, "Please don't do it." Then he screamed, "Carbo, no!"'

Vespillo felt like a bucket of ice-cold water had been thrown over him.

'Say that again,' he whispered. But the woman babbled on.

'Then his cries were cut short pretty quick. But the boy carried on screaming. My daughter was crying her eyes out. Then he screamed even louder, then he stopped. And that was it.'

'He said Carbo? You're sure? It couldn't have been something else? Like Cilo? Or Cato?'

'No,' she said firmly. 'Definitely Carbo. Clear as a bell. I'll remember that man's last words to my dying day.'

–

Carbo's fitful sleep was punctuated by horrible visions of normality. Sitting in the tavern with Marsia. Having a drink with Vespillo. His arms around Rufa. Each time, he woke with a start, the brief lingering happiness that the scenes engendered deep inside evaporating as memory crashed back upon him. The windowless room gave him no indication of the passing of time, so he had no idea whether it was midnight or midday when he was woken fully by a heavy banging at the door. The oil lamp had long since guttered out, and the small cubicle was pitch black.

He stared towards the door, then rolled over and closed his eyes. The hammering came again, and a familiar voice yelled, 'Carbo. Open up. I know you're in there.'

He blinked hard, sat up, rubbed his palm across the growth of stubble. How long was it since he had last shaved anyway?

'Carbo!' More hammering.

He felt around for his tunic and pulled it over his head, then staggered over to the door. He fumbled with the bolt and then opened the door to let a crack of daylight in. Although the light was filtered, having first passed through the tavern beyond, it was bright enough to make him squint at the bearded face before him. But of course he knew who it was. Who else?

He turned his back and returned to his bed, flopping down onto it, facing the wall. The door creaked open to its full extent, flooding the room with an illumination that even pierced his closed lids.

'Get up, Carbo. I need to talk to you.'

'Fuck off, Vespillo. I don't need your pity and I don't need your help.'

'Carbo,' said Vespillo more firmly. 'Get up.'

Carbo frowned at the tone. It didn't sound pitying or solicitous. He swung his legs over the edge of the bed and sat with his head in the palms. Hunching forward squashed the skin on his chest and the self-inflicted wound stung suddenly. It felt good.

'Carbo, I'm sorry about what happened to you…'

'Save it.'

'I need to know where you were last night.'

Carbo looked up at his friend sharply. Now that his eyes had had time to adjust, he could focus on his features more clearly. The expression was not that of one who had come to lend a fallen friend a helping hand. There was worry yes, but something else. Suspicion?

'What's it got to do with you?'

'Answer my question. Where were you? Were you drunk?'

'Not drunk enough,' said Carbo. 'I was here.'

'And before you were here?'

'I don't know. I walked. I had just been thrown out of my home. You know that, right? I had just had everything taken from me. I wasn't keeping notes about which streets I wandered down.'

Vespillo pursed his lips. 'What time do you think it was when you got here?'

'How the fuck should I know? My portable sundial doesn't work at night!' Carbo was irritated by the stupid question. The day was divided into twelve equal hours spanning sunrise to sundown, so the length of the hour changed with the seasons. The night was similarly divided, but unless someone was paying particular attention to the movement of the celestial objects, time at night was an imprecise and uncertain measure.

'Don't be smart,' said Vespillo, voice tight. 'I just meant roughly. Did you see the position of the moon when you got here?'

'No I didn't. Why would I? Listen, just tell me why you are here, or get the fuck out.'

Vespillo took a breath, then said evenly, 'There were more murders last night.'

Carbo frowned. 'And? I'm not really in a position to help you with an investigation Vespillo, even if I had the inclination. I have enough to worry about.'

'Witnesses at this and the previous killings saw a big man with dark hair and a limp leaving the scene.'

'Well that narrows it down. I can't imagine in a city of a million people, full of veterans and cripples, that there would be many tall people with a limp.'

'Last night was different. A witness heard the victim cry out before he died. He said, "Carbo."'

Carbo stared at Vespillo, uncomprehending. Carbo was not a particularly common name. He was aware that there had been a family of Carbo's that had held various offices a hundred years before, but they fell out of power in the convulsions of the end of the Republic. Carbo didn't know if they were distant relatives, or if he had a slave ancestor who had been given their name on his manumission. He liked to think it was the former, but he suspected the latter. There were certainly a handful of Carbo's around in Rome with a variety of skin tones and body types suggesting that at least some of them were the descendants of freedmen of the old family rather than directly from the noble Carbos.

But the name was rare. Carbo didn't even have any family. Father long dead. Mother more recently. A half-brother that his mother had produced, some time after the death of his father, also dead now.

'The witness misheard,' said Carbo.

'She doesn't think so,' said Vespillo.

Carbo cocked his head to one side, unable to believe what he was hearing.

'Let me get this straight, old friend' – he emphasised the word 'friend' sarcastically – 'you think I did this?'

Vespillo ran his hand through his hair.

'I don't know what to believe, friend.' Unlike Carbo, Vespillo used the word sincerely. 'But this is a real mess. The last fellow who was murdered was important; An equestrian's son. Someone who matters, as Pavo puts it. This isn't going to go away. I just need to look into your eyes and hear you tell me it wasn't you.'

Outrage washed across Carbo.

'Are you serious? After all we have been through together?' He stood, stepped forward, towering over Vespillo. 'You really think me capable of that?' His voice was rising in his indignation.

Vespillo took a step back and his heel clanged against something metallic. He turned, bent down, and picked up Carbo's gladius from the floor where it had been discarded the previous night. He held it by the hilt and angled the blade into the light so he could see it clearly.

The congealed blood along the edge was clearly visible, spattered like someone had spilled redcurrant jam over it.

'Oh, Carbo.'

Carbo stared at the blood, mouth open. 'That's not... I mean...' How could he explain the desire to inflict a wound upon himself to Vespillo. He would never understand, even if he believed him.

'Listen, come with me to the station. I'll pop you in a holding cell. It will be safer for you. People are angry about this.'

'Vespillo. You can't possibly think this was me.'

'What am I supposed to think, Carbo? Look at the state of you. And now we have witnesses – your appearance, your name, and a sword covered in blood. Let me take you in, and we can see about getting you a light sentence, after all you did for the city. I'm sure we could get Sejanus to commute the death sentence to exile.'

'I haven't even had a trial, and you have convicted me already!'

'Carbo...'

'No! You call me friend, and then accuse me of murder. Give me my sword back, and get the fuck out!'

Vespillo shook his head sadly. 'I can't do that.' He held the blade before him, not pointing at Carbo, but ready to strike if there was trouble. A black anger overwhelmed Carbo. Vespillo must have seen the change in his eyes, and raised the sword.

Carbo struck like a snake. For such a big man he could move with amazing rapidity. One hand grabbed the wrist of Vespillo's sword hand, slamming it against the wall, while his other reached for Vespillo's neck.

But Vespillo was no stranger to a tussle. A veteran of many years in the legions, and almost as many in the vigiles, dealing with the violent criminals of Rome's underclasses, he knew how to fight dirty. He batted Carbo's outstretched hand aside with his forearm, then brought his head sharply forward. His thick skull smashed into Carbo's face, who turned aside just enough to take the blow on his cheekbone and avoid the broken nose that would have inevitably resulted from the head-butt.

Carbo grabbed Vespillo's thick hair in his fist and slammed his head back into the wall. If the partition had been solid brick, the impact would easily have knocked Vespillo out cold, if not killed him outright. But in fact it was made of thin, dry, partly rotted planks of wood, and Vespillo's head went straight through it, protruding into the tavern, where the startled owner was cleaning a stew pot.

Vespillo brought his knee up sharply, and though he didn't find the target between Carbo's legs, his kneecap drove into Carbo's thigh, causing the leg to buckle. Vespillo shoved hard, and Carbo staggered backwards two steps, releasing Vespillo's sword hand.

Vespillo whipped the sword round in an arc, aiming at Carbo's neck, a killing blow. But at the last instant he altered the aim and pulled the power, so the edge sliced into Carbo's shoulder, a stinging wound, but not dangerous.

'Stop this, Carbo,' said Vespillo, panting heavily. 'We shouldn't be fighting.'

Carbo looked at the blood trickling down his upper arm. The pain kicked in a moment later. It felt different when it was inflicted by someone else. Not satisfying, releasing, but enraging.

He put his head down and charged at Vespillo like a bull. His shoulder smashed into Vespillo's chest and he wrapped his arms around him. Vespillo flew backwards, Carbo holding him in a tight bear hug. Both crashed through the partition wall which disintegrated into a cloud of flying splinters. Vespillo landed heavily on his back, his breath leaving him in a whoosh. The sword skittered across the floor. The tavern owner leaped back with a shriek, clutching the clay pot before him like it could provide him any sort of protection.

Carbo sat up, straddling Vespillo, and reached for his neck with both meaty hands. Vespillo boxed him hard in both ears, then bucked, tipping Carbo sideways.

Vespillo put an arm underneath himself, trying to rise off the ground. Carbo kicked the arm away, so Vespillo fell backwards, then lunged for the sword. As Vespillo struggled to get upright, Carbo leapt to his feet, and stamped on Vespillo's chest. There was the sound of a rib cracking, and Vespillo slumped back with a cry, clutching at his side.

Carbo towered over him. He held the gladius above his head in both hands, the sword pointing directly down towards Vespillo's heart. His grip on the hilt was so tight, his knuckles turned white. The sword point trembled. Carbo breathed hard through gritted teeth, eyes wild. Vespillo stared up at him helplessly. Then, resigned, he closed his eyes.

A moment passed, and he opened them again.

Carbo hadn't moved.

'What are you waiting for?' said Vespillo. 'Look at you. You can't control yourself. You're a wreck. Come on, killer. Do it.'

Lucidity returned to Carbo. He looked at the sword in his hand as if not recognising what he held. He stared down at his supine friend, who was waiting beneath him for the killing blow. For a moment, he wondered if he was everything Vespillo had accused him of. Was he a killer? Could he have done these things, and had no memory of them? It didn't seem possible. But then, it didn't seem possible that he had lost everything, and yet that was true.

He tossed the sword aside in disgust. Vespillo let out a relieved breath. Carbo reached out a hand to help him up, but Vespillo ignored it, and struggled to his feet under his own power, one arm clamped across his injured side. Slowly, he limped over to the fallen sword and picked it up. Carbo didn't move, didn't try to prevent him.

'Come with me, Carbo,' said Vespillo, his voice full of sadness. 'You're a danger to yourself as much as to others.'

Carbo hesitated. It was so tempting. He could let his friend take him away, and then await whatever Fortuna had in store for him, be it exile or death. It would all be out of his hands then, he could just surrender to fate.

But somewhere deep in his guts, a spark of pride, nearly extinguished, still glowed faintly. He hadn't done these things, he was sure. And the world thought he had. It wasn't right.

He turned his back on Vespillo and limped painfully out of the tavern. Vespillo made no move to stop him.

'Shouldn't you go after him?' said the tavern-keeper.

Vespillo let out a laugh that was cut off sharply, replaced by a grimace of pain.

'Go to the nearest vigiles station. Get them to send a couple of lads here. And a medicus.' He slumped onto a bench by the wall.

'And get me a really big cup of wine.'

Chapter Eleven

The tomb of Eurysaces the baker was situated just outside the pomerium, the ancient sacred boundary of Rome. The inscription read, 'This is the monument of Marcus Vergilius Eurysaces, baker, contractor and public servant. Obviously.' And it was obvious. The tomb stood over thirty feet high, and was a very different style to the classical tombs in the city. Among its stand-out features were the circular holes that represented kneading basins, just the right size to hold a unit of grain. There was a frieze below the cornice showing all the steps of baking, by which the eponymous baker had accumulated his riches.

None of this mattered to its current occupants. The spacious tomb had become a shelter for the destitute and homeless, and though the weather in Rome was not as inclement as it had been in Germania at this time of year, it was still no fun to be out all night. In the middle of winter, the temperature would occasionally fall low enough to freeze the fountains and water troughs, and on a rare year, snow might even fall. It was cold enough to kill those not in shelter, especially the very old, the very young and the infirm.

So huddled into the resting place of Eurysaces was a motley collection of the lowest strata of Rome's population. Even many slaves looked down on these people, and thanked the gods that, however bad their lot in life, at least they weren't one of them.

Some of the derelicts here were in fact former slaves. Some were freed in the wills of their former owners, some generously freed after a long service for the most altruistic reasons. Some were cynically thrown out when they became too old to be of use, and manumission then meant one less costly mouth to feed, one less body to house. For many former slaves, freedom was a sentence of destitution, starvation and death.

Others residing in the tomb had been born free. A variety of quirks of fate had led them to this place and situation. Born into poverty, orphaned, too ill to work, invalided out of the legions, too fond of wine and chariot racing. A score of unfortunates huddled together, sharing the shelter, sharing too in each other's company. Being homeless could be a heart-rending and lonely experience, the have-nots begging on the streets looking longingly at the haves in their family groups and households, meeting their friends for drink and food or a gossip around the fountain.

But even in the company of all these other people, Carbo felt completely alone. The other vagrants had some sort of community. A pecking order. A veteran with a scar running up from his forehead and disappearing under his hair-line, one arm ending in a stump just after the elbow, was clearly in charge. Though he may not be much use for manual labour, he was big enough and dangerous enough that none of the others would challenge him if he gave an order.

A straggle-haired, gap-toothed woman, nursing an infant, clearly belonged to him. He made an obvious show of ownership whenever Carbo looked over, kissing her hard, putting an arm around her, squeezing a breast, all the while defiantly challenging Carbo with a hard stare to try to take her away from him. Even if Carbo had had any interest in women since Rufa, he didn't think he could keep his lunch down if he found himself in any sort of intimacy with her.

He couldn't remember when he last ate. Although his stomach contracted and gurgled, he felt no motivation to find something to eat. He sat on his own, gazing blankly at the wall, avoided by the others who knew a dangerous beast that should be left alone when they saw one. His nostrils flared at the stench of unwashed bodies, urine, faeces, rotting food and dental decay. He clenched his fist and unclenched it. Over and over. Over and over.

He hadn't chosen this sanctuary at random. This was the place to which Rufa had fled when pursued by the soldiers who had been working for the mad priestess Elissa. It was here that Carbo had found her, hiding with little Fabilla, shaking in the aftermath of a sexual assault.

Lucky for her assaulter that she had already killed him when Carbo arrived. He would have made him suffer far worse than death.

Though Carbo hadn't paid much attention to the other denizens of the tomb at the time, apart from to castigate them for their lack of aid when Rufa was in need, he thought that the occupants were different. The homeless population of Rome was ephemeral, constantly changing. Some moved on, a rare few pulled themselves up out of the streets, some joined criminal gangs, most died. Life expectancy was short, food scarce even for those who qualified for the corn dole. Violence, starvation and disease ravaged the population mercilessly.

He didn't know if any of them recognised him. His size, his thick dark hair and his limp marked him out for those that knew of him. No one approached him, or used his name, or gave any indication that he mattered in any way. That was as it should be, he felt. He could just stay here, with the others who Fortuna and Providentia had turned their faces from, and just fade away. No one would notice. No one would care. And one day, maybe soon, he would just be another body swept up by the public slaves, thrown into a cart and dumped in a mass grave outside the city walls. And then at last there would be an ending.

He closed his eyes, and despite, or maybe because of his misery, sleep overwhelmed him.

–

He woke with a thick tongue. He could smell his own breath, stale and sour. He felt an overwhelming desire for something to drink. Something stronger than water. Sunlight filtered through a gap in the roof, just enough illumination to see by. He realised with surprise that he had slept through the whole night. He looked around his fellow tomb-dwellers. Some were still asleep. Others were stirring. Some had already departed. A small girl holding a dirty, moth-eaten rag doll stared at him with unblinking eyes above the filthy thumb that was deep in her mouth. A sudden, guilty thought of his abandonment of Fabilla hit him like a punch in his gut. He looked away.

Did any of these creatures have any wine? It seemed unlikely. He got painfully to his feet, put his hands to the small of his back, and tried to stretch the cramps away. He was hungry and thirsty. How did you get food and wine in a city, when you had no money?

He pushed past an elderly man who was dithering in his path, and walked out through the broken doorway that provided the ingress to the tomb for its living inhabitants. There were few clouds in the sky that morning, and he looked up, blinking at the bright blue. The gentle warming of the distant winter sun did nothing to improve his mood.

He stumbled to a nearby fountain, where a jet of water spurted from the mouth of a nymph to collect in the basin below. Slaves and women filled buckets for their households, others washed faces, bodies and clothes, or just drank the liquid they had scooped up in their cupped hands.

Carbo pushed aside a large slave woman who was bending over the fountain, her ample backside blocking access. Her curses faded in his ears as he plunged his head under the surface.

The icy water sent a shock through him, and it hurt and felt good. He opened his eyes, seeing a blurry view of the bottom of the basin, green with algae, shiny with offertory coins, punctuated with dark leaves of lead on which were scribbled prayers and curses.

He lifted his head back up, water streaming in chilly rivers down his back, and gasped a deep breath. He drank deeply, the liquid quenching his thirst but accentuating how empty of food his stomach was. He looked around.

The tomb was located at the junction of the via Praenestina and the via Labicana on the Esquiline. Much of the housing on the Esquiline was at the luxury end of the scale, but as with most parts of Rome, there were also shoddily constructed buildings for the poor, and of course the homeless and destitute wandered freely through the streets.

He looked along the busy street heading west back into the centre of the city. That way lay the Subura, and he didn't want to go anywhere near his old haunts. He didn't want anyone to see him like this, but more importantly, the vigiles might be on the lookout for him.

He found a dirty piece of cloth on the street, ragged and full of holes. He wrapped it around his head in a makeshift hood to disguise his hair, then set off walking, trying not to limp, though it worsened the pain from his leg.

He wandered east a short way, then having no real purpose, he sat, back against the wall between a fish-monger and a potter's shop.

The fishmonger shouted at him to move on, but Carbo ignored him and drawing his knees up to his chest, closed his eyes. He heard some customers at the stalls, haggling for goods.

'I'm not paying that for a week-old turbot.'

'That's slander. Caught last night that was.'

'Doesn't smell like it.'

Another customer: 'I'll have some sole, but if it makes me throw up like the last lot, I'll be coming back to have words with you.'

And at the potter's shop: 'I'll take it off your hands at half price. It's got a crack in the lip.'

Carbo let the words and arguments wash over him, his world comprising only the emptiness inside, phys-ical and spiritual. His stomach clenched in a particularly vicious hunger pang. He opened his eyes, and looked up at a wealthy looking man studying the wares of the fishmonger.

He opened his mouth. Closed it again. Not quite believing he was going to say the words.

'Spare a coin for a veteran, sir?'

The rich man glanced at him, then turned back to the fishmonger as if he hadn't spoken.

'Sorry about him, sir. Next time the Urban cohorts do a patrol I'll have him moved on.'

The wealthy man made his purchase and walked away. But having debased himself once already, it was easier the second time. The next customer looked like a well-cared for slave, maybe the steward of a rich household.

'Spare a coin, for a soldier who Fortuna has turned her face from?'

The steward looked at him with pity. 'I would, but it's my mistress' money, and she insists every as is accounted for. I'm sorry.'

It was his fifth attempt, a Roman matron shopping with her maid in close attendance, that tossed him a copper as. She walked away and made some comment to her maid, who put her hand over her mouth and let out a shocked, high-pitched giggle.

Carbo looked down at the blue-green, partly corroded copper coin. It bore the profile of a young-looking Augustus and the legend 'IMP CAESAR DIVI F AVGVSTVS IMP XX.' He got slowly to his feet and walked a short distance down the road to where a baker was selling gorgeous-smelling loaves of freshly baked bread. He looked at the goods for a moment. Then he turned his back and approached the tavern opposite.

The tavern-keeper took one look at his filthy hood and dirty face and wrinkled his nose at the smell. 'Move along,' he said.

'Wine,' said Carbo, offering him the coin.

The tavern-keeper hesitated, and them more in pity than avarice, took the coin, filled a cup and passed it to him.

Carbo drank deeply. The taste was sour, little better than vinegar, and it sat in his empty stomach, burning. Still, it took a bit of the edge off. He walked back to his place between the fishmonger and potter, much to the tradesmen's chagrin, sat, and extended his hand. The next coin he was given, he resolved, would buy bread.

He actually used the next three coins to buy more wine, enough that he started to feel more relaxed even as his stomach ache grew worse. But a kindly shopper, an older man, gave him bread instead of coin, and thereby provided his first meal of the day. He tore the firm loaf with his teeth and swallowed large chunks hungrily, almost choking in his hurry. Then he felt suddenly sick. He put a hand over his mouth, willing the bread to stay inside him, to not waste it by spewing it onto the streets.

'Hey, if you're going to chuck up, do it somewhere else,' said the fishmonger. 'I have enough people claiming my food makes them sick without a visual reminder.'

But Carbo kept the food down. Mildly drunk, and fractionally satiated, he sat in morose silence and watched the people go about their business.

He had nowhere to go. He had no family. His best friend thought him a murderer.

He thought about leaving the city. But what could he do? It would have been easier if he still owned the farm, but moving to a country retreat was no longer an option. Maybe he could offer his services with a sword to someone as a bodyguard. Or even join the bandits who preyed on the travellers down the via Appia.

But any of those things would require him to get off his backside, to have a desire to somehow change or improve his lot. What was the point of any of it? Better just to rot away on the streets of this city that he called home. At least Rome itself had not turned her back on him.

He put his hand out again.

'Spare a coin for a veteran of Germania?'

He woke up to a gentle shaking; a hand on his shoulder rocking him softly.

'Carbo. Carbo, wake up.' The voice was soft, high.

He didn't open his eyes. He was still in that half-state where it is uncertain whether the last dream was real or not. In Carbo's case, that last dream had involved sitting in a tavern with Vespillo, dicing and drinking and laughing. The reality of his situation returned with a crash, and he started and opened his eyes.

A face swum before him that he couldn't immediately recognise through his sleep-blurred vision in the gloom of the tomb. He blinked hard, rubbed his face, squinted.

He had been living in the Baker's tomb for about a week, though he was not keeping any strict track of the passing days. The generosity of strangers in providing food and coin, as well as some petty theft, had kept him fed enough to stay alive, and just drunk enough to stop him collapsing into a trembling ball. It wasn't really living. He doubted if it was really enough for him to survive for any meaningful length of time. But he wasn't dead yet.

He stared hard at the face. A young girl. Kind of familiar.

'Carbo. It's me. Sica.'

For a moment, Carbo couldn't connect the name to the presence of this person before him now. It was too incongruous.

'Sica?'

'Yes.' She held out a hand. 'Get up. We go get you sorted.'

'I don't understand.'

'Don't need to. Take hand.'

Carbo hesitated then grasped the outstretched hand. It felt tiny as his sausage-like fingers closed around it, but she pulled with surprising strength, and despite the aches in his back and knees, he came upright. He towered over the young girl.

Wordlessly, she led him out of the tomb, a dozen pairs of eyes following them with mild curiosity. It was night, and the Esquiline streets were bathed in white moonlight. The air was chill, a wind whipping through the streets and through the holes in his tunic, so it seemed to penetrate into his very marrow.

'Where are we going?'

'My home. Shelter. Warm.'

She led him through the dark streets. They were full of night traffic as usual, but she skirted the busiest streets, and took a long route round, avoiding the Subura. Carbo marvelled at her knowledge of the city, but he supposed he shouldn't have been surprised – she had been resourceful and a quick learner since he had known her.

He peppered her with questions, but she put a finger to her lips. At last they crossed the Tiber into the Transtiberim area of the city. He kept his head down as they walked over the narrow bridge, but it was too dark, and people were too concerned with their own business, for anyone to recognise him, even if there had been anyone in this region that had known him.

Sica led him to an insula a short distance from the main docks area. The ground floor shop was a laundry, and there was a strong smell of urine, the cleaning agent of choice, so important that hard up Romans could sell their waste liquid for cash to the fuller.

Sica's apartment was on the first floor, accessed like many by an external staircase. The stairs led up three more storeys, and Carbo was impressed that the young freedwoman lived in one of the better flats in the block. He assumed at first that she had found herself a moderately comfortable tradesman, and that the apartment was rented or owned by him.

But when she unlocked the door and led him inside, there were no other occupants. She lit an oil lamp, and he saw a single chair and table, an unlit brazier, and a few clay figurines and other decorations. One in particular held pride of place on a shelf on the wall, a terracotta statuette of a man wrapped in a cloak and holding a horn overflowing with fruit and corn.

Sica bowed to it, and whispered a few words in her native Dacian language. She turned to Carbo. 'Derzelas,' she said by way of explanation. 'God of my people. Make you healthy.'

Carbo nodded, then bowed reverentially to the statue.

'Sit,' said Sica, gesturing to the chair. 'Wait.'

Carbo did meekly as he was told, still completely bemused. Sica disappeared out of the door, leaving Carbo alone. He looked out of the window at the street below. He could see the docks, ships unloading throughout the night as they did during the day. Slaves trudged on and off gangplanks, loaded down for the most part with the

171

sacks of grain that were constantly brought from the fertile grounds of Sicily and Egypt to be poured into the starving maw of the city. But other goods were plentiful too – fruits, vegetables, salted meats, earthenware, herbs, spices and raw materials like stone and marble. It was like looking down on an ants' nest, the drones hurrying backwards and forwards, the work never-ending.

Sica returned, and in her arms she carried a bundle of freshly laundered clothes, with the handle of a bucket of water looped through her elbow.

'Clothes off,' she said.

Numbly, Carbo obeyed. It wasn't the first time he had been naked before the young ex-slave, and it felt as unerotic as the first time, when they had been forced to strip under threat of the whip of the overseer of the mines.

Sica placed the bucket on the floor beside Carbo, and taking a clean but rough rag, she scrubbed at his chest and arms, his armpits, even between his legs, with all the detached care of a young slave girl performing toilet duties for an elderly mistress. He submitted meekly to her rough ministrations, and when she had towelled him dry, she pulled a clean tunic over his head.

Still not done, she produced a razor-sharp knife and took it to his stubble, scraping it away with sufficient precision to not leave a single nick. He rubbed his face, and it felt smooth even though the dry shave had left it stinging. Now she attended to his hair, rinsing the worst of the muck out in the bucket, then taking a comb to it to remove the tangles.

When she was finished, she stepped back and looked him up and down, then gave a satisfied nod.

'Better.'

It was a strange feeling. Even before he lost the tavern, he hadn't been looking after himself, and had rebuffed any attempts from Marsia to care for him, much as she had protested it was her duty. He was now clean for the first time in as long as he could remember.

'Thanks, I guess,' he said, running fingers through his dark hair. 'Do you have anything to drink?'

Sica nodded and handed him a cup of water.

He looked down at it and wrinkled his nose. 'I meant wine.'

'Know what you meant. Drink.'

Carbo did as he was told, and finding he was more thirsty than he had realised, he downed the cup in one long draught. Now his hunger hit him. Before he could ask Sica handed him a small loaf and a dish of nuts. He ate greedily, and looked for more. Sica shook her head.

'Enough. Build you up slowly.'

Carbo suddenly felt overwhelmingly tired. He sat back in the chair, closed his eyes.

He opened them again, and felt a strange disorientation. The sun had come up and the apartment looked sufficiently different in the daylight that it took him a moment to work out where he was. Strangely he found himself lying on Sica's small bed, his legs bent since they were too long for the small space. He stretched and yawned, marvelling at how much better he felt. No hangover. No aches and pains from sleeping on hard, cold floors. He even smelled better.

He rose, and saw that Sica had left him a small breakfast, some more bread and some dates, and a large cup of water. He sat, ate and drank, and was just clearing up the last of the crumbs when Sica returned.

'You look better,' she said.

'I feel better,' he said. 'At least, physically. Sica, I don't understand. How did you find me?'

'Came to visit your tavern. Wanted to know how you were. You never came to see me.'

'Oh, I…' He didn't really have an excuse. They had formed such a close bond, but when they had returned to Rome he had left her to her own devices. She was resourceful, and he had never been worried for her, but now he realised how indifferent he had been to her welfare. Young, female, foreign. Vulnerable. Anything could have happened to her. He had been so self-obsessed, he had thought of no one else. Not Sica, not Marsia. Not even Fabilla. Shame rushed over him, and he put his head in his hands.

Suddenly, he couldn't hold back the tears, and he cried, guilt, sadness, despair driving his sobs. Sica put an arm around him and let the storm blow itself out. When he was done, he wiped his eyes on his tunic and looked up at her.

In the daylight he could see her clearly. She was the same slight, young girl, long dark hair and wide green eyes. But there was a little more substance to her now. Not just a fleshing-out from better nutrition, but something inside. She seemed to have changed from a defiant, sharp-toothed mouse to something more self-assured, a fox strutting through the city streets, alert for danger but confident in its ability to fight or flee, to survive whatever fate threw. He smiled sadly, reached out and touched her face gently.

'I'm sorry, Sica. I let you down. If it's any consolation, I let a lot of other people down too. Not least, myself I think.'

'Yes, you did.'

He didn't know if he had been expecting words of comfort, but he was quickly disabused of that idea as Sica continued.

'This isn't the man that saved me in the mines. That fought those bandits. That man brave. Didn't give up. This man here is – what is the word? Broken.'

Carbo couldn't disagree. That was exactly how he felt.

Sica took the statuette of Derzelas off the shelf, and after a moment's hesitation, she handed it to Carbo. He took it carefully, respectfully, looking at her, uncertain what she wanted him to do.

'Look at it,' she said.

He turned the figurine over in his hands, and saw now in the better light that it had a crack through its midriff. He rotated it and saw that the crack went right to the other side. At some point the statuette had split in two.

'Broken,' said Sica. Then firmly, 'Mended.'

Carbo stared at the figurine. It was a simple analogy. But this was something that Sica cared deeply about. And she had fixed it. He nodded and handed it back to her. As he did so, he noticed that where it had been damaged there was a small chip in the fault line. A piece missing.

He didn't mention it to Sica as she placed the sacred statue back in place.

–

Sica told him that she had to work, and that she would return in the evening, and then they would talk. She made him promise not to leave, just to eat, drink and rest. He did as he was told, but as soon as she had left, he felt anxiety creeping up on him again, like a demon stalking him, just behind him, always out of sight. He tried to think of pleasant thoughts, but he had so few that were not tied to sadness. He could not think of happy times with Rufa without the fact and manner of her death bursting in. He could not think of good times in the legions without remembering terror and torture and slaughter. He could not even recall his mother, without thinking about coming home and finding her gone.

He thought about his half-brother. They hadn't been close, the age gap had been too big. And Carbo had resented the new arrival, offspring of a different father. Most of the time, he had been beneath his notice, a bit of an embarrassment when Carbo was trying to make bonds with the older lads on the streets, or woo the neighbours' daughters.

And yet there had been regular family meals. Shared games when Carbo had been bored – ball games, hide and seek, or wrestling which inevitably ended with Carbo holding him down and tickling him until he shrieked so loudly that their mother screamed at them to shut up.

And he remembered the boy bravely holding back the tears when he had left for the legions, and vowing to follow in his steps when he was old enough. He supposed it had been some twenty-five years since he had seen the kid. He had had occasional updates in letters from his mother over the years; enough to know that he had indeed joined the legions and been killed in action. He had mourned briefly, paid for a mason to carve a funerary stele with a brief epitaph that could be placed in the grounds of the legions headquarters, then returned to his duties. He hadn't even taken leave in Rome to check on his mother. Just more people in the list of those he had let down.

So much for happy memories. And he couldn't bear to contemplate the future. So he sat and stared out of the window, trying to stay distracted by the porters, travellers and tradespeople working at the docks. Watching the constant flow of cargo ships, coming and going in a carefully choreographed dance was strangely relaxing, and it kept his anxiety at bay until Sica returned.

She smiled when she saw him, walked straight over to him and hugged him. She smelled of urine.

'Thought you might have run.'

Carbo shook his head. He wasn't sure if it was bravery or cowardice that had kept him there all day. It didn't really matter.

She had brought some hot food with her, a sausage each and a meat pie to share, and they ate and drank together. When they had finished, Carbo said, 'So, I'm guessing you're a fuller.'

Sica nodded. 'Bought business with money you gave. When you freed me.' It explained the smell of urine and the supply of freshly laundered clothes. He wondered how Sica would explain their loss to their owners when they came to collect them.

He gestured at the apartment. 'It seems you are making a success of it. It's impressive. A young woman in a strange city. I would think that men would have tried to muscle in.'

Sica shrugged. 'Had some offers. Had some threats. No one threatened twice.'

Carbo could imagine how she had dealt with an overly persistent suitor, a thug trying to get protection money or a rival trying to put her out of business. A knife in the dark once or twice, and word would quickly get around that she was not to be messed with.

'Sica, you still haven't explained how you found me. You said you came to visit. Visit where? The tavern?'

She nodded. 'Yes. Sorry you lost it. Marsia told me everything.'

Carbo felt a pang at the mention of her name. 'How is she?'

Sica looked down. 'Not well.'

'She's ill?'

'In spirit.'

Carbo swallowed, said nothing.

Sica hesitated then continued. 'He treats her badly. New master.'

Carbo took a breath, let it out slowly. Anger stirred inside him, mixed with frustration and impotence. A master could do whatever he liked with a slave. Beat her, abuse her, humiliate her. Kill her if it pleased him. He should have freed her long ago, then she at least would have been spared the consequences of his weakness. He hadn't even checked how she had been since he had lost her. After all Marsia had done for him. Just another to add to the long list of people he had let down.

'She told you where to find me? How did she know?'

'She remembered where Rufa had hidden. Place where people without homes go.'

'It was a lucky guess. The streets of Rome are full of the poor. Under arches, in temples, in the doorways of shops.'

Sica shrugged. 'If you not there, would have kept looking.'

Carbo narrowed his eyes. 'But why?'

'Oh Carbo.' She stepped forward and hugged him hard. 'Sad that you don't know. You not remember who you are.'

He accepted the hug, the platonic act of comfort an almost forgotten pleasure. She stroked his hair and he held her close.

She stepped back, hands on his shoulders and looked him straight in the eyes.

'People still love you, Carbo. Me, Marsia, Fabilla, Vespillo.'

At the mention of Vespillo, Carbo frowned, and the memory of their last meeting passed through his mind.

'Vespillo thinks I'm a murderer.'

'Are you?'

Carbo's mouth dropped open.

'Carbo. Look me in eyes. Tell me. Are you a murderer?'

He fixed his gaze hard on her, and said firmly, 'No!'

Sica nodded, satisfied. 'Good.'

Carbo watched her expression in surprise. 'You didn't know what to believe until just now? And yet you did all this for me?'

'You are my friend. Through good and bad.'

Carbo shook his head. What had he done to deserve someone like her? Nothing he could think of.

'Sica. I don't know what to do.'

She gestured at the little idol. 'We fix you. Then fix everything else.'

It sounded so simple. But she was right. He needed to get a grip on himself, before he could do anything about the rest of his problems. He gritted his teeth, and made a little promise inside his head to Rufa that he would try harder. He would try to mend, and become whole again.

He looked at the benign face of Derzelas, gazing down on them. Then his eyes settled on the missing piece.

Chapter Twelve

Marsia swept the floor with a birch-handled besom. The dirty straw, mixed with spilled wine and ordure from the city, accumulated in soggy piles before she ushered it out of the door onto the street. When she had finished, she fetched a pile of fresh straw and tossed it out in handfuls, the way a farmer spreads his seed.

Vatius sat in his usual corner, drinking slowly and reading from an unrolled scroll. He squinted in the dim light of the tavern, running his finger along the tatty papyrus as he deciphered the words. Myia sat curled in his lap, apparently asleep. But every time the door opened, she lifted her head and pricked her ears, only to slump back down with her chin on her paws when she saw that it was not Carbo coming through the door.

There were few other customers. A couple of regulars. Two legionaries that Marsia hadn't seen before. Their loud conversation was all about the hardship of army life on the northern frontier, and how fortunate they were to have been part of a vexillation sent to Rome to accompany a provincial official at the end of his tenure.

Business had not picked up after the moody and unpredictable Carbo had been evicted. In fact, the reverse. Carbo still had some friends who had continued to patronise his establishment from loyalty. With him gone, they had, probably with some relief, moved to other taverns with more welcoming atmospheres and no doubt better wine.

Everything felt pointless. The world looked grey. Food and drink was as tasteless as ash. She had felt like this before, when she had first been taken into captivity, out of the forests of her beloved Germania and into the smelly and dirty capital of the Empire, her freedom yanked away, servitude her life. But when Carbo became her master, she had started to gain some self-respect. Yes, he had always treated her like a slave, and as she developed her love for him, he had never returned it. But he had always treated her like a human being, not a domesticated beast.

Olorix was different, she knew it already. He had owned her over a week, and had done nothing overtly abusive, yet. But he had visited the tavern a few times, and his salacious comments, made with knowing winks and sly smiles to his bodyguards filled her with dread. She kept thoughts of him from her mind as best she could, but the anxiety kept creeping in at the edges when she let her mind drift.

To keep herself occupied, she did a round of the customers, asking if there was anything she could get them. The soldiers ordered another cup of wine each, which they accepted from her without thanks, or indeed pausing their conversations at all.

Vatius was more politely grateful for his cup of pomegranate juice, nodding to Marsia and smiling sympathetically.

'What are you reading?' she asked.

Vatius furrowed his forehead, his thick white eyebrows closing together.

'*Oedipus*, by Julius Caesar. Have you read it?'

Marsia shook her head. She had some literacy, her master before Carbo having educated her to help him with his book-keeping, and she had greedily absorbed everything she could find about law, philosophy, history and politics. But she had no interest in fictitious accounts of figures from Roman and Greek mythology. Her people had their own culture and folklore, and the tales of the exploits of Donner and Woden her father had told her around the roundhouse fire had thrilled her as a child. She didn't know if the Roman deities were as real as her Germanic gods, but she had no desire to learn more about them.

'Well, I shouldn't bother,' said Vatius. 'It's not very good. Caesar had undoubted talents in many fields, and his *Of the Gallic Wars* is a fascinating, if self-aggrandising account of his campaign. This play though? Hmmm. I somehow doubt it will stand the test of time.'

Marsia nodded, but could think of nothing to contribute to the conversation. She fussed Myia's ears, and went back behind the bar to stir the pot of stew which bubbled softly over a low flame.

The door opened, and cold winter air blew in. She turned to admonish the newcomers about the draught, and then froze.

'Marsia!' said Olorix. 'How is my business?'

Marsia bowed her head. 'Last night we had eleven customers who spent a total of seventeen denarii and three copper asses. We finished an amphora of lora, and most of the stew which I...'

'Enough!' said Olorix. 'I didn't come here for an audit.' He went over to an unoccupied chair and sat down heavily. Two bulky bodyguards joined him, one either side. 'What's the best wine we have in stock?'

'We have some posca and some mulsum. Not much, our stocks are running low...'

'Fine, posca will do. Three cups.'

Marsia dispensed three full cups worth of the second-rate wine, far-removed from the strong and expensive Falernian that they had once stocked, but better than lora, which was made from soaking the skins of grapes that had already been twice-pressed in water for a day, and fermenting whatever juice and flavour leeched out. She carried them over on a tray to Olorix and his men. The bodyguards drunk them deep without complaint, but Olorix took one sip and wrinkled his nose.

'Disgusting. Make sure we have some Falernian beneath the counter for next time I come to visit. For my sole use, understand?'

'Yes, master.'

'And some fresh olives. And grapes. Apples. Honey-cakes. I get hungry.'

Marsia couldn't help dropping her eyes to Olorix's vast belly. She kept thoughts about the benefits of maybe staying a little hungry to herself – she was often outspoken, but she wasn't stupid enough to risk a beating for no reason.

Nevertheless, Olorix saw the direction of her gaze and frowned. He gestured towards the cubicle at one side of the room. Its tatty curtain was drawn back, and the stone bed within had no mattress.

'The bed doesn't seem to be made.'

'It is not in use, master,' said Marsia.

'You mean we have no whores working here?'

'We used to. A young boy called Philon. But he died...'

'And you aren't offering yourself because...?'

'I don't do that, master.'

Olorix let out a short bark of laughter.

'Who told you that?'

'My former owners. Both of them. They said I did not need to provide this service.'

'Well, that changes now. Put up a sign. You obviously don't have much experience and you aren't that much to look at, but you aren't too old, and you're healthy. I would say four copper coins a go sounds about right.'

'No, master.'

Olorix stiffened. 'That's not a word I here very often from a slave. Unless it is in answer to a question, such as, "is there any reason I shouldn't punish you severely for disobedience?" But I think I will show my kind side and pretend you didn't speak. You start tonight.'

'No, master. I will not.'

Olorix sighed. He looked around the room, and his eyes lit on the broom, resting in a corner. He stood with an effort, and picked up the broom, gave the floor a little swish. He nodded to one of his bodyguards.

'Bend her over the bar.'

Before Marsia could move, the bulky henchman grabbed her arm and dragged her towards the bar. She struggled, hissed, scratched and tried to bite. Her finger-nails raked a bloody gouge in the man's forearm, and he cursed and smacked her round the side of the head. It did little to calm her, so the other bodyguard joined in, taking her other arm. Together, they forced her face onto the bar. She turned her head to one side, her cheek pressed against the granite surface, and she could see the grime around the rim of the one of the depressions which held the big pots of soup and stew.

She heard Olorix swagger up behind her, and then felt him grasp the hem of her tunic and yank it up around her waist. Her bare backside was exposed to all the onlookers. She squeezed her eyes shut, bracing herself for what was to come. She had never felt so vulnerable and helpless, and terror of what he was about to do to her welled up inside. He drew the moment out, and her horrified anticipation heightened, as she imagined him abusing her with his member, or even with the broom.

When the handle of the broom cracked across her buttocks, it was almost a relief.

Until the pain hit her.

She had taken beatings before, but Olorix seemed particularly skilled. He paused long enough between each stroke for the pain to crescendo, peak and start to fade, before the next stroke fell. The guards held her firmly, but did nothing to stifle the screams coming from her.

It seemed to continue forever, but in fact was around a dozen swipes of the broom handle. Abruptly, the guards let her go. Her legs gave way, and she slumped to the floor, curled up and sobbing. She pulled her tunic down to protect her modesty as best she could, but when the material touched her buttocks it felt like fire, and she had to hold it away from her skin.

She looked up at Olorix, who was standing over her, through tear-misted eyes. He was breathing heavily, and she could see the bulge of excitement sticking out against his clothing from under his bloated gut. She wondered why he hadn't taken her himself. But Olorix, for all his crassness, thought of himself as belonging to the higher echelons of society, and she presumed he didn't want to put that side of himself on public show, lest it damage his carefully cultivated reputation.

'Starting tonight,' he said. 'Four asses.'

She looked down, her defiance ended. Olorix looked at her contemptuously, then turned to leave. A croaky voice arrested him for a moment.

'You know, I've always fancied a turn with her myself.'

Marsia stared at Vatius in horror. Had she heard right? Did the kindly old teacher really say those words?

'Really?' said Olorix, looking at the old man with a half-smile.

'Oh yes,' said Vatius. 'She has a shapely calf. And a delightful bosom.'

'Well,' said Olorix. 'Pay your money and you can take your turn.'

'Ah, well there is my dilemma,' said Vatius. 'I'm not very good at sharing.'

'That isn't really my problem,' said Olorix. 'Take your turn or don't.' He reached for the door.

'How about I make you an offer?'

Olorix grasped the handle but waited. 'I'm listening.'

'How about I have her to myself for two weeks? I'll pay five sestertii a day.'

Olorix quickly did the maths. 'That's twelve and a half copper asses. She could earn me that with three men in one hour.'

'She could,' conceded Vatius. 'But would she? There are a lot of prostitutes in Rome. Can she have three customers per day guaranteed? As you said, she isn't much to look at. And don't forget she has other duties. If she is on her knees in that cubicle, she won't be serving the customers their wine.'

'Hmmm.' Olorix stroked his double chin. 'I had rather hoped to see Carbo's precious slave used by all and sundry, night in night out. But maybe having her taken by a geriatric old duffer like yourself would be just as humiliating. And business is business. You have a deal, old man.'

'You're too kind,' said Vatius, and reached out his hand to seal the bargain. Olorix took it, pumped it once, then with one last leer at Marsia, he took his leave.

Vatius smiled at Marsia, who looked at him in horror.

'Well, my dear, no time like the present. Come on.' He put Myia on the floor, stood painfully, put both hands in the small of his back and stretched. Then he held out a hand to Marsia. She took it in a stupour, and allowed herself to be led to the cubicle. The soldiers watched them disappear behind the curtain with envious glances. In spite of Olorix's and Vatius' unkind words, Marsia was a handsome woman. Firm of jaw and thick of brow, not the typical picture of Roman beauty, but attractive in her way.

She looked at Vatius with profound disappointment. All this time, had the kindly old man being looking at her with lust? Dropping his eyes to her bust or buttocks when she wasn't looking? Imagining her naked, in his bed? It felt like a betrayal. How a rich man must feel if he overhears a best friend saying that he only tolerates his company because of his money.

She swallowed to keep the sickness from rising. Then she knelt down and put a hand on his leg.

Vatius reached down and pulled her gently back to her feet.

She looked into his eyes uncertainly. He wanted something else? She closed her eyes and leaned forward to kiss him. Her lips met only air. Vatius had stepped back. She opened her eyes again. Vatius was gesturing to the bed.

'Sit please, Marsia.'

She did as she was told, shifting on the stone bed gingerly to try to minimise the pain from her backside. Vatius sat beside her, pulled out his battered copy of Caesar's Oedipus and began to read. After a moment, he glanced at her, and smiled sadly at the look of confusion on her face.

'Oh my dear. What do you think of me?'

'I don't… understand.'

Vatius sighed and put the play down.

'Marsia, you are an intelligent woman. But sometimes you don't think. Look at me. I'm old. It's been a long time since I was able to enjoy myself with a young woman. Not that I don't appreciate beauty, and regardless of what Olorix, and indeed I, said earlier, you are a beautiful woman.'

'So, you paid for me just so you could look at me? You could do that in the tavern for free.'

'Oh Marsia. I understand why you find it hard to think the best of people. But you must realise, I did this for you.'

Marsia swallowed, and suddenly tears welled up. She put her arms around him and buried her face in his shoulder and sobbed quietly. Vatius patted her head and stroked her hair, until she recomposed herself.

'But why the pretence? Why bring me back here? You could have just said you would pay for me not to be whored.'

'Olorix would never have accepted that. He doesn't need the money. His sole purpose was to hurt and humiliate Carbo. Everyone knew that Carbo wouldn't sell your, um, feminine services, for any price. He wants to show how completely he has triumphed over your former master.'

'But why? Why does he hate Carbo?'

Vatius patted Marsia's knee.

'I have known men like Olorix all my life. They have power, or money, but deep inside they are weak. Men like Carbo scare them. Men who are innately powerful. Physical and strong and self-reliant. And of course, well-liked. Or at least, he once was. So Olorix saw Carbo's current situation, and spotted a chance to take advantage.'

Marsia nodded. Viewed that way, Olorix's actions made more sense. He was never interested in Carbo's material possessions. He wanted to break him spiritually.

'But he would never have had the chance if Carbo hadn't made those stupid bets. If that stupid Camilla bitch hadn't talked him into it.'

Vatius stroked his chin. 'Yes. I had presumed that Olorix had just capitalised on Carbo's bad fortune. But what if he had engineered it?'

Marsia frowned, then her eyes widened. 'You think maybe Camilla and Olorix are in it together?'

'It has to be a possibility, doesn't it?'

Marsia looked away. 'I should have stopped him somehow. Tried harder to warn him. I knew she was trouble.'

'You can't blame yourself. Carbo has been in no mood to listen to anyone since he returned to Rome. Not Vespillo, not you, and certainly not an old fool like me.'

'But it's all too late anyway, isn't it? Even if we found out that Olorix had cheated, what could Carbo do about it?'

'If there was real proof, then Carbo could use the courts to try to reclaim what he had lost. There would be no guarantees, and the winner would probably just be the one who bribed or intimidated the jury the most successfully. But it is all irrelevant. Wherever Carbo is now, he can't return here. Vespillo will have him arrested, and he will be tried and executed for these murders.'

Marsia grasped Vatius' hand. 'You don't think he really did those horrible things, do you? Surely not Carbo.'

'I would like to think not. But when a man is at his limits, who knows what he is capable of. Vespillo certainly thinks he did it. Or at least feels it is his duty to believe it.'

'He didn't,' said Marsia firmly. 'I know him better than anyone does. He couldn't. It's not in him.'

'I admire your loyalty, dear, and I hope you are right.'

'Vatius, what am I to do? How am I to help Carbo?'

Vatius shook his head sadly. 'Just because I know the works of the great philosophers by heart, doesn't mean I possess their wisdom.'

'You're the wisest man I know.'

'Then you need to widen your circle of intellectuals, my dear.'

'Vatius, what will happen to me? I appreciate your generosity, paying to stop me... to stop...' She waved her hand at the bed. 'But I know you aren't a rich man. You can't do this for ever.'

'No. And Olorix probably wouldn't allow it indefinitely either. He will get bored and want some new entertainment.'

'Then what am I to do?'

'I'm sorry, Marsia. This small thing I have done for you is all that is within my means. All we can do is pray that Fortuna, or whoever is your German god of luck, smiles upon you.'

Marsia stared at the wall, and a sense of hopelessness crushed her like a collapsing house.

Marsia flinched whenever the tavern door opened, terrified that Olorix was returning to humiliate and punish her further. This time though, it was just a small woman, barely more than a girl, unaccompanied. A faint smell of urine wafted around her.

'We're not open yet,' said Marsia and turned back to her task, scrubbing the grease from the bar where it had slopped over the side of the stew pots the previous night. Then she looked up sharply.

The girl was still framed in the doorway, the light of the morning sun behind her making her features hard to see. Marsia squinted.

'Sica?'

Sica stepped into the tavern. Marsia held her clenched hands to her chest, hardly daring to breathe.

'Did you find him?' Her voice was a whisper.

Sica nodded. Marsia let out her breath in a sob. Her shoulders slumped forward and she pressed one hand to her forehead.

'I thought he was... he had...'

Sica stepped forward and took her hands, then threw her arms around Marsia. They hugged each other tight, then broke apart and looked into each other's misty eyes.

Marsia gestured to a table. 'Sit, please. I'll bring you some wine and food.'

Sica sat, but said, 'Just water please.'

Marsia brought her a cup of water and stood beside her. Sica frowned. 'You don't sit as well?'

Marsia shook her head, a sharp, jerky motion. Sica opened her mouth to question, then shut it again abruptly. Marsia knew that Sica was not a slow girl, and that she had been a slave herself. She knew intuitively what had happened. Casually, Sica got to her feet, and leaned against a wall. Marsia appreciated the gesture, allowing their subsequent conversation to be less awkward.

'How is he?'

Sica pursed her lips.

'Bad.'

'Sick? Injured? Sad? Scared? Tell me, Sica. What's going on?'

Sica held up a hand to stop the flow of words. Sica's Latin was much poorer than Marsia's and she needed time to parse coherent sentences.

'Like he is broken. Too much wine. Too much grief. Too much hating himself.'

Marsia's face fell. It wasn't news to her, but the words were like dagger stabs.

'But,' said Sica. 'I help. He get better. Slow.'

Welcome as the words were, she couldn't help but feel a pang of jealousy. Hadn't she tried to make him better? Why had Carbo listened to this young girl who he had known for such a short space of time, rather than her, his sole slave, who was beside him all day, every day? She could rationalise it, knowing that Carbo had reached a point where he couldn't get any lower, and needed to either accept help or die. But still it rankled.

'No more wine. No more gambling. Clean clothes. Give him back some…' she looked for the words.

'Self-respect?' suggested Marsia.

'Yes. Dignitas? Is that what the Romans call it?'

'It is. It's a good start, Sica. But it isn't enough. How can we make him the man he was?'

'We can't,' said Sica. 'But he can.'

Marsia looked into Sica's eyes, then gave a smile. She knew what Carbo was capable of. She had seen the kind of apparently invincible enemies he had defeated. Now he had to overcome his most powerful threat. Himself. And only he could to that.

But he had friends. Sica and Marsia, at least.

'What about these killings, though?' said Marsia. 'As long as he is wanted for murder, he can do nothing to restore his fortune.'

'You think he did it?'

Marsia frowned at the suggestion. 'Of course not. Do you?'

'No. So we need to find out who did.'

It seemed impossible. And yet, for the first time in so long, Marsia felt a stirring inside. What was that unfamiliar feeling? Hope? Purpose? Maybe there was something they could do. And, if Carbo became Carbo again, if he saved himself, just maybe he could save her.

Sica hesitated, then took Marsia's hand. 'How bad?'

Marsia swallowed. 'Bad. But Vatius stepped in to prevent the worst. Though he can't keep... that sort of thing... away forever.' She explained what had happened the previous night, what Vatius had done to help.

'Don't worry. We help Carbo. Then Carbo help you.'

Could it really be that simple? But it was something to cling to. Carbo had proved his resilience. He could do it again. She just had to keep her faith in him.

'So what should we do first?' It felt strange to Marsia to ask for advice from one so young. But Sica was giving off an air of confidence that was inspiring.

'I know you stuck here. Just listen. See what people say.'

'And you?'

'I speak to Vespillo.'

–

'It's good to see you looking so well,' said Vespillo. 'You're a fuller now, I hear.'

'All day deal with shit-stains,' said Sica. 'Like you, yes?'

Vespillo laughed. 'Glad to see you haven't changed. Yes, maybe our jobs aren't so different. And we both have to get our hands dirty to do them well. So to what do I owe the pleasure?'

'Pleasure?' Sica looked suspicious.

'Why are you here in my office, Sica?'

'Oh. Need to talk about Carbo.'

'Not to see my smiling face, then? I guessed as much. I don't know what there is to say to you.'

'He no do it.'

Vespillo sighed and gestured to a chair on the other side of his desk. Sica ignored the offer, so Vespillo had to look up at the girl from his seated position, small as she was.

'I want to believe that. But the facts point another way.'

Sica shook her head emphatically. 'He no do it,' she said, even more firmly.

'Listen. A man fitting his description has been seen walking away from the scene of more than one of the murders. A witness heard one of the victims call out Carbo's name. And I found Carbo's sword covered in blood.'

Sica looked uncertain, but only for the briefest moment.

'He no do it,' she said again. 'He can't. He is Carbo.'

'Sica, Carbo is probably my closest friend. We have been through a lot together. I know his character better than you. He is an honourable man, and a heroic one. He has the blood of men like Horatius Cocles running in his veins.'

'Who?'

'The man who single-handedly held the Pons Sublicius against the invading Etruscans five hundred years ago. When all else had fled, he defied the Etruscan army, enabling the Romans to destroy the bridge behind him and save the city. That's the sort of thing Carbo would do.

'But he also has a temper. I've seen him lose control and beat men to the point of death in his fury. And he is a wreck of a man. Damaged by his time in the legions, and broken by the loss of Rufa.'

Sica was shaking her head, trying to deny the truth in his words, but Vespillo continued.

'I love him like a brother. But I think the gods have taken his wits. He has become a danger to the people of Rome. People I have a duty to protect. I must find him, and I must stop him. Even if it means his death.'

'You no friend to him,' said Sica bitterly. 'Friends stick by each other, always.'

'Not always,' said Vespillo, his voice laden with regret. 'Some things come before friendship. Like duty and honour.'

'Nothing comes before friendship,' said Sica, the words spat into Vespillo's face.

'Sica,' said Vespillo, his voice low, coaxing. 'Do you know where he is?'

The flash of guilt across her face told Vespillo the answer, even as she denied it.

'I know nothing. I just know he in trouble. And he my friend.'

'Sica, you must tell me where he is. If you don't more people will die.'

Sica put her hands on Vespillo's desk and leaned forward, so her face was close to his.

'Thought better of you,' she said. Then she strode out of his office.

Vespillo sighed, rubbed his hand over his beard, then called out, 'Plancus.'

The slight secretary hurried in, drew himself erect and saluted. Though he still showed signs of his previous timidity, his brave actions in the fight alongside his fellow vigiles against the thugs trying to rule the district had given him a newfound confidence.

'Yes, sir, how can I help, sir?'

'Fetch me Taura.'

Plancus looked deflated that he wasn't being given a more dangerous task, but he slipped out with good grace, and moments later returned with Vespillo's deputy. True to his name, Taura was built like a bull, barrel-chested, and carried a constant air of barely repressed anger.

Taura gave a firm salute, though his expression suggested resentment at being disturbed. 'Sir?'

'Do you know of the fullers owned by Sica, by the docks?'

'No, sir, but I can find it.'

'Go there, keep a watch. I think that's where we might find Carbo.'

'Ummm, on my own, sir?'

Vespillo smiled inwardly. Few things scared Taura, but the thought of handling Carbo alone was clearly one of them.

'No, take a couple of the lads.'

'Sir,' said Plancus. 'That region is not in our jurisdiction.'

'I realise that. I want you to take a message to the station commander there. I know him; good man. He'll understand, and probably be relieved we aren't asking him to sort it out for us.'

'And what am I to do if I find him?' asked Taura hesitantly.

'Bring him to me.'

'Right,' said Taura. 'I see. Very well. Anything else you want me to do? Has Jupiter broken the law? Or Mars? I could fetch them for you too.'

Vespillo sighed. 'Sarcasm doesn't suit you, Taura, and you aren't very good at it. Carbo isn't the man he was. You should have no trouble.'

Taura's eyes betrayed his disbelief.

—

'Carbo!'

Abandoning her usual reserve, Marsia ran to him the moment he set foot in the tavern and threw her arms around him. She hugged him so tight that for a moment he couldn't breathe, despite their marked differences in size. He squeezed her gently back, then prised her arms from him, and held her at arm's length, looking into her eyes.

'Marsia. How are you?'

She opened her mouth to speak, then burst into tears and buried her face in his shoulder as she cried. When she had recovered, Carbo took her hand and led her to the back room.

He looked around. It was odd. There were still things that had belonged to him, a vase taken instead of payment from a needy customer, a statuette given by a grateful shop owner whose business he had saved from thugs. Yet now it was all owned by Olorix. Including his former slave.

He sat on a three-legged stool, and gestured to Marsia to sit too. She did so, slowly, shifting her weight to try to find a comfortable position, pursing her lips as she tried to cover the pain.

Carbo's eyes narrowed. 'He did that?'

She bit her lip, then nodded once. Carbo clenched his fists.

'What else?' he asked.

'Nothing, yet.'

Carbo looked at her quizzically.

She hesitated, and he could see she had more to tell. 'Go on.'

'He… He wants to make me a whore.'

Carbo took a deep breath and let it out slowly so it whistled through his teeth.

'He already has, in a way,' she continued. 'But Vatius has purchased my services exclusively. For now.'

'Vatius! How could he!'

Marsia leaned forward and put a hand on his arm. 'It's not like that. Vatius has only done it to spare me. He sits with me and we read. But it can't last. It amuses Olorix, but he will get bored, if Vatius' money doesn't run out first.'

'I'll make it right,' said Carbo, and knew as the words came out of his mouth that he had no idea how to do that.

'Please don't make promises you can't keep,' said Marsia. 'Spare me that, at least.'

Carbo's eyes misted suddenly. Marsia was his slave yes, but she was so much more. Friend, companion, sister and mother, all contained in one tough Germanic body.

Tough, but not invulnerable. And he had abandoned her, allowing her cruel new master to exploit her vulnerability.

When he didn't reply, Marsia said, 'Sica is looking after you?'

'She is. She found me and took me in. I don't know what she thinks she can achieve. But she obviously sees some hope in me yet.'

'She isn't the only one.'

Carbo tilted his head to one side. 'You, too? After everything?'

'You're Carbo,' said Marsia simply, as if that said enough.

Carbo looked away. With all the pain, physical and emotional, he had put her through, she still had faith in him. Faith he was sure had no foundation. It was almost too much to bear.

She squeezed his upper arm. The wine, bad diet and lack of exercise had taken a toll on his physique, but he was still a big, well-muscled brute of a man. He flexed his thick bicep under her grip, a small gesture to remind them both of who he once was. She gave him a half smile.

'Marsia, I...'

The door to the tavern opened, and a voice yelled out, 'Marsia. Where are you? Are you neglecting your duties?'

Marsia's face paled, and Carbo clenched his jaw and stood. She clutched at him. 'Carbo, don't. You will only make it worse.'

He gently prised her grip off him and walked into the public bar room.

Olorix was standing by the bar, flanked on either side by two bulky thugs, a huge, long-haired German and an equally big bald-headed Syrian. Olorix's appearance was in sharp contrast to his bodyguards. Where they were tall, he was short, where they went out, he went in, and vice versa. Yet it was Olorix who held the power, and his stance, legs apart, belly thrust forward, showed he knew it.

Olorix's eyes widened when he saw Carbo.

'Well. An unexpected guest. You are of course welcome to purchase food and drink here. If you have coin to pay. But I must ask you to stay out of the private areas of this establishment.'

'I was invited there, by Marsia.'

'I'm afraid my slave overstepped the bounds of her authority. She will be punished for it.'

'No,' said Carbo. 'Leave her alone.'

'Why should I do that?' asked Olorix, sounding genuinely surprised at the suggestion.

'Because I am telling you to.' He took a threatening step forward. The two bodyguards stepped in front of Olorix, faces like stone. Olorix put his hand on the Syrian's shoulder and whispered in his ear. The bodyguard nodded once, gestured to the German, and they both stepped out of the tavern, closing the door behind them. The room was empty now except for Carbo and Olorix, and an anxious Marsia, standing at the back, hands clasped together.

Olorix gestured to a table with two chairs. 'Please Carbo, sit. Let's talk.'

Carbo looked uncertain.

'I have dismissed my bodyguards as a sign of good faith. Please, join me.'

Carbo reluctantly sat with Olorix, who flicked his fingers at Marsia.

'Two cups of wine, slave.'

'Water for me,' said Carbo. It felt strange to say, not least because inside he was desperate for the solace that a strong drink could bring. But it would seem like weakness, to drink in front of this man. And it would feel like he was letting Sica down. He was attempting to stop disappointing people.

Marsia brought them a cup each and placed it on the table, then retreated when Olorix waved her away.

Olorix drank deeply. Carbo picked up the cup, just for something to do with his hands, though he didn't touch the insipid liquid.

'What do you want to talk about?' asked Carbo eventually, when Olorix hadn't spoken.

'Well. I wanted to talk about our new relationship.'

'What new relationship?'

'The balance of power around here has changed now. Before, you emboldened people. They knew that if say, a local businessman demanded his rightful payment, and threatened them with just sanctions if they refused, that they could run to you, and you would take care of them.'

'I never said I would do that. I was just keeping to myself. I'm no one's protector.'

'Oh, I know that,' said Olorix. 'But they didn't. Your mere presence was enough to make them feel they could get away with anything. It was starting to impact my livelihood.'

'If I gave the people of the Subura a sense of freedom, I'm glad for them, but it wasn't my intention.'

'Your intentions are irrelevant. Only the outcome matters. But of course, now the situation has changed. Until recently they saw a Carbo struggling with his sadness, and they made allowances while they waited for you to find yourself once more. Now, they see a man bankrupted by his own folly. Humiliated. His property forfeit. His beloved slave turned into an old man's whore.'

'I don't care what they think.'

'Oh, but I do. Now, they see what happens to someone who thinks themself above retribution. Too powerful to be challenged, because of your strength and your friends among the vigiles.

'Already, outstanding debts are down. No one tries to avoid payment. Everyone respects me. And the tavern, and the slave's degradation, will remain as a reminder of who has the real power around here.'

A thought entered Carbo's head, unbelievable at first, but increasingly obvious as he examined it.

'Camilla? She works for you?'

Olorix sat back and smiled.

'The horse race. It was fixed, but not the way she claimed?'

'Please, Carbo. Give me some credit for knowing what goes on in the shady world of the chariot teams. And indeed, having some influence there. Don't look at me like that. You tried to cheat the system, tried to cheat me, by taking advantage of the situation. Unfortunately, you were misled about the true nature of the fix.'

Carbo squeezed his eyes shut. He had been taken in so easily. He could scream at his own stupidity. When he opened his eyes again, Olorix was wearing a broad grin.

'So you see, Carbo. It has worked out very nicely for me. I own a new tavern. I removed a problem. And I have shown the locals where true power lies.'

'Listen Olorix. I don't care about the tavern. I don't care about myself. But please, leave Marsia out of your game. You don't need to punish her because of me.'

'You aren't listening, Carbo. Everyone knows you care about her. And while her shame is on public display, it will remind them all what it means to defy me.'

'I won't let you...'

'You? What can you possibly do? You're a shadow of who you once were. The locals don't support you. Your friends in the vigiles certainly aren't going to help you, since they are pursuing you for murder. Yes, I know about that, too. You're the prime suspect.'

'The murders? That was you as well?'

Olorix laughed. 'Give me some credit, Carbo. "Rome will be cleansed." What nonsense is that? Not my style at all. I actually thought it was you. I wonder now, from your reaction.'

'I didn't kill those people.'

'That doesn't really matter to me. But the vigiles will catch up with you soon and you will be executed. A tragic end to a tragic story.'

Carbo heard the door to the tavern open and Olorix looked over his shoulder.

'Oh, what a coincidence.'

Carbo turned in time to see four vigiles march into the tavern. Their tunics were grimy with soot and ash, and in one case some dried blood, unwashed from the previous night's duties. They were armed with axes and clubs, tools of their trade, useful in fighting fires and criminals alike. The leader blinked, eyes adjusting to the gloom of the poorly lit room. Then his gaze settled on Carbo and he strode forward.

'Carbo. Please come with me. Don't make this difficult.'

'You summoned the vigiles while you kept me talking?' Carbo asked Olorix. Olorix just smiled.

Carbo stood, squinted at the watchman, trying to place the face. He noticed that the arm that loosely held the watchman's axe was crooked, the bones of the forearm broken and healed askew.

'Pinarius,' said Carbo. He nodded at the arm. 'Still give you pain?'

Pinarius glanced down. 'Sometimes,' he conceded.

Carbo reached down and rubbed his right leg. 'This one still hurts, all these years after a German stuck his spear in it.'

'Carbo...'

'We fought the great fire on the Caelian side by side, didn't we? We saved the city. Did you get credit for your heroism?'

'I'm an optio now,' said Pinarius. 'And you were a hero, too. But that was then. This is now. Things have changed. You have changed.'

'Maybe I have, but I didn't do those things they say.'

'That's not for me to decide, Carbo. You can give your defence in court.'

Carbo looked at the other vigiles.

'You only brought three with you? Has your respect for me fallen that far?'

Pinarius glanced behind him at his comrades, and in that instant Carbo struck. Shoulder down, pushing off with his good, left leg, he charged Pinarius in the midriff. The optio folded around the blow, axe flying away, bundled back into two of the men behind him. All three fell to the floor in a tangled heap of limbs. The fourth watchmen stared in shocked indecision for a moment, then heaved his club at Carbo's head.

Carbo ducked under the wild, poorly aimed blow and punched, an uppercut with the force of a hammer that caught the unfortunate watchman in the jaw. His eyes rolled upwards, his legs gave way, and he crumpled to the floor, knocked out cold.

'Stop!' Pinarius was reaching for his axe. Carbo wasted no time and rushed to the door. He wrenched it open, and cast one quick look back. Olorix was standing, yelling at the vigiles to get to their feet and stop him. The vigiles were struggling to rise. Marsia was standing by the bar, something in her hand.

'Carbo, catch.' She tossed the piece of iron to him, and he caught it in one hand, looked down into his palm.

It was the door key.

He looked at her in gratitude. 'I'll make it right,' he said, then dashed out onto the street. He yanked the door closed, placed the hefty key in the lock and turned it. The mechanism slid into place.

It wouldn't hold them long. At night, the door was barred from the inside to discourage burglars and other miscreants from attempting to gain entrance. Even that was not enough to stop a determined intruder. The lock was mainly for when the tavern was left unattended during the day, to deter casual theft. But it gave him a chance.

He turned to run and found himself face to face with Olorix's big Syrian bodyguard. Behind him, blocking escape, was the hairy German. Both had their clubs drawn.

Hard thumps on the tavern echoed out into the street. Passers-by looked at the commotion in alarm and retreated to a safe distance to spectate.

Carbo squared up to the Syrian, who grinned at him, patting his club in his hand. The long piece of wood had two nails hammered at right angles to each other through the tip. Swords were technically forbidden in Rome, but one blow in the wrong place with that weapon would be just as fatal.

Carbo clenched his fists, preparing to strike. The Syrian smiled. Despite Carbo's words to Pinarius about respect, Carbo knew he looked out of shape. And it was true. But that didn't mean he wasn't still as powerful as an ox and as dangerous as an asp.

Carbo dropped to his knee.

The German's club swished through the space his head had been a moment before. Carbo punched hard, and his fist connected with the German's lower chest-bone. He might have struck it with a brick, such was the force behind the blow. It knocked the wind out of the bodyguard, who dropped to the floor, clutching his midriff and gasping for breath.

The Syrian reacted quickly. He swung his spiked club downwards, and Carbo threw himself sideways. The club smacked into the ground, one of the nails splitting a cobblestone in two. Carbo rolled and regained his feet, staggering slightly as he put too much weight on his damaged leg, then recovering his balance. The Syrian was already swinging the club upwards, trying to catch Carbo under the chin. If it made contact, it wouldn't knock him out, as Carbo had just done to the watchman. It would kill him.

Carbo swayed to the side, and as the club passed him, he struck forward, a straight jab to the middle of the Syrian's face. Cartilage split, and blood spurted from his nose. The bodyguard staggered back. But he was made of sterner stuff than the watchman Carbo had rendered unconscious. He shook his head then swung the club back over his shoulder, ready for another hefty sweep.

Carbo stood up to him, as if he was preparing to accept the blow.

From within the tavern came the sound of axes splintering timber. The door shook and shards of wood sprayed out into the street.

The club came round.

Carbo stepped forward, inside the arc of the blow. He gripped the Syrian's wrist, twisted his body, and with one leg extended, threw the bulky man over his shoulder. It was a trick a legionary who was something of an expert wrestler had taught Carbo years ago and it had saved his skin in many brawls.

The Syrian landed heavily, still clutching the club. He put a hand beneath him, ready to get up again.

But Carbo would not give him that chance. He kicked the Syrian hard in the side of the head with his booted foot. The Syrian fell back, and this time didn't move.

An axe-head crashed through the tavern door. Carbo looked up and down the street, then ran. Behind him the door flew off its hinges, and he heard shouts.

'There he is! This way!'

Carbo risked a glance behind him. The three vigiles who remained conscious had emerged from the tavern, and Pinarius was pointing in his direction. Carbo put his head down and sprinted down the street. His war-wounded leg screamed in complaint at the abuse each time it impacted the hard cobbles, but he gritted his teeth and ran on.

The Subura was a maze of narrow streets and alleys. Carbo's knowledge of the local geography was passable. He had explored the area exhaustively as a child in search of entertainment and adventure. But Rome was a vibrant, living city, and its houses, especially in the poorer areas, were shoddily built. Regular fires and collapses, together with ambitious building projects aimed at packing ever more people into tighter spaces meant that the topography of the Subura was in constant flux. And since his return from the legions, Carbo had done little exploring for its own sake. He knew where the best taverns and gambling dens were, but would struggle to locate a single shop selling kitchenware or furniture.

So after turning two corners, Carbo was already in unfamiliar territory, and dodging down two more side streets got him thoroughly lost. The vigiles pursuing him spent every night pounding these streets and knew them as well as the lines on the palms of their hands. Coupled with Carbo's lack of fitness and his war wound, they were soon gaining on him.

He risked another look back at the corner of a dangerously leaning insula and saw that only two vigiles were still giving chase, a bare score of yards back. For the barest of moments he believed he had shaken one off, until he turned the corner and saw Pinarius charging towards him from the other end of the narrow street. He had obviously cut down a side street to head Carbo off, and now Carbo was trapped.

He slowed down, looking for a way out, an alleyway or cut through between the houses, as the vigiles closed in on him from front and back. But he was confronted on either side of the street by shop after shop, cheek by jowl with no gaps between. All manner of merchants and tradesmen sold their wares and plied their trade, cheesemongers beside cobblers, potters next to butchers, perfumiers nestled up against barbers. The men, it was mainly men, working behind the counters or sitting on stools waiting for customers watched Carbo with dispassionate curiosity, waiting for the unfolding of the drama that was building to a climax before them.

'Carbo, in here.'

The voice was a loud hiss, and he turned to see a white-haired, crinkle-faced old lady beckoning him into her fruit shop. He hesitated, but without any other options he ducked inside, past the displays of apples, pears, plums and pomegranates and into the interior of the shop, where crates of produce were stored. The air in the room smelled fresh and sweet, in contrast to the usual odours and stenches of the Subura streets.

He peered at the lady who was still beckoning him, ushering him out of the back. He didn't recognise her.

'Who are you? How do you know me?'

'There is no time,' she said. 'I saw you were being chased. I don't know why and I don't care. Just follow me.'

She hurried into a small backroom, and pointed to a backdoor.

'There are stairs outside that lead to the roof. You can get away that way.'

His leg gave a spasm as he thought of climbing the steps, but he heard shouts from outside. He pulled the door open, grabbed hold of the stair rail and hauled himself onto the first step. The old lady shuffled back inside, holding the door handle, about to pull it shut.

'Why are you helping me?'

She pursed her lips in exasperation at his questioning. 'I used to have to pay Manius more than I could afford. You stopped that. Thank you. Now go!'

She slammed the door shut. He heard raised voices inside the shop, demands from the vigiles, protests from the old lady. She wouldn't hold them up for long, but he thought Pinarius to be a basically decent person, and he would try to persuade her to let him pass without hurting her.

He climbed, left leg up two steps, right leg pulled up level, left leg up another two steps. He was soon even more out of breath than from the running, and he cursed his fitness levels. If he got away, if he cleared his name, if everything went back to normal, he swore to all the gods that he was going to go to the baths every day and exercise in the gymnasium until he was back in shape.

He reached the top of the stairs and found himself at the door of the top floor apartment. The roof was not high, and there was a protruding beam which he used to drag himself up. The tiling was patchy, but that was an advantage since he could see where the underlying rafters ran. He stepped out, feeling tiles crack beneath his feet. But the rafters took his weight. Tentatively, he made his way across the rooftop, balancing only on the beams, where he could see them or predict their path, until he reached the edge.

The insula walls leant out at an alarming angle, and it likely wouldn't be long before this building, like so many others, collapsed from its poor construction and substandard materials. But for Carbo now, it was a boon, since the roof leant across the street, near to the insula on the other side. The opposing building was also a little lower. So Carbo, despite his lack of fitness and injury, should be able to leap across.

He hoped.

He took a deep breath, stepped back from the edge to take a short run-up. He hesitated. But the sound of the vigiles stomping up the staircase and yelling his name forced him into action. He took two strides forward and leapt.

There was no way the roof of the building across the street was going to take the weight of a big, hurtling body. He crashed straight through the tiles, bouncing sideways off an unyielding rafter, and thumped to the floor of the top storey apartment. For a moment he couldn't suck air into his chest, his muscles locked in defence against the damage from the impact, and it felt like he was suffocating.

As the spasm eased, he gasped sweet lungfuls of air, and then slowly sat up. The room had two occupants, a man and woman, frozen in shock. The woman, short, wide, held the handle of a saucepan with both hands, the pan over her shoulder ready to swing it at the man's head. The man, skinny and balding, was backed against the wall, one arm held defensively before his face.

Carbo got painfully to his feet.

'Sorry to intrude,' he said, voice tight but apologetic. He went to the small window overlooking the street and looked up. Pinarius was standing with the other two vigiles on the edge of the roof opposite, silhouetted against the fading light of the early evening sky. Pinarius was pointing at the hole in the roof, and the others were shaking their heads emphatically. In their fire-fighting capacity, they would be familiar with heights and shoddy constructions. Clearly they felt the risk of the leap across the street, with an unfirm footing at the leaping-off point and an uncertain landing, was too great for the reward of apprehending one fugitive.

Pinarius noticed Carbo at the window and put his hands on his hips, a dark look on his face. Carbo gave him an exaggerated shoulder shrug.

'We'll find you, Carbo,' he yelled.

'I'm glad we didn't have to fight,' Carbo called back. 'I didn't murder anyone. Please believe me.'

Pinarius returned Carbo a mirror image of his shrug. Carbo sighed and ducked back inside the room. The woman had dropped the pan and was now cowering behind the man Carbo presumed was her husband. The husband had his arms spread protectively, to keep Carbo from molesting his wife. Carbo smiled inwardly at the thought of this slight man being any impediment to him, or at the thought of having the slightest design on his wife. But he didn't mock them.

'I am very sorry. When it is within my means I will pay for the damage. If I haven't been thrown to the beasts first.'

He went to the front door of the small apartment, drew back the bolt, and went out onto the staircase. He hurried down, conscious that the vigiles might try to continue the chase. But when he reached ground level, he stopped and listened. There was no sign of pursuit. He wended his way through the alleys and narrow, grimy streets, until he found somewhere that looked familiar. Then he squared his shoulders, dipped his head to hide his face as best he could, and headed back towards the docks.

Chapter Thirteen

Olorix stared at the demolished door, his cheeks white with fury, comically accentuating his big red nose. Marsia stood with folded arms, a smug grin fixed on her face, a feral joy inside her chest. After a few moments, his two bodyguards limped back into the tavern. The Syrian had a duck-egg sized bruise on the side of his temple, and the German was breathing heavily, holding his ribs. Olorix gaped.

'You let him get away?' His voice was high, squeaky, like an alarmed girl.

The bodyguards hung their heads, not answering the obvious question. Olorix swung round to Marsia, then advanced slowly on her. She stopped smiling and backed off, the triumph quickly evaporating to be replaced by an acute sense of danger.

Olorix jabbed a finger in her face. 'This is your fault. You helped him.'

'He didn't deserve…'

'Silence slave! Have you forgotten who your Master is? It is I, Olorix. Not Carbo, that pathetic criminal.'

'Master, I…'

'I said silence! It sounds like you need reminding who holds your leash. Boys, hold her down.'

She made a rush for the door, knowing it was pointless, but the instinct to flee too great to meekly submit. The two big bodyguards grabbed her arms, and dragged her to the bar, bent her forwards. Just like the last time. Her buttocks still ached, and she clenched her teeth at the thought of them taking more of a beating.

But Olorix had other plans. He grabbed the back of the collar of her tunic and yanked downwards. The woollen material bit painfully into her neck before it gave way, and the tunic ripped all the way down. He threw it open, so she was fully exposed from behind. She squeezed her eyes shut, clenched her legs together. Was this the time when he would force himself upon her?

The sting of the lash was so excruciating, so unexpected, she didn't even scream. Not the first time. She opened her mouth, but nothing came out. The pain was like nothing she had ever experienced. And it was only the first stroke.

By the time Olorix had finished, and the bodyguards released her arms, she was barely conscious. The torment had seemed to transport her to another place, a world filled solely with a rhythmic crack, and accompanying agony. She slumped to the floor, curled up, knees drawn up to her chest, her face a mess of snot and spit and tears. Twelve lashes had ruined her back, long bloody lines intersecting like a macabre map of the Subura.

'Next time you defy me,' said Olorix, breathing heavily from his exertion, 'I will have you crucified.'

He left her lying on the tavern floor, in no doubt that he meant what he said.

—

Carbo hoped Marsia would not suffer for aiding him. Though it seemed likely she would. He clenched his fists in impotent rage. How could he have put her in this situation? How could he have let her down so badly?

He couldn't let things stand the way they were. Not for Marsia. Not for himself. He didn't yet know what he would do, what he could do, but there would be a reckoning. First though, he had to do something about the threat of arrest hanging over him. How could he clear his name? Finding the real killer would be the obvious answer, but if the vigiles had tried and failed, what more could he do? That said, the vigiles had stopped searching. They thought they had their man.

He was so lost in thought, he almost bumped into the scruffy, snot-nosed urchin who blocked his way.

'Are you Carbo?'

Carbo looked down at the small boy.

'Who wants to know?'

'Are you Carbo?' said the boy again.

Carbo looked around, checking for a trap, an ambush. Something the vigiles had set up? Olorix? But if there were others lying in wait, they were too well-hidden for him.

'Maybe,' he said, suspiciously.

'If you're Carbo,' said the boy, 'I've got a message for you. From a woman with a funny accent. Name was Sica.'

'Sica!'

'She gave me a coin and said to wait here for a big man with dark hair and a limp, called Carbo. I reckon that's you.'

'It's me,' conceded Carbo. 'What's the message?'

'She says the vigiles are watching the front of her insula. Go to the chandler in the insula next door. Say Sica sent you.'

'That's it?'

The urchin held out his hand.

'I thought you said Sica paid you?'

'Yes but…'

Carbo smiled despite himself and tousled the boy's head. 'Come and find me in better times and I'll see what I can do. For now I can only give you my thanks.'

The boy sniffed, wiped his nose on the back of his tunic sleeve, and disappeared off down the street. Carbo reflected that he was starting to build up debts again. But none so big as those he owed Marsia and Sica.

He skirted the insula, avoiding the surveilled front door, and approached the chandler's shop just as he was pulling down the shutter.

'I'm closed,' said the chandler, and let out a wheezy cough.

'Sica told me to come here.'

The chandler looked him up and down. He would have been equal to Carbo's height – though not build – if he hadn't been so stooped.

'Carbo is it?'

Carbo nodded.

'Very well, follow me.'

The chandler pulled the shutters down behind them, shutting out the external light. The shop was illuminated by half a dozen candles rather than the ubiquitous oil lamps, not surprising given the nature of the business. Each was held upright by a rolled lead sheet, and Carbo could make out reliefs of warriors and mythic beasts in the flickering flame. The walls of the shop were coated in soot, and there was an overpowering odour of animal fat and smoke which made Carbo want to gag and cough simultaneously. The pollution from burning the tallow made it obvious why people generally preferred olive oil lamps to candles, though there was still a demand for the chandler's wares from priests and those who had an aesthetic preference for the light of the candle.

The chandler picked up a candle stick and beckoned Carbo onwards. He led him into a back room and down some stairs into the cellar. The thin light from the candle showed Carbo huge vats of tallow, and though the atmosphere was less smoky, the sickly smell from the rancid lard almost overwhelmed him.

Fortunately, he didn't need to stay there for long. The chandler located a door in the furthest wall, and lifted off a bar.

'Years ago, the same person owned the chandler and the fuller and he knocked the cellars through to make it easier for him and his slaves to move between the two shops. Now they are separate businesses, this door is usually barred from both sides. But Sica said she has unbarred it her side.'

He gave the iron ring door handle a gentle tug.

Nothing happened.

He pulled harder. The door remained firmly closed.

The chandler looked at Carbo. 'Maybe she forgot.'

Carbo frowned.

'I don't think she would. Let me try.'

The chandler stepped aside, and Carbo grasped the door handle and gave it a huge jerk. Years of moisture had swollen the timbers of the door and its frame, wedging it shut. But Carbo's strength shifted something, and the door moved inwards an inch. He braced his foot against the door and pulled with all his strength. The wood groaned and squeaked, the handle protested, then the iron ring came off in his hands with the sound of damp, rotted wood giving way.

Carbo flew backwards, the handle still in his hands, knocking into the chandler behind him. Both fell onto their backsides, Carbo sitting between the surprised chandler's legs as if they were rowers on a galley. The candle fell to the floor and the flame sputtered. Almost complete darkness fell.

The chandler snatched up the candle and breathed wheezily on the dying spark. It glowed brighter orange, faded as he ran out of breath, then glowed brighter again as he huffed on it once more. The flame caught, and Carbo looked up to see the door was standing half an inch open.

He could just fit his thick fingers into the crack, and he pulled, opening the old door with the creak of unoiled hinges and the scrape of warped wood against stone flooring.

A new scent filled his nostrils to replace the sickly-sweet tallow smell.

Urine.

Not exactly an improvement, but he knew he was in the fuller's now. He could make his way up to Sica's apartment unseen.

He turned to the chandler.

'Thank you,' he said.

The chandler looked down at the iron ring still clutched in his hands. Carbo handed it to him sheepishly.

'I'll pay for the damage,' he said.

—

Marsia watched the men troop in and out of the brothel. She shivered, sickened as she watched them enter with animal hunger and leave with satisfied swagger. All sorts paraded past her, young and old, fat and thin, smooth-cheeked and purulent and pock-marked. How long would it be until she had to start servicing them? How long until Vatius couldn't pay Olorix any more, or Olorix got bored with that arrangement?

Finally there was a gap. A man left, and none was queuing to take his place. Marsia took a breath, and stiffly entered.

The atrium smelled sickly sweet – cheap perfume, wine and sex. The walls were frescoed floor to ceiling with pornographic imagery, partly designed to titillate and stimulate the customers, but also, with numbers written beneath many of the varied positions, acting as a price list.

The leno, a skinny, greasy-haired man, sat in a chair, his back to the wall and his feet up on a stool. He held a finely embossed silver cup which was halfway to his lips when Marsia walked in. He stopped in the act of taking a sip, eyebrows raised in surprise.

He looked to his bodyguard, a tall, scarred man with the air of a veteran gone to seed, but still enough about him to sort out any patrons that got out of hand. The bodyguard shrugged.

'Client or employee?' asked the leno.

'I'm sorry?' asked Marsia, momentarily non-plussed by the environment and the abrupt question.

The leno, picking up her accent, said loudly, slowly and clearly, 'Do you want a job or a fuck?'

'Oh,' said Marsia. 'Neither.'

The leno frowned. 'Then what do you want?'

'I just wanted to speak to Camilla.'

The leno turned to the bodyguard with a questioning look.

'The freelancer, boss. Second floor.'

'Oh, her. Well, she is working. And she pays me a decent percentage of what she earns, so I don't want anything to interfere with my cash flow.'

'Is she with someone now?'

'Well, no. But you never know when a customer will walk through that door.'

'Please, sir. I just want a few moments with her. I'll leave straight away if she is… required.'

The leno stroked his stubbly chin. 'Why do you need to see her?'

'I'd prefer not to say.'

'Then the answer is no. Get out of here.'

'Sir, I beg you. I can't get away from my master for long. I don't know when I will get the chance next. And he will beat me so hard if he knows I am here.'

'Who is your master?'

'His name is Olorix.'

'Olorix? The bookie?'

Marsia nodded.

'That fat, cheating bastard. He stiffed me at a dog fight just last week. I found out he had given poison to the hound I bet on. The poor beast barely made it into the ring before he keeled over.'

'That sounds like him, sir.'

'Well, I don't know what you want, but the fact you are doing it behind Olorix's back gives me some satisfaction. Up the stairs, two flights, second cubicle on your right.'

'Thank you, sir, so much.'

'Hurry up. Who knows how long her break will last.'

Marisa bowed her head in gratitude and hurried up the stairs. Some of the cubicles had doors half open and as she passed them she saw a variety of girls, all shapes and sizes and skin tones, some attending their make-up, some staring blank-eyed at the walls, one curled up in a ball and sobbing quietly.

The door to Camilla's cubicle was closed and she knocked tentatively.

'Come in, darling.' Camilla's tone was light and inviting.

Marsia opened the door and found Camilla sitting on the edge of a cheap bed, cheeks rouged, eyes accentuated with kohl, lips bright red, wrapped in a pristine white toga.

'Marsia!' Camilla couldn't keep the surprise out of her voice.

Marsia closed the door behind her and stood with her back to it. Now she was here she was uncharacteristically uncertain what to say. Her eyes dropped to the toga, the elaborate folds concealing much more than they revealed. Camilla noticed the direction of her gaze.

'Well, prostitutes are supposed to wear togas in public,' she said. 'To show the world what kind of women we are. Though we mostly don't bother. But I find that here in private, some men like it.'

'Really?' Marsia didn't understand, but then, much about men was a mystery to her.

'I think some like to unwrap me, like a Saturnalia gift. Some like the message it shows, that I am no prim, Roman matron in stola and palla. And I think some actually like to imagine I am some rich young boy. It takes all sorts.'

'How can you do it?' asked Marsia, her fears forcing the words out before she could stop them.

Camilla frowned, but considered the question. 'I think it helps that I am free. I get to choose my clients. I can refuse who I want. I can refuse to do anything I don't want to do. And I don't have to put up with beatings from an angry master or leno for not doing as I'm told.'

Marsia flinched at this, closed her eyes, and took a deep breath before opening them again. Camilla was looking at her curiously.

'Marsia? What's wrong? Why did you come here?'

Marsia swallowed. Now she was confronted with the question, she wasn't sure. What could she hope to gain from this self-absorbed girl? Would she show any remorse at all?

'Did he pay you very well?' she asked.

'Who?' asked Camilla.

'Olorix.'

'Oh.' Camilla looked down. Marsia shifted her weight from one leg to another. The stinging pain from her back seemed to have barely abated, and she thought that the walk to the brothel had pulled off some scabs as they rubbed against her clothing. She hoped her dark tunic wouldn't show up the blood.

'I was born free, you know,' said Camilla. 'Born free, but I would have been better off a slave.'

'You are never better off a slave.'

'I had no food other than what I could beg for. My mother would get drunk and beat me. I never had a father. I was cold every winter, and hungry every day. My mother started hiring me out to men when I was thirteen years old.'

Marsia looked at her, sympathy warring inside her with anger at what she had done.

'My mother died when I was fifteen. Her lungs, they said. I think she just didn't want to go on. It doesn't matter. For me, that was when I started living. Taking control. I told myself I would be rich, any way I could. And when

I had enough money, I was going to buy a farm in the country, and have slaves of my own, and grow grapes and make wine, and never be hungry or cold again.'

'Any way you could? No matter who got hurt along the way?'

'Hurt? I've made a lot of men happy. And I've never killed anyone.'

'Maybe not with your own hands. But how many have you cheated, like Carbo, who went on to take their own lives?'

'Carbo? He didn't...'

'No, thanks be to Nerthus.'

'Then, what's the problem?'

'Camilla, he lost everything to Olorix, because of you.'

'Everything?'

'He was already a humbled, broken man before you got your claws into him. The things he had suffered – the pain and loss. It's no surprise that he took to gambling and drinking. But you never knew the man when I first met him. Damaged yes, but a hero. And because of your scheme with Olorix, what little he had left has been taken from him. Now he has no business, no home and the vigiles are after him for murders he didn't commit.'

'I heard about the murders,' said Camilla. 'It wasn't him?'

'Of course not!'

Camilla sighed. 'Yes,' she said.

Marsia frowned at the non sequitur.

'Yes, what?'

'Yes, Olorix paid me very well. It's the only reason I did it. Getting me closer to that prize, to my farm. I have nothing against Carbo. I actually liked his company.'

'Then help me make it right.'

'How? What can I do?'

'I don't know,' said Marsia helplessly. She had hoped something would occur to her, or that Camilla would volunteer something. But the truth was, she was completely without a plan. The goals were clear. Prove Carbo's innocence. Restore his fortune. Help him heal. But the path there was shrouded in fog.

'Look, I have no love for Olorix. And I feel bad for Carbo. If there is something I can do, I will. I just don't know...'

There was a loud banging at the door.

'Time's up!' came the leno's voice. 'You've got a customer downstairs, Camilla.'

'Give me a few moments,' Camilla called back.

'No,' said the leno. 'He asked for you, but if you keep him waiting he will choose one of the others. And you aren't using my room for social callers. Either pay your way, or get out.'

Camilla looked helplessly at Marsia. Marsia nodded her understanding.

'Come to me, at the tavern. It's hard for me to get out. Olorix would... hurt me again.'

Camilla nodded. 'I'll come. I promise.'

'Camilla!' yelled the leno, knocking hard again.

Marsia pulled the door open so suddenly that the leno nearly hammered her on the nose. She brushed past him and down the stairs. In the atrium a man old enough to be Camilla's grandfather was pacing up and down. She gave him a contemptuous glance, then hurried back out onto the street, heading back to the tavern as fast as her injuries would allow.

–

Rome never slept. Even at this time of night, a few short hours before sunrise, the streets were full of the wheeled vehicles that were banned during the day, taking their produce to the various markets throughout the city. Criminals prowled, vigiles patrolled, and groups of drunken young men staggered around looking for beggars and semi-conscious inebriates to toss in a blanket or throw in the river for sport.

Nevertheless, the streets were dark, illuminated only by the moon when it peeped out from behind the scudding clouds, and the light of braziers and oil lamps shining out of unshuttered street-facing windows. It was an ideal time for Carbo to sneak out of Sica's apartment, utilising the secret route through the cellars, and also an ideal time to visit his old tavern, empty of customers and in no danger of a visit from Olorix.

Though being out on the streets made him nervous, it was easy enough to avoid the vigiles and any others who might recognise him, especially accompanied by Sica, who scouted ahead to warn him of any dangers. They reached the tavern uneventfully, and after giving a soft knock, were admitted by Marsia.

Marsia gave Carbo a long hug, then Sica a much shorter one, and ushered them to sit around a small round table. Camilla was already present. The room was lit by one small oil lamp, but Carbo could see the anxious expression on her face as she looked up from her seat. She looked like she was about to bolt at the slightest sign of anger from him.

And he did indeed feel a rush of fury at the sight of her. It was her fault that he was in this situation, skulking around like a thief, sneaking into his own tavern, with not a copper as to his name.

But it wasn't her fault, was it? If he hadn't been looking for the thrill of the bet, if he hadn't been desperate to pay off debts because of his drinking and gambling, he would never have been taken in so easily. She was just like a thief who sees a silver cup on a window ledge, and makes off with it before anyone sees. The fault belonged just as much to the fool who left his treasure negligently unguarded, didn't it?

Besides, what was she doing here, if it wasn't to make amends?

Camilla was looking at his hands, and he realised his fists were clenched into tight balls. With an effort, he willed them to relax. He ran one hand through his thick hair, then nodded to her.

'Camilla.'

'Carbo,' she said.

He sat at the table, across from Camilla, and Sica and Marsia sat on either side of him. For a moment no one spoke.

It was Sica that broke the silence. 'Well? What we going to do?'

Marsia looked to Carbo for an answer, maybe out of habit, but he pursed his lips and waited. Marsia had arranged this meeting, and while he appreciated it, he didn't know what it was meant to achieve.

Marsia sighed. 'Let's establish some basics. Is there anyone here that believes Carbo committed these murders?'

Sica shook her head emphatically. Camilla hesitated, then said, 'No. I don't.'

'Good,' said Marsia. 'So we have two problems to solve. Firstly, we need to either prove Carbo couldn't have committed these crimes, or find out who did.'

'Agreed,' said Camilla.

'And secondly, we need to prove Olorix cheated Carbo when he took his tavern and his farm.'

Camilla looked doubtful.

'We can take him to the law courts. If you testify that he fixed the bets, we can sue him for the lost assets, and damages too.'

Even in the dim light Carbo could see the thought of this scared Camilla.

'No,' she said. 'Who would believe someone like me? It would be my word against Olorix's. That's if I ever made it to court. More likely Olorix would have me murdered and my body cut up and dumped in the cloaca maxima.'

'She's right,' said Carbo. 'Besides, suing someone costs money, which is just what I don't have.'

'I am saving a little,' said Sica hesitantly. 'But my business is new and I...'

Carbo put his hand on hers. 'You are already doing so much for me,' he said.

Marsia looked at Camilla, one eyebrow raised. Camilla bridled at the unspoken implication.

'If you think I am dipping into my savings for him, you can think again. I feel bad for Carbo, but not that bad.'

'It's fine, Camilla,' said Carbo. 'As you said, it's pointless anyway. We need harder evidence, multiple witnesses of impeccable character, or something in writing.'

'And Carbo can't take anyone to court while he is wanted for murder,' said Marsia.

This gave them all pause for thought.

'So that is first,' said Sica. 'Catch the killer.'

Camilla laughed. 'You make it sound easy.'

'Not easy,' said Sica. 'Things worth doing never easy. But must be done anyway.'

'How?' asked Carbo. 'How do we find this madman?'

'What do we know of him already?' asked Marsia.

'He crazy,' said Sica.

'That's helpful,' said Marsia. 'What else?'

'We know he is my height and build. Dark hair like me. Walks with a limp.'

'The appearance is unusual, but not unique,' said Camilla. 'But the limp too? That's strange.'

'What are you saying?' asked Marsia, her tone ominous. 'You said you didn't think Carbo did it.'

'I don't,' said Camilla. 'But what if the limp isn't real?'

'You mean, pretending?' asked Sica. 'Why?'

'To look like Carbo.'

They were all silent. The implications were stunning.

'But that means...' said Marsia.

'That means he is deliberately trying to frame me,' said Carbo.

'Why?' asked Sica. 'Who would do that?'

Marsia laughed without humour. 'Carbo has been making enemies since he first returned to Rome. The list is long.'

'But why now? And this way?'

'Someone I offended recently? Someone who is also a bit crazy?'

'Not Olorix,' said Marsia. 'He looks nothing like you, and anyway, he seems satisfied that he has shown his superiority over you already.'

'What about that strange guy who was with you at that wrestling match?'

Carbo frowned. 'Who?'

'Is that the one who you were rude to the following day?' asked Marsia. 'When you were hungover?'

'I don't really remember.'

'Tall, dark hair, but scarred face and a haunted look. He was very jumpy whenever there was a loud noise. Eyes always darting around. Terrible teeth.'

'Yes, that's him,' said Camilla.

'I've seen him in the tavern a few times,' said Marsia. 'He could definitely be mistaken for Carbo in the dark. His size and build. Maybe even something about the shape of his face, if it wasn't for the broken teeth and scars. And if he put a limp on too...'

'But why?' asked Carbo. 'Because I was rude to him?'

'We don't know it is him at all,' said Sica.

'And even if we thought it was him, we need to prove it.'

Carbo scratched his chin. He wished Vespillo was here at his side, his friend rather than his adversary. He could really do with his advice. Then he looked at the three women seated around the table, and realised that Fortuna had just maybe turned her smile back on him. All three of them were clever, resourceful and cunning. He didn't need Vespillo. He had them.

'How do we draw him out?'

'He leaves messages saying "Rome must be cleansed." People say he is killing off those he doesn't approve of. The weak and the immoral. The beggars. And the prostitutes.' She looked at Camilla.

'Oh no,' said Camilla. 'You had better not be going to suggest what I think you are.'

'Please Camilla, think about it. You are the sort of person he is targeting. And what's more, you have a connection to Carbo, who he is trying to hurt. You may be in danger already.'

Camilla sat back. 'Maybe I am in danger. All the more reason for me to keep my head down. Maybe I'll just go to the country for a few weeks until this all dies down, he gets caught or gets bored, or Carbo is captured and executed.'

'I thought you wanted to help,' said Marsia.

'Help yes. Die, no.'

'How close to getting your farm in the country are you?' asked Marsia abruptly.

Camilla narrowed her eyes. 'I still have some way to go. Why?'

'Carbo had a farm. If we could clear his name, get his properties back maybe...' She looked at Carbo.

'The farm would be yours, Camilla,' said Carbo without hesitation.

Camilla swallowed. He could see the calculation behind her eyes. Risks and rewards.

'What would I have to do?' she asked.

Chapter Fourteen

Cicurinus stomped through the streets of the Subura, irritable and frustrated. Ever since Carbo had disappeared, and that fat bookmaker had taken over the tavern, the mood to kill had not been upon him. Actually, he wouldn't have minded putting a knife in, what was his name, Olorix. Carbo was his prey. But Olorix had come along and taken Carbo's business and his slave, and Carbo had fled, the Allfather Woden alone knew where.

So now, his mission seemed less clear, less purposeful. Yes, Rome still needed to be purified, but he wanted Carbo to be able to appreciate his achievements, as well as take the blame for them. If Carbo had left the city, if he was staying with someone who could vouch for his whereabouts, and Cicurinus committed another murder, it would be obvious even to the dumb vigiles that Carbo was not the killer after all. And that would not do.

He wished Veleda would advise him. But she had disappeared too. Maybe she had gone to find Carbo for him. Maybe she had other plans. She confided little in him.

He felt crushingly alone. Carbo, who he had thought could have been the fraternal companion he craved, had first rejected him, then vanished. Veleda, who guided him, was gone too. And he could not bring himself to seek social comfort with the lowlifes of the Subura.

So he stomped up and down the busy streets all day, ate when he was hungry, slept when he was tired. And he waited. For Veleda. For Carbo. For something.

And then, it happened. He saw him.

The big man with the dark hair was limping down the road arm in arm with that prostitute who had been by his side, that first time he had encountered him on his return to Rome. Quite blatant, for all the world to see. As if he cared nothing for propriety.

It was bad enough when a man skulked around brothels or took advantage of whores in back alleys. To be so unmindful of what it meant to be a Roman... it was upsetting. He knew Carbo had fallen far from the hero he had once been, but this was too much.

And yet still he would not kill Carbo. That would bring him no satisfaction.

The prostitute though...

He followed them, and after a short distance, the girl pulled Carbo up against a wall, and encircled her arms and one leg around him, kissing him deeply on the lips. Carbo clearly wasn't mindful of picking up the cold sores that were so commonplace in Rome this winter.

That brought back the memory of his own lapse, the prostitute that he had been careful not to kiss. But even that was Carbo's fault. That evening – when they had drunk and gambled together – was a seduction where a need for companionship, strong wine and the city's open arms had dragged him down. He knew now that he needed none of that. He needed only his purpose, and Veleda. Where was that priestess?

'Kill the girl.'

The sweet, soft whisper contrasted with the harsh words. He turned quickly, shocked. Veleda was standing under the awning of a spice seller's stall, deep in the shadows. Despite her unusual appearance, her white robe, her barbarian hairstyle, she was concealed enough in the shadows that no one paid her attention.

'Veleda. Where have you been?'

'No concern of yours. Go quickly. Don't lose them. And make sure the whore dies.'

With that, she was gone, slipping into the crowd and immediately disappearing from his sight. He turned back to Carbo, and found they too had vanished. He searched for them among the packed masses in the street, heart thumping and guts clenching at the thought of finding him and losing him so quickly. But both Carbo and Cicurinus were above average height, and after a few moments he spotted the top of Carbo's head, fifty yards away.

Cicurinus elbowed and shoved his way forwards, ignoring the curses, gestures and filthy looks he received as smaller people, both in stature and importance, stumbled out of his path. Soon he was at a range where he could hang back, confident of keeping them in view, not wanting to get too close, not yet. Murder in the broad daylight of this late afternoon, in full view of the populace of Rome, was not his style, nor his plan. The whore would die somewhere quiet, and Carbo, who was clearly attached to her, would watch. They wouldn't be walking the streets forever. Soon they would find somewhere to be alone together, to indulge Carbo's disgusting needs. A tavern room, an apartment, a brothel room, a back alley even.

That was when Cicurinus would strike.

The young watchman breathed hard and his words came out in a jumble.

'Taura sent... Carbo... hurry...'

'Take a breath, Musca' said Vespillo, forcing a calmness into his voice that he didn't feel. The lad had obviously run to the station as fast as he could, but was now unable to talk. 'That's it. In through the nose. Out through the mouth. One more. Good. Now try again. What is it?'

'Taura sent me, sir. He's found Carbo.'

'By the docks?'

'No, sir. The Subura.'

Vespillo frowned. 'Taura is supposed to be staking out Sica's place in the Trans Tiberim region.'

'Yes, I know, sir, but he had his contacts looking for Carbo across the city. Informers and beggars and street children.'

'And?'

'He was told he was at the baths of Agrippa. With a woman. Taura has gone there, but he sent me to get you.'

'Not keen to deal with Carbo on his own?'

'Who would be, sir?'

'Fair point. Fetch half a dozen of the boys, just the ones who are ready to leave this instant. Go!'

Vespillo grabbed his belt and fastened it around his waist, then took his axe from the corner of his office and thrust the handle through his belt. In a gratifyingly short space of time, Musca returned with a motley selection of vigiles.

'Boys,' said Vespillo. 'We've found Carbo. We're going to go get him and bring him back. You all know how dangerous he is. We are going to attempt to capture him, alive and unharmed. We all have great respect for his actions in the past, and he is a personal friend to many of us, not least myself. But understand this. He is a killer. He has killed barbarians in the legions, he has killed criminals in Rome. And now he has started killing innocents.

'We will not take any chances with him. If he doesn't give himself up, or we can't subdue him safely, then we put him down. Permanently.'

Vespillo looked into the vigiles' eyes one by one, and they nodded grim agreement.

'Let's go, before we lose him again.'

—

Carbo felt distinctly uncomfortable, and not just because of the heat in the laconicum. He had never before been self-conscious of his scarred body, but the fresh, self-inflicted wounds felt shameful. Worse, Camilla sat beside him, the clouds of steam emanating from the brazier whenever someone splashed water over the hot coals doing precious little to hide her attractive nakedness. Despite his reduced circumstances, despite his general uninterest in women since the death of Rufa, despite the danger they were risking, he felt an unbidden stirring of desire. He had a sudden fear of an unwanted tumescence, and the humiliation that would bring, both from Camilla and the other bathers. Fortunately, anxiety about the possibility quickly dampened the possibility of the occurrence.

'Are you sure this is the best place to try to lure him to?' asked Camilla.

'I have no weapon,' said Carbo. Camilla glanced down at his lap with a smile, and Carbo covered himself with his hands, blushing like a little girl. He coughed and tried again. 'I have no blade, nothing to defend us with apart from what you see before you now.'

Camilla giggled but Carbo ignored her and pressed on.

'Maybe he won't come for us here. But we will give him every chance, because if he does, he will be as unarmed as myself.'

He looked around the steamy room, assessing where the hard edges and solid surfaces were, where anything that could be used offensively might be. He assessed the other bathers for threats, but was reassured. These baths were free, and tended not to be frequented by the rich with their bodyguards, who were more likely to bathe in more expensive or private facilities. There were a couple of old ladies, seated by the door to the tepidarium, wrinkled and droopy, gossiping in loud voices that the rest of the room couldn't help overhear. Near the entrance was a pot-bellied man with a grizzled beard and a receding hairline. He had his eyes closed, as if he was trying to tune out the noise from the rest of the baths; the screams from the customers of the armpit hair pluckers, the grunts from the gymnasium, the splashes and shouts from the pools, the shouts and cries advertising the services of the masseurs and physicians.

It was early evening, and soon the bath attendants would be coming round to shoo the customers out, so they could close for the night. But not quite yet. There was time.

There was no mistaking the man when he entered, even through the misty atmosphere. Black haired, tall, broad-shouldered. More wiry and less muscular than Carbo, though his frame could have borne more brawn. Terribly scarred, from head to feet. Totally naked.

Carbo stood slowly. They looked at each other, eye to eye. Now he was seeing him, really seeing him, rather than just being aware of the presence of a drinking companion, as was the case previously, there was something familiar about him. He narrowed his eyes.

'What's your name?'

Cicurinus let out a single bark of a laugh. 'You seem to have trouble keeping that in your head. My name is Cicurinus.'

Carbo frowned. He had a vague recollection that was the name this man had given when they met, but he had not known anyone by that name in the past. Maybe his sense of past familiarity was a mistake.

'Just tell me why?'

Cicurinus looked around the room, at the old ladies and the middle-aged man, who were watching the exchange with curiosity and some nervousness.

'Get out,' he said to them, his voice brooking no argument. All three hurried out rapidly. Camilla stood to leave as well, but Cicurinus pointed at her. 'Not you. Sit.' Camilla looked to Carbo, who nodded, and she reluctantly sat back down on the warm stone seat.

'Why what?' asked Cicurinus. 'Why the killing? Or why pretend to be you?'

'You can tell me both. In whatever order you like.'

Cicurinus seemed to consider for a moment. Then he spoke, and his voice was strangely flat.

'I fought in Germania, like you. I killed the so-called barbarians, hated them even while I admired their courage and nobility. But I was just a young soldier, doing what soldiers did. Whoring, drinking, gambling. I don't need to tell you about that, do I?'

Carbo said nothing and Cicurinus continued.

'And then I was captured. Just a routine patrol, ambushed. I hadn't even been a legionary for that long. A year or so. Enough to think I knew it all, not long enough to realise I knew nothing.

'They took all of us who survived the ambush prisoner, and intended to sacrifice us all in honour of Tywaz, their god of war. They did in fact, nail the rest of my comrades to trees and then slice open their bellies. They made me watch.'

Still his voice held no emotion.

'But their priestess, a young woman called Veleda, saw something in me. She told me that Frigg, wife of Woden, had spoken to her. Told her that one day I would make a difference. Be someone.'

'I guess you are still waiting for that day?' interjected Carbo, but Cicurinus carried on as if he hadn't spoken.

'It was a long time coming. Veleda put me through many trials. To prepare me. Sometimes she treated me with kindness. Often it was pain. You might even call it torture. For years.'

Carbo had no comeback to that, but his eyes roamed over Cicurinus' naked body, which told its own story in the scars of burns and cuts and healed fractures.

'And then the Romans came again. A raiding party led by a Centurion of the XXIst Rapax, curse him. He destroyed the German village where I was held. Killed them all, women and children. He rescued me, or so he thought. But no legionary ever welcomed me back. They stared when they thought I wasn't looking, looked away when they thought I might catch their eye. I didn't care. Veleda taught me what mattered.'

'And what is that?' Carbo couldn't help wanting to hear the story, even as he itched for the fight to begin.

'The pure life of the savage. The Germans are at peace with the world, the forests and the hills and the rivers, the birds and animals and fish. Their warfare is noble and honest. They are true warriors.'

Carbo thought of the treachery of Arminius in the Teutoberg forest, that had led to his own brief capture. He shuddered at the thought of what he might have become if, like Cicurinus, he had been unable to escape.

'And look at Rome. Beggars. Drunkards. Whores. The empire is in decline, and soon will fall to the warriors at its gates.' Cicurinus was becoming more animated now, accentuating his words with conviction and righteous anger.

'You don't think that's a good thing?'

'Germans and Romans both need strong enemies. Corculum knew it, back when Cato was arguing for Carthage to be destroyed, and Corculum said it must be saved. A strong Carthage would have meant a strong Rome. But that ship has sailed. Now it's the turn of Germania to be Rome's foil. They keep each other powerful. But if Rome continues its decline, then the German tribes will soon follow, just as the Romans did after the destruction of Carthage.'

'So this is your purpose? Your mission? This is why you write "Rome must be purified" at the scenes of your crimes.'

'I can't rid Rome of all the degenerates, there are far too many. But Veleda tells me, if they see the consequences of their ways, then fear may complete my work for me.'

Carbo cocked his head on one side. 'The German priestess is here in Rome?'

'Of course. She is my guide. She tells me what is right and wrong.'

'And me? Why try to make it look like I committed these crimes? Because I am one of the degenerates your Veleda despises?'

Cicurinus shook his head, and his pitying smile revealed his new wooden dentures. 'You really don't know do you?'

'Then tell me.'

'Enough. You have had the benefit of Veleda's wisdom now. Maybe you will come to understand, as I do. Before the end. But I didn't come here to talk.'

'You're here to kill me then,' said Carbo, his voice matter of fact.

'Actually, no,' said Cicurinus. 'Not you.' His gaze drifted sideways and down to where Camilla sat. She shrank back from him.

'Carbo,' she said in a small voice.

'Don't worry, Camilla. I won't let him hurt you.'

'So Carbo the hero is still in there somewhere?' Cicurinus' tone was mocking. 'I thought he had vacated your body in favour of Carbo the drunk, Carbo the gambler, Carbo the beggar.'

'What makes you think you know anything about me?'

Now Cicurinus laughed with genuine amusement. Then he lunged forward.

He was quick. He was a little smaller and a lot younger than Carbo which allowed him to put his mass into motion more quickly than Carbo could.

But Carbo was no slouch. He had always had quick reactions, and with no wine in his belly, they were not dulled. Cicurinus reached out for him with both arms spread, but Carbo ducked under the embrace, pivoted to one side, and punched Cicurinus in the side of the head.

Cicurinus rocked with the punch, and the impact was slight. He followed up with a blow of his own, spinning sideways with elbow out, so the pointy bone jabbed into Carbo's ribs. It stung but did little more.

But now they were close, too close for sparring and feinting. Cicurinus moved again to grapple with Carbo, but Carbo's body was slick with sweat, and he couldn't get a purchase. Carbo brought his knee up, aiming for between Cicurinus' legs, but the other man twisted so the blow caught his outer thigh. It was clearly painful, maybe enough to deaden the leg, but that only put Cicurinus on equal terms with Carbo given the battle injury that stiffened his own leg.

They wrestled, attempting head-butts, kicks, trips. Carbo tried every trick he knew from his brawling days in the legions, and on this account he had the upper hand. But Cicurinus was younger, had not been abusing his body with wine and poor diet like Carbo, and further, Carbo had spent more time in the hot room than him. Quickly, Carbo found himself gasping for breath, heart racing, and knew that he would not be able to fight on for long.

He grasped Cicurinus' wrist, turned his body swiftly, and attempted to throw him over his shoulder in the classic wrestler's move.

A combination of his old injury and the slick concrete floor let him down. His leg buckled, then slid from under him. He crashed heavily onto the flagstones, turning his head to one side at the last moment to avoid smashing his face in. But he landed prone, with Cicurinus' weight on his back.

The air rushed out of him, and for a moment he couldn't draw breath. The impact and the pressure from

Cicurinus compressed his chest, and panic hit him as he tried to gasp in air.

Cicurinus took immediate advantage of the situation. Unharmed by the fall, cushioned as he was by Carbo, he was able to grab Carbo's wrist, and before there was any chance to resist, twist his arm behind his back. A wrestling trick from Cicurinus, this time.

Carbo struggled as he gasped, but it was impossible. Exhausted, winded, armlocked and unable to suck in air, he was helpless.

Cicurinus leaned close to Carbo's ear, and the smell of rotten gums washed over him.

'I'm not here to kill you,' he hissed. 'I'm here to kill your whore friend. While you watch.' He grabbed the hair on the back of Carbo's head, pulled it back, then smashed it forward into the ground. His forehead hit the stone, and his vision filled with sparks, while the room blurred and darkened.

The weight abruptly lifted from his back, but he was too dazed to move. He could hear screaming. He panted hard and got to his hands and knees. The room spun around him dangerously. Then he heard shouts, yells, from far off, getting nearer.

The screaming stopped. Carbo slumped back to the floor, rolled onto his back. A face appeared above his, out of focus. Bearded. Craggy. Kind-eyed.

'Good evening, Carbo,' said Vespillo. 'What are you doing down there?'

Chapter Fifteen

Carbo held onto the bars of his cell, and shook them again in frustration. They were solid, well-made, not a speck of rust. He should have expected nothing less from anything in the headquarters of the second cohort of the vigiles, run as it was by the ever-thorough Vespillo. Taura and Pinarius stood guard outside the locked door, but their presence was superfluous. There was no way Carbo could escape, and he had no friends in the city who were capable of attempting a rescue.

'Please,' he begged them again. 'You have to let me go. You don't understand.'

'Shut your mouth,' said Pinarius. 'You're going to get what's coming to you. You know, one of those girls you killed had a baby boy. Who will care for him now? He'll probably just be exposed on the dung heap.'

'I didn't do it!'

'Stop talking to him,' said Taura. 'He isn't even man enough to admit to what he's done.'

'Where's Vespillo? I must speak with him.'

The vigiles studiously ignored him.

Carbo turned away in exasperation, and thumped the wall of the cell. He dislodged a small puff of dust, but the only significant damage was a graze to his knuckles. He leant forward and pressed his forehead against the brick-work and tried to control his breathing. When he had regained some measure of composure, he took to pacing the cell, like a tiger in the holding cages behind the arena, all pent-up energy, waiting for release.

Eventually, with no outlet for his frustration, he sat on the floor and closed his eyes, clenching and unclenching his fists and his jaw rhythmically.

'Wake up,' came Taura's voice. 'Visitors.'

Carbo was on his feet in an instant. 'Vespillo?'

'No, Carbo. It's Tribune Pavo.' Taura stepped aside, and two men stood before the cell, peering in at Carbo. One, Carbo recognised as Pavo, the Urban Cohort tribune who had been so incompetent and obstructive in the lead-up to the great fire on the Caelian hill. The other, older, floppy-haired, looking down his aquiline nose, was unfamiliar.

'Is that him?'

'Yes, sir,' said Pavo. 'This is Carbo.'

The man's expression held fury and contempt, but his voice was tight and controlled.

'Do you know who I am?' he asked.

Carbo looked to Pavo uncertainly, then shrugged. The man now looked affronted as well as angry.

'I,' he said haughtily, 'am Titus Servilius Ahala.'

Carbo looked at Pavo, wondering if the name should mean something to him.

'I am a very rich and powerful man!'

'I'm pleased for you,' said Carbo. 'You came here to tell me that?'

Ahala's composure disappeared now. 'You murdered my son!'

Carbo looked down.

'I'm sorry for your loss. But I had nothing to do with it.'

'You're a liar as well as a murderer? Do you have no shame?'

'I've never even met your son.'

'His name was Quintus. And he was a good boy. He had his… idiosyncrasies, but who doesn't fool around in their youth? He didn't deserve to die. And in such a way, so violent, so humiliating…' Ahala broke off and swallowed hard. Pavo put a supportive hand on his shoulder.

'What will happen to him?' asked Ahala.

'He will be tried and quickly found guilty.'

'You'll give me the names of the jurors so I can make sure they are properly rewarded for their work?'

'Of course,' said Pavo. 'Although it is hardly necessary. The evidence against him is overwhelming. And he has no resources to… incentivise the jury himself.'

'Nevertheless, I want to be sure.'

'I'll make sure you have the information.'

Carbo stared in disbelief. He knew that bribery was commonplace in the Roman judicial system, but to discuss it so openly, in front of not only the defendant, but his gaolers, showed a level of arrogance and entitlement that was way beyond what the vast majority of Romans would ever know.

'And when he is found guilty?'

When, not if, Carbo noted.

'There are options,' said Pavo, as if he was discussing the menu for a banquet. 'Thrown to the beasts is one. They may put him up against a Thracian or a retiarius in the arena armed only with a wooden sword. Something to entertain the masses.'

'It needs to be painful,' said Ahala. His voice had turned icy now.

'Well, there will be plenty of time to dream up something imaginative. I'm sure if you talk to the Urban Praetor, he would be happy to take your suggestions on board.'

Carbo shivered, from the coldness of the cell, and fear of the punishment. Not for the likes of him the quick and merciful death of a beheading or garrotting. If he was to die horribly in the arena, he hoped he would go with honour and dignity. But he doubted it. He had seen enough death to know how few faced it in the manner they would wish.

He tried one more time. 'Please,' he said. 'I didn't kill your son. You must believe me.'

'You disgust me,' said Ahala. 'You go on this killing rampage, and my son gets caught up in your madness, and you don't even have the decency to admit what you did. I will take great pleasure watching you die.'

He strode off, footsteps echoing on the flagstones. Pavo looked Carbo up and down one last time, then followed.

Taura and Pinarius took up their places on guard once more. They kept their backs to Carbo, carefully avoiding eye contact with him, or with each other.

-

Carbo sat on the floor of the cell, staring at the wall, contemplating the punishment awaiting him. He could see no way out, whichever angle he looked at the problem. The evidence, Vespillo's probity and the enmity of the powerful Ahala combined to make a cage as escape-proof as the brick and iron one in which he was currently incarcerated. On top of that, he worried for Camilla. Cicurinus had been intending to kill her. Had she escaped? Was she safe now?

'Carbo.' Vespillo's voice was full of sadness. Carbo turned to see his friend's mournful face at the cell door. 'I'm sorry I couldn't come sooner. There was a big fire on the Viminal and they pulled crews in from all the stations. It's under control now, but I think this one will burn for a day or two.'

'Vespillo, listen to me. You have to let me go.'

'You know I can't do that, old friend. You can't know how sorry I am that it has come to this.'

'Camilla is in danger.'

'Who?'

'The girl I was with.'

'Carbo, there was no one in that room apart from yourself.'

'Vespillo. I found the killer. He came for me. And for the girl. He wants to kill her, to punish me.'

'Why would he want to punish you?'

'I don't know,' Carbo said helplessly.

'Carbo, we found you on your own. You had slipped and hit your head. I think you had been in there too long, got a bit too much heat.'

'No. The killer was there. His name is Cicurinus. Camilla witnessed it. There were others too who saw him, a couple of old ladies and a middle-aged man.'

'When we got there, the baths were closing. There was no one there who had seen anything untoward, though one or two heard the sound of your voice and the impact when you fell. You were seen going in with a girl, this Camilla I guess, but she must have pushed off when you injured yourself. I guess she realised she wasn't going to make any money off you last night.'

Carbo gripped the bars of the cell in frustration.

'Please. If our friendship meant anything. This isn't just about me. Marsia is in trouble; she is being used badly by Olorix. Camilla is in danger. I can't do anything for either of them while I'm stuck in here.' Or if I'm dead, he thought. The idea chilled him further.

'I'll look in on Marsia,' said Vespillo. 'Make sure she is all right. Put a bit of pressure on Olorix if necessary. He won't want me paying too much attention to his business.'

'He'll do what he wants to her when you aren't looking. And what about Camilla?'

'I'm sure a girl of her... status... can look after herself.'

'Vespillo, this man is crazy. Who knows what he is capable of?'

'Is there anything you need, Carbo? Anything I can do to make you more comfortable? Food, blankets?'

'You're not listening to me.'

'I am listening, Carbo, but it changes nothing. But I will do everything I can to make everything as... easy as possible.' He shook his head and sighed. 'What happened to you, old friend?'

'I'm aware I have been behaving badly, but you know me. You know I couldn't do those things.'

'I know what the witnesses told me. I know there was blood on your sword.'

'I can explain that...'

'Save it for the trial. I haven't slept and I'm exhausted from the fire-fighting, and dealing with the mess you have made. I'm going home to my wife, and to Fabilla, who I hope will forget you very soon.'

'Vespillo...' The words and the lack of faith from his friend were as devastating as any punishment he might have to face. He dropped his head, turned his back, and did not look around as Vespillo walked slowly away.

It took Veleda's best efforts to calm Cicurinus down. He had had Carbo and the little whore at his mercy. Moments more and the girl would have been dead, and Carbo covered with her blood.

But no, his friends in the vigiles had to come and save him. He couldn't believe they hadn't arrested him already. How much more could he do to make them believe Carbo had committed all those murders? They were all corrupt. Just more turds in the sewer that was Rome. But the death of the prostitute would have made it indisputable that Carbo was to blame.

He had thought of going ahead, even as he heard the shouts from the entrance to the baths. How long would it take to strangle her, to break her neck? Too long. If he was spotted, everything would be ruined.

He had slipped out of the door leading to the tepidarium, doubled round to the changing room, grabbed his tunic and boots from the changing room and strolled nonchalantly away from the baths, outwardly without a care, inwardly seething. He even nodded to one of the vigiles who was standing guard at the entrance to the baths. The watchman didn't give him a second glance.

He had caught sight of Camilla fleeing down the street, barefoot, clutching her stola around her. He had thought to give chase, but it would have drawn too much attention. Instead, he had returned to his apartment, where Veleda had been waiting for him.

He had expected admonishments, recriminations, but her words were surprisingly soothing, even as he raged and swore.

'All is well, Cicurinus. Everything is as it should be. You will find the girl and kill her. There are many witnesses placing her with Carbo. When they finally believe he is the killer, when his lack of dignitas and pietas is on display for all of Rome, when the common people have seen what happens to degenerates, then you can step forward, and show them there is a better way. They will plead with you to allow them to follow you.'

Cicurinus took a deep breath, let it out slowly. He clenched and unclenched his fists, letting the emotion wash out of him. She was right. These people needed more than just retribution. They needed an example, a light to guide them to a better path. He could be that light.

He looked at Veleda, who smiled at him beatifically. 'You can be the saviour of both worlds, German and Roman,' she said. 'You, Sextus.'

Cicurinus frowned. That wasn't quite right. 'My name is Cicurinus.'

Veleda bowed her head. 'As you wish. Now go and do your duty, and take your rightful place in the world.'

-

She had been tempted to flee Rome, the experience in the bathhouse had shaken her so thoroughly. Take what money she had accumulated and start afresh somewhere else. Ostia for example, the port city, thronged with sailors with purses and ball sacks full and waiting to be emptied. Or maybe she should be thinking further away. Baiae, the resort town, where the rich went to escape the city and enjoy the warm weather and the beach. But the competition there would be intense. And was it far enough? Maybe she should consider Regium, at the tip of the Italian peninsula. Or another country. Britannia or Syria.

But Camilla was nothing if not stubborn and self-confident. Once she had collected herself, sitting on the bed in her small, private apartment between the Subura and the Viminal, a feeling of determination and anger had settled over her. Who was this man, to threaten her, to make her feel small and scared? She had lived off her own wits for so long, and she didn't intend to change now.

She had a plan, and she would stick to it.

She couldn't honestly say prostitution was a job she enjoyed. But there was a big difference in the working conditions for the free and the enslaved. Slaves had no rights, no choices. They were forced to have sex with whoever and however many their masters required, in whatever manner was desired. And beyond the act itself which could be more or less unpleasant depending on who was involved, was the absolute loss of all sense of humanity. Slaves were tools, toys, domestic animals, and were treated as such. Some masters developed a fondness for their slaves in the same way as they may favour a beloved dog. Others viewed them as cattle, with no regard for their welfare beyond what was necessary to keep them useful and profitable. Enforced sexual degradation was about as bad as it got, in Camilla's mind.

She, by contrast, had control, agency. If she didn't like the look of a client, she refused him. If a client treated her badly, she never allowed him near her again. By working mainly through established brothels, she benefitted from the protection of the brothel owner and his doormen. Of course she was expected to pay her way with a certain level of customer throughput. But she still had choice, and that was what made the difference.

And so, she chose to return to work, and not let the crazy bully intimidate her.

That said, she wasn't foolhardy. So she returned to a regular haunt, where she trusted the leno and his muscle.

The greasy pimp greeted her with a friendly smile.

'Good to see you back, Camilla. I hope you are here to work, and not to receive social calls today.'

'Get lost, Villius,' she said good-naturedly. 'Usual room?'

'Cleaned specially for you.'

'When, last month?'

Villius grinned, revealing a mix of yellowy-brown teeth and wooden dentures. 'Becoming fussy? Go and get yourself ready, girl.'

Camilla headed for the stairs, then turned back.

'Oh, if a big, dark-haired man, scars and a funny look in his eye comes asking for me, I'm not here, right?'

'Whatever you say, beautiful. As I say, you're getting fussy.'

Camilla shook her head and went to her room. It was a small cubicle, a dozen feet by six. By one wall was a wood-framed bed with a cheap straw mattress and a couple of wool blankets. She sat on the edge of the bed, pulled her toga out of her woollen bag, shucked off her tunic and wrapped it around her, taking care to fold it just the way a proud senator would. Once she was done, she took out her bottle of kohl, the dark eye make-up made of antimony and ashes, and a rounded bone applicator. She applied it carefully around her eyes, then darkened her eyebrows and drew them towards the centre in the fashionable way. Then she applied chalk power to whiten her face, and rouged her cheeks with wine dregs. One day she would be able to afford red ochre, but for now, economy was the watchword. Finally, she applied some perfume behind her ears, and tipped a little breath-freshening powder into her mouth, enjoying the fizzy, sweet taste on her tongue before swallowing it.

'Visitor, Camilla,' called Villius up the stairs. 'You ready yet?'

'Send him up,' she called back.

Her third client of the evening, a regular named Manlius, was making so much noise that she almost didn't hear the noise that came from downstairs. She moved her head to one side trying to tune out his groans. There it was again. Raised voices.

'Stop,' she said.

Manlius seemed not to hear, lost in his own world. She heard a shout this time, though her client was oblivious. She put both hands under his shoulders and shoved upwards.

He levered himself into a kneeling position, looking at her in surprise and irritation.

'Didn't you hear?' she said. 'There is some trouble downstairs.'

'Just a visitor being quarrelsome,' he said. 'Drunk or unable to pay. The leno and his bodyguard will sort them out.'

At that point a scream of pain and fear echoed up to them. Camilla grabbed a sheet from the bed, wrapped it around her, and ran to the door. She opened it a crack, and saw other doors on the same floor were open too, the frightened faces of her co-workers peeping out. From the ground floor came the sounds of violence, yells of rage, crashes.

Suddenly, Villius came running up the stairs, face a mask of terror. He saw Camilla and yelled to her.

'Help me! He's killed my man. He's coming.'

Camilla slammed the door shut in his face and locked it. She leaned her back against the wood, heart racing, breath coming fast and shallow. Villius hammered on the door.

'Camilla, let me in. Please, I beg you. Oh gods.'

Manlius was staring at her in disbelief.

'What's happening?'

Camilla looked around her desperately, ignoring his questions. There were no windows and no other exits. The room held no weapons; that would be foolish in her line of work. The only piece of furniture was the bed.

'Help me move this,' she snapped. She grabbed one end of the bed, and after a moment's hesitation, Manlius grabbed the other. They manoeuvred it over to the door, then upended it, so its weight was braced against the wood.

'Listen,' said Manlius. 'Let me go out there. I am a veteran. I know how to handle myself.'

Camilla shook her head. 'You don't know who is out there. We just need to pray the vigiles or urban cohorts come before he finds me.'

'Finds you? Why would he want you?'

'No, stay back!' It was Villius' voice from the hallway. High-pitched and panicking. She heard him hammering again, a different door this time. Clearly all her colleagues had taken the same option as her and barricaded themselves in their rooms.

'Where is she?' The other voice was deep, hoarse, full of menace. 'Where is Camilla? I know she is working here today.'

Villius had never struck her as one to whom bravery and self-sacrifice came naturally, but maybe there was something about being threatened in his own territory, maybe he knew he was about to die. Whatever his thinking, Camilla heard him say in a voice that quavered despite the defiant words, 'You will have to come through me first.'

'So be it.'

Camilla tried to picture what was happening right outside her room, from the crashes, cries and gurgling noises. Whatever the reality, it was short-lived. Moments after it started, all was quiet. Then the gravelly voice came again.

'Camilla? Where are you?'

Her skin went cold as if an ice wind had blown across her.

'I know you're here. I asked around.' She heard him pacing up and down. 'You're brave, I'll give you that. I think most would have hidden or fled, after our last encounter. I thought it would take a long time to find you. But no, not you. You are too full of pride to run. Pride. Ha. You should be too ashamed to show yourself in public ever again.'

There was a crash, the sound of splintering wood. A woman's scream.

Camilla flinched, but it was not her own door caving in. A man's voice, a yell of outrage cut short with a thudding sound. More screaming, then sobs, then chokes, then quiet once more.

Manlius had a face as white as her toga, unable to comprehend what was happening.

'Is it him?' he asked her in a whisper. 'The madman who has been doing this killing?'

Camilla nodded, tears trickling down her face. Where were the vigiles? The legionaries from the cohorts? When would they arrive?

There was a thump at her own door, and the boards creaked, and the bed gave a few inches. Without prompting, Manlius helped her shove the brace back into position, and leaned against it.

'Ah, you're in this one, aren't you? Why delay the inevitable? You can't escape. And no one is coming to save you. There is no Carbo here today.'

'No Carbo?' whispered Manlius, puzzled. 'But I heard it was Carbo that…'

Another crash, and the door lock burst apart. Manlius and Camilla were thrown back into the room. Quickly, they rushed back to the improvised fortification. But more impacts followed. The door planks broke apart, meaty hands tore then away, and now Camilla saw Cicurinus' face, a mask of fury.

With the door in pieces, it was trivial for Cicurinus to grab the bed and hurl it into the room. He stepped into Camilla's chamber, and she saw he held a short knife that looked tiny in his meaty hands.

Manlius stepped forward. Whether he felt bravery or terror was irrelevant. It was clear that he had to fight or die.

Camilla backed to the far side of the room as the naked Manlius confronted the much bigger Cicurinus. Cicurinus looked down at him with sneer. Manlius threw a punch, a firm jab, whose speed took Cicurinus off guard. Cicurinus' head snapped back, and he retreated a step. The punch had landed on his cheek, and Cicurinus explored the developing bruise with his fingertips.

Then, faster than Camilla would have thought possible for a man of his size, he thrust his blade into Manlius exposed abdomen. The naked man had no time to react, to dodge or flinch. His eyes and mouth flew open wide, and he stared down at the hilt protruding from just under his rib cage.

Cicurinus drew the blade savagely downwards, opening him from sternum to groin. Slippery, glistening ropes of guts spilled out onto the floor accompanied by a shower of blood and intestinal contents. Manlius dropped to his knees, then pitched onto his face.

Camilla had her back to the wall, staring in absolute terror. At some point, she hadn't noticed when, her bladder had let go, and the inside of her legs were wet with urine.

'Why?' she whispered. 'I don't understand.'

'No,' said Cicurinus, and his voice held a tinge of sadness. 'I don't suppose you would. Your face is buried too deep in the filth of the gutter to be able to look up and see the stars. Just know that each death of one such as you takes Rome and Germania further on the path back to greatness. And there is the added bonus of killing you that it implicates Carbo even further. That's why I came for you in the baths. You're a well-known associate of Carbo. Your death is the final nail in his crucifix. Everyone will believe he finally snapped and killed you as well.'

'But,' said Camilla desperately, 'That won't work. Carbo, he…'

In the dim, flickering light of the oil lamp, the knife flashed.

Camilla fell to her knees and he watched her bleed out, her sentence unfinished.

Chapter Sixteen

'What do you mean it wasn't him?'

Pavo sounded both petulant and exasperated. He looked at Vespillo from behind his desk, his palms pressed down onto the wooden surface.

'It can't have been. He was locked up when these new murders took place. In my cell, under guard the whole time.'

'And the details are the same? Same sort of people? Same graffiti on the walls?'

'Well,' said Vespillo. 'Same sort of people, certainly. It was a killing spree inside a brothel. The leno, his bodyguard, prostitutes and clients. But no, no graffiti this time.'

'So it may have been unrelated? Someone else, with a grudge?'

'Who goes to a brothel and slaughters everyone there on the basis of a grudge?'

'So he had an accomplice. There are two of them.'

'Does that really seem likely?'

'Likely or not, you hold in your station the man that Titus Servilius Ahala believes murdered his son, and that man will be the one that pays the price.'

'Even if he's innocent?'

Pavo spread his hands placatingly. 'Look, Vespillo, I know this Carbo is your friend. But you have to be professional about this...'

'Are you questioning my integrity?' said Vespillo, his voice rising. 'I imprisoned my friend because I believed him guilty. I was prepared to hand him over for execution because I thought that was right. Don't you dare question my professionalism.'

'Now, now, calm yourself. I'm just saying that he must stand trial. If he is innocent, as you say, then the courts will find him so.'

'Even with Ahala's money in the jury's pockets?'

'Careful now, Vespillo. Those sort of allegations can be very damaging without proof. To the person making them.'

'I need to release Carbo.'

'You shall do no such thing. He is pending trial. You can release him after that, if the jury so decide.'

'This is wrong, Pavo, you know it.'

'Since when has the law been concerned with right and wrong, Vespillo.'

–

Carbo was sitting on the floor when the cell door opened. He looked up and saw Vespillo enter, looking sombre.

'Come to give me more good news, old friend?' asked Carbo sarcastically.

'Mixed,' said Vespillo. 'You're free to go.'

Carbo got slowly to his feet, regarding Vespillo with suspicion. 'Don't mess about with me. That's not worthy of you.'

'I mean it. I don't believe you committed these murders any more.'

Amazement, disbelief and relief warred inside him.

'What's changed?'

Vespillo rubbed his hand over his beard, hesitated, then said bluntly, 'Camilla's dead.'

The air left Carbo's chest in a rush. It felt like he had been punched. Of course that was why they were letting him go. Because the killer had struck again, while he had a rock solid alibi. And of course it was Camilla who had died. Just as Carbo had predicted.

'I warned you,' said Carbo. 'I told you she was in danger!'

'I know. I'm sorry. Look, let's go to a tavern. I'll buy you a drink.'

'You think that is enough of an apology?' spat Carbo. He looked at the open door. 'You said I can leave.'

Vespillo nodded.

Carbo strode to the exit, looked back at Vespillo. 'Fuck you. I hope your conscience can handle this.'

He swept past Taura and Pinarius, who stepped back hastily to get out of his way.

–

With his head down, Carbo marched out of the vigiles station, mind whirling. His footsteps led him automatically into the heart of the Subura, and before he even realised it, he was standing outside his old tavern.

He looked up and down the street. It was busy, but few were considering starting drinking at this hour, mid-morning, and he knew from his time as an owner that it was usually empty around now. He eased the tavern door open a crack and peered inside.

He saw Marsia bustling about, and a figure sitting at a table. As his eyes adjusted to the gloom, the man's face resolved itself into Vatius' distinguished features. Carbo let out a sigh of relief and eased himself inside.

Vatius saw him first and lifted a hand in greeting.

'Carbo, what a pleasant surprise.'

Myia, who had been asleep on Vatius, jumped down and barked excitedly for a few moments, jumping up on her back legs and running in tight circles. Carbo reached down to fuss her head, and when she had checked his hands for treats and found none, she scuttled back to the comfort and warmth of Vatius' lap.

Marsia stared at him with an expression of guarded joy. Her eyes continually darted to the door, to the back room, as if something was going to happen, someone was going to come and take him away again.

Carbo stepped forward and put his arms around her, crushing her against him, and she hugged him back tightly.

When the embrace broke, she stepped back and looked searchingly, anxiously into his eyes. 'How are you here? Did you escape?'

Carbo gave her a half smile. 'Vespillo released me. He doesn't think I am a murderer any more.'

Marsia seemed to sag in relief, a tension visibly departing her.

'But how? What made him change his mind?'

Now Carbo's expression was grim. 'More murders. While I was locked in Vespillo's cell.'

'A fine alibi,' commented Vatius happily. But Marsia could see the pain in Carbo's eyes.

'Who?'

Carbo pursed his lips, let out a breath. 'Camilla.'

Marsia put her hand to her mouth and turned away. Carbo stood helplessly, looking at her back. She blamed him. He blamed himself.

'I know you are angry with me, Marsia. It's all my fault, and I put her in danger to save my own skin.'

Marsia turned back and her expression was resolute. She gripped his arm. 'No, master. She had much to pay for, for her part in your ruin. It was only right that she try to make amends. It is very sad that it cost her life. But the guilt is with the killer. Not you.'

The words were like a sip of water to a man dying of thirst. Not enough to quench the awful feeling, but a drop of comfort nevertheless.

Marsia took Carbo's hand and ushered him to sit. She sat opposite him, leaning forward, not releasing her grip on him.

'What happened?' she asked.

'You don't know?'

She shook her head. 'All I heard was that you had been arrested, and Camilla went missing at the same time. I had no idea.'

Carbo glanced over at Vatius, who was well within eavesdropping range.

'Don't worry about Vatius,' said Marsia. 'He is absolutely trustworthy.'

Carbo nodded, then recounted what had happened in the baths, his arrest, his meeting with Pavo and Ahala, and his release.

Marsia took it all in, not interrupting to question. When he had finished, she asked, 'What do we do now?'

'Do?' asked Carbo. 'What do you mean?'

'About the killer. What are you going to do about him?'

'Now they know I am innocent, I think I should leave Cicurinus to Vespillo.'

Marsia let go of his hand and sat back in surprise.

'You aren't serious?'

'Why would you think that?'

'Master, look at what he has done. Leaving aside the many people he has killed, people we have bumped into in the streets, served drinks to, gossiped with, think of what he has done to you personally. Impersonated you, to make the authorities think you were the culprit. Attacked you. And murdered Camilla. Yes, she had her faults. But she died because she was trying to help you. So don't tell me you are going to do nothing.'

Carbo flushed. 'Well, I… Of course I'm going to do something.'

'If you are hesitant,' put in Vatius, clearly listening to every word from his seat a dozen feet away, 'think of this. Vespillo may be convinced of your innocence, but from what you have said, the dead noble boy's father, this Ahala, thinks he has his man, and is likely to need a lot more to convince him not to make sure you are punished for the crime. And no doubt he has Pavo in his pocket.'

'I said I would do something,' snapped Carbo. Then he ran his hand over his face and looked down. 'But I have no idea what.'

'You need to catch him,' said Marsia firmly. 'Show him dead or alive to the witnesses, to Pavo, so they can see it was him who did the killings and not you. It will prove your innocence once and for all, and stop the murders.'

'But how do I find him? I tried to draw him out before, and look what happened. Besides, he will be wary of me now.'

'Well, what do we know about him?' asked Marsia. 'What is driving him to do these things?'

'He's mad,' said Carbo, simply.

'So are many men,' said Marsia, 'but they still have motivations.'

Carbo thought. What had Cicurinus told him?

'He said that he is being urged on, coached, by this German priestess, Veleda. He respects the Germans, wants both Rome and Germany to keep each other strong and pure, noble opponents, like, I don't know, famous gladiators or mythological heroes.'

'So he respects Germania and the German gods?'

'I would say so, yes.'

'So if someone was showing the German people and their deities disrespect, he would be angry?'

'Yes, and so would Veleda.'

'So, we need to find someone to be rude about Germania, and see what he does about it.'

'Maybe,' said Carbo. 'But who would we ask to do such a dangerous thing?'

'I'll do it,' said Marsia immediately, but Carbo shook his head vehemently.

'Out of the question. I will not put you in any more danger.'

Marsia opened her mouth to protest, but it was Vatius who spoke next.

'Have you ever read Ovid's *Metamorphoses*?'

'No,' said Carbo, at the same time as Marsia said, 'Yes.'

'Of course you have,' said Vatius to Marsia. 'I would have been disappointed if you had answered otherwise. You remember Tiresias?'

Marsia looked up, trying to recall. 'He was the man who had to settle the dispute between Jupiter and Juno about who got the most pleasure from sex? Because he had been turned into a woman, and lived as a woman for many years, so had experienced it from both sides.'

'Quite so,' said Vatius. 'And for the record, he confirmed that women get more pleasure from the act than men.'

Marsia rolled her eyes, but Carbo cut in. 'Vatius, this really isn't the time for one of your lessons…'

'Marsia, do you remember why he was turned into a woman?'

'He… hit two snakes with a single stick?'

'Exactly.'

'I'm not following,' said Carbo, but Marsia was nodding slowly.

'It seems to me,' said Vatius, 'that you have two problems, Carbo. One is Cicurinus, and all the threat he still holds for you. The other is Olorix, who took everything from you. Including Marsia, who suffers terribly for it.'

'Two snakes, one stick,' said Marsia thoughtfully. 'I think I have an idea.'

—

The smack across her face knocked Marsia to the floor. She had actually started to throw herself before the blow landed, both lessening the physical while accentuating the dramatic impact. She had quickly learned that Olorix liked to see his chastisements have an effect, and stoicism only heightened his anger.

She stayed on the floor for a moment, lying on her hip, hands planted in the clean straw that she had only just spread out. Hidden by the hair drooping down over her face was a half-smile, as she thought of what was coming his way.

'Get up, useless slave,' spat Olorix. Slowly, with exaggerated stiffness, Marsia got back to her feet.

'Now explain to me again why takings are so poor.'

'Master,' said Marsia, keeping her voice timid and respectful. 'Men do not visit. It is all the former owner's fault. He drove them away, and now they have all found other places to drink. They have no reason to return.'

'Maybe I should have you flogged naked in the tavern every evening. That might draw a crowd.'

'Master, if I may be so bold, I do have an idea.'

Olorix looked at her suspiciously. But he was nothing if not avaricious, and if his slave had come up with a moneymaking plan, he would want to hear it out.

'Get me a cup of unwatered wine and tell me what you have in mind.'

Marsia hurried over to get him his drink and proffered it to him where had now settled his considerable bulk.

'Well?'

'I was thinking…'

'On your knees, slave. I'm not looking up to you while you talk to me.'

Marsia sank to her knees and looked up at him submissively, waiting for permission to speak.

Olorix took a sip of the wine and grimaced. 'No wonder people don't want to drink here. But the quality of the wine can't be improved until we have more customers paying for it. Interesting conundrum. Anyway, let's hear it, slave.'

'Rome has many soldiers. Veterans who have fought in the legions. Legionaries in vexillations on duty in the city, or on leave.'

'This isn't news to me.'

'I was thinking, what if we held an event. A festival, like one of the city-wide holidays, but this would be confined to the tavern.'

'What sort of festival?' asked Olorix cautiously.

'A celebration of the legions and their victories.'

'Well, there hasn't been anything major for a while.'

'Then we can celebrate the battle of Idistaviso. When Germanicus defeated Arminius once and for all, and finally revenged the Teutoberg forest massacre.'

'That was eleven years ago. And was not fought in the winter. People will wonder why we celebrate it now?'

'No one would care why, if there was entertainment and liberal amounts of wine.'

Olorix nodded thoughtfully. 'It could work.'

'And if we provide the wine cheaply, and many men attend, then hopefully they would become regular visitors. It could even be a place known for welcoming legionaries, and they always have money to spend.'

'You're German. Why would you want to celebrate victory over your people?'

'I am a slave of Rome, master. And I am your slave. I want the tavern to do well, so you will think kindly of me.'

Olorix stroked his chin. 'It could work. We can make it hugely patriotic. Celebrate our heroes and gods, and mock the German ones, like, like...'

'Like Woden and Frigg, master?'

'Yes, and that traitor Arminius. And we can dress you up like a prisoner taken in battle. How will that make you feel?'

'If it is for my master's benefit, I am happy.'

Olorix looked at her with suspicion for a moment, then nodded, apparently satisfied she was not being sarcastic or disrespectful.

'If this works,' said Olorix, 'I will be pleased with you. If not...' He let the threat hang in the air. Then he finished his drink and put his cup down. 'I'll leave the arrangements in your hands. Then there is no one else to blame for the event's success or failure. Do you understand? This is entirely your responsibility.'

'I understand, sir.'

Hope welled up inside Marsia, for the first time in a long time.

–

Centurion Brocchus of the XXIst Rapax sipped his wine, then took a deep breath through his nose. There was something comforting about the air of the Subura. He had been born in Rome, and for a long while as a child had lived in this poor but vibrant district, before, as so many did who dreamed of escape, joining up in the legions. He had been stationed in Germania for a dozen years or so now, and while he understood why the fresh air of the hills and forests in the province was favoured by some, he couldn't help but feel nostalgic for Suburan odours. Street vendors selling roasted chickens, sizzling sausages and piping hot pies flooded the atmosphere with mouth-watering scents, which mingled with the smells of perfumiers and make-up sellers, tanners and fullers, not to mention the mixture of human and animal wastes that ran down the deep grooves in the streets ground down over the years by the wheels of transport vehicles, and the stench of rotting carcasses abandoned where they died, mainly beasts of burden, but occasionally human.

It was a heady mix, and someone unused to it might struggle to cope. It was why the elites lived on the hills up above the city, particularly the Palatine and Esquiline. But for those to whom the Subura was home, the smell was as comforting as mother's hair or grandfather's musty tunic.

He looked up and down the street, savouring the moment. He was only in Rome for a few short days, part of a small vexillation detached from his legion to escort the legate who had official business with Sejanus of some sort – he hadn't enquired further. For him, it was a rare chance to relax in his home environment, and maybe see if he could track down any old friends.

Something fluttering in the gutter caught his eye and he bent down to pick it up. It was a pamphlet made of cheap papyrus, covered on both sides with untidy but large handwriting. Some ox dung had obscured the odd letter, but overall its message was clearly legible.

> *Come to Olorix's tavern to celebrate Rome's victories over the Germans.*

Brocchus frowned. It had been a good few years since there had been a major battle in Germania, but as he was well aware, skirmishes, scuffles and police actions were commonplace. He wasn't sure why they had decided to have a party in honour of them now, but he was curious enough to read on.

> *Girls. Dice games. Cheap wine. Legionaries and veterans especially welcome.*

The reverse side of the pamphlet gave the street, the time, which was from mid-afternoon till late at night, and the date, which was tomorrow. He stroked his chin. Some of the lads that had come down with him, like Gratius, his optio, might enjoy the event. Girls, gambling and booze were always welcome, and finding them in a place that was not only welcoming but encouraging legionaries, and celebrating their work would be great for morale. He resolved to reconnoitre the place beforehand, as any good soldier should. He tucked the pamphlet inside his tunic and finished his wine. Then he stood, oriented himself and headed in the direction of the street indicated in the notice.

It was only a short walk as the crow flies but a long one in the Subura's twisted and crowded streets. Soon, though, he was at the tavern. A couple of drinkers were sitting at a table on the street directly outside gambling and arguing good-naturedly.

He opened the door and entered.

It was an unprepossessing venue. Tired, old furniture. Cracked plaster on the walls. Faded frescoes. Timbers pitted with woodworm holes. But it was clean. Dry, sweet-smelling straw on the floor, surfaces wiped down, the stew in the serving pots on the bar looking fresh, not just reheated from the previous night.

He approached the bartender, a barbarian-looking slave. The odour from the stew made his belly rumble, and he ordered a bowl full. The slave ladled out a portion and handed it over, taking his coins and stowing them under the bar.

It was scalding hot, so he took a spoonful, blew on it, then tasted it. Chicken meat and vegetables. Not bad at all.

'Wine, too, slave.'

'Yes, master. Any particular variety?'

'Nothing too cheap, nothing too expensive.'

She nodded and poured him a cup of red liquid. He smelled it, tasted it and grimaced. Rough as sandpaper, but it had a kick. It would do the job.

He pulled out the pamphlet and waved it at the bar slave.

'So what's this party all about, then?'

She smiled at him, professional charm, and he didn't care that it was obviously insincere. She was nice enough to look at that he wasn't bothered if she was only pretending to enjoy his company.

'It's a celebration of our brave legionaries, and their battles fighting against the evil Germans.' Her Germanic accent was not lost on him, and his eyes twinkled as he returned her smile, acknowledging the irony.

'But why now?'

She looked around her, then leaned in conspiratorially. 'To be honest, sir, the tavern hasn't been doing too well of late. This was just an idea to drum up business, get some more bodies through the door.'

He nodded. 'It's a good idea. Legionaries do like to be acknowledged for their hard work, and if that acknowledgement involves booze, dice and girls, then there's not too much to think about.'

'Would I be wrong in thinking you are a legionary yourself, sir? Even though you are in civilian dress, you have that bearing, and you are too young and in too good health to be a veteran.'

She had the charming patter finely honed, he noted, though there was still a reserve that suggested she was happy to serve him food and drink, but there was nothing else on the menu.

'You're quite right. I'm Centurion Brocchus, of the XXIst Rapax, stationed at Castra Vetera in Germania Inferior. Here in Rome on duty, though with a couple of days leave to enjoy the best that the city has to offer.'

'I'm glad you are choosing to spend your time here. You know, my former master served in the legions in Germania. This was his tavern. Maybe you would know him?'

'I doubt it. Many thousands of men serve under the eagles on the northern frontier.'

'I understand he was quite well known. His name is Carbo.'

Brocchus paused, his cup halfway to his lips.

'Carbo? He was the owner of this tavern? What happened to him?'

'He fell on hard times, sir.'

From the sorrow in her voice, he could tell she had a genuine affection for him.

'I'm sorry to hear that. It is a constant fear to all of us in the legions. Much as we might desire our freedom from the hard life we lead, most of us worry what life will be like when we are no longer surrounded and supported by our comrades, fed and paid by the army. Will we be able to cope with normality? Many don't.'

'His experiences serving under the eagles have weighed heavily on him, that is for certain.'

'Do you think a visit from someone like me, who knows what he has been through, would be a comfort to him?'

Marsia looked at him in surprise, and hesitated. Brocchus spread his hands in a gesture that seemed to withdraw the offer.

'Stupid suggestion. I'm sure the great Carbo has plenty of friends he can rely on for support. Why would he need to see the likes of me?'

'Fewer friends than you might think, sir. And I only hesitate because things are... precarious for him, right now.'

'Well,' said Brocchus. 'If you think he would like a friendly face to chat to, I'll be staying at the Castra Praetoria. Nice new barracks for the Praetorians, those lucky bastards, but at least I get to stay there for a couple of days and not have to find myself a billet in the city like the rest of my men. If you see him, tell him to come and visit and we can chew the fat together.'

'I will, sir, thank you.'

'In any case, I'll bring my men over to your little bash tomorrow.'

'You will all be most welcome.'

–

The Castra Praetoria had the feel of a building where the cement had not yet set. Only four years old, the permanent camp of the Praetorian guard had been ordered to be built by Sejanus, the Praetorian Guard Prefect and de facto ruler of Rome during Tiberius' self-imposed exile to Capri. It was situated on the high ground to the north-east of the city, and had the layout of a standard provincial barracks, but with a much finer and less ephemeral construction; the walls built from pink and red bricks and the streets between the camp buildings neatly cobbled.

Carbo queued at the gates, waiting to be seen by the immaculately attired Praetorian on guard duty. He wondered if he was making a mistake. But when Marsia had told him about this Brocchus, it had got him thinking. If there was to be a group of battle-hardened men in the tavern during the party, ones who didn't owe their allegiance to the Urban Prefect or the Prefect of the vigiles, then it might make sense to have them on side, or at least make sure they weren't going to intervene in what might be about to happen.

The man in front of Carbo in the queue was a baker with a sackful of honeycakes on his back. The guard ordered him to dump the sack on the ground, then he rummaged through it to ensure there were no weapons or other contraband. Satisfied, he took a cake for himself, bit into it, and jerked the thumb of his free hand over his shoulder to indicate the baker could enter. The baker grabbed his sack and hurried inside with head bowed.

When Carbo stepped up, the Praetorian looked up at him and frowned. Men in positions of authority often took an instant dislike to Carbo, and he suspected it was purely on the basis of the intimidation caused by his imposing physical presence.

'State your business,' said the guard brusquely.

'I'm here to see Centurion Brocchus.'

'There are no Praetorian Centurions by that name. On your way.'

'He isn't a Praetorian. He is with the XXIst Rapax, on temporary assignment to escort his legate from Germania to Rome. He has been quartered in the Praetorian barracks.'

The guard looked doubtful. 'And what's your business with him?'

'Personal.'

'Not good enough.'

Carbo sighed inwardly, willing himself to appear outwardly calm, not to clench his fists or push his chest forward, or to step forward threateningly.

'I'm an old friend of his,' Carbo lied through tight lips. 'He invited me to see him while he is in Rome.'

The guard pursed his lips. 'What's your name?'

'Vatius,' said Carbo, the first that came into his head. Though the vigiles no longer believed him guilty, the Urban Cohorts' position was less clear, and though the Praetorians considered themselves to be above mere policing of crime, if pressure came from someone powerful like Ahala, they might be forced to step in. A false name at this point seemed prudent.

'You a veteran?'

'I am.'

'Lift your arms up,' said the guard. Carbo did as he was told, and stood passive as the guard patted him down for concealed weapons. When he was satisfied, he stood back.

'Fine. The temporary accommodation is at the far end of the cavalry barracks. Take the second left, and then follow your nose – you can't miss the smell of horse dung. But if I hear you have caused any trouble, I'll come for you and rip your balls off.'

'Understood,' said Carbo, aware that the much smaller man would need a number of allies to carry out his threat, but happy to let it pass.

He walked into the camp, looking around him at the fine buildings, so much more ornate than any structures found in even permanent military fortifications in the provinces. Functional camps of necessity concerned themselves with function over form. But the Praetorians, the best remunerated, most highly trained soldiers in the legions, always had to have the appearance of superiority. It was typical of their reputation among the rank and file soldiers that served throughout the Empire under the Eagles. The Praetorians were over-paid, over-admired and under-experienced. Mainly used to make the Emperor look good and feel safe, they had little battle experience, and the other legions held them in contempt, while secretly jealous of their privileged lives.

It was clear as Carbo walked through the camp, though, that Praetorians considered themselves a breed apart from most mortals. Those that were marching in units, training or on their way to some important destination, kept their eyes fixed firmly ahead, paying Carbo no attention, to the extent that he had to leap out of their way more than once to avoid being trampled under their polished boots. Those that were not on duty or training shot him contemptuous glances as he passed.

When he reached the cavalry barracks, he found a young decurion hovering anxiously by the side of the farrier, who was bent over, paring a hoof with a sharp knife from a stoical pony.

'Will she survive?' said the decurion, ringing his hands.

'It's just an abscess,' said the farrier, not bothering to hide his frustration with the close attentions of the cavalry officer. As he spoke, his knife dug into the infected cavity. The horse flinched, and there was a spurt of dark, foul-smelling pus. 'There. She'll be fine now. Get your orderly to poultice it three times a day for five days. Walk her out on her lead twice a day. Then call me and I'll pop her shoe back on, and she will be good to go.'

'I can't thank you enough!'

The farrier grunted, and began packing up his tools.

'Excuse me,' said Carbo. 'I'm looking for Centurion Brocchus. He is staying in the temporary accommodation.'

The relieved decurion seemed in a good mood, and directed him to a low building beyond the cavalry barracks.

Carbo pushed the door open and entered. Inside were rows of beds, all carefully made, sheets and blankets folded precisely. At the far end was a table where two bored-looking men sat playing latrunculi.

Carbo approached, and they stopped and looked at him with mild curiosity.

'Centurion Brocchus?'

One of the men, tough and scarred, looked him up and down.

'And you are…?'

'My name is Carbo. My slave, my former slave, told me you had invited me here.'

'Carbo, of course.' Brocchus looked around to offer Carbo a seat, but the table had only two chairs. He moved towards another table, but Brocchus' companion got to his feet.

'Don't worry, you can sit here. I'm going to push off Brocchus, and find something to eat in the mess tent. Thanks for the game; hope I can relieve you of some more of your pay before too long.'

Brocchus gave him a sour grunt, then a good-natured slap on the arm, and gestured to Carbo to take the newly vacated seat as his erstwhile companion departed.

There was an awkward moment where both of them looked for something to say.

'So, you're in Rome on escort duties?' began Carbo tentatively.

'Indeed. Legate had a meeting at the palace, though he is also grabbing the opportunity to take some leave in Rome. The higher-ups start to pine if they are away from the city for too long.'

'You don't?'

Brocchus shrugged. 'I miss the old place, of course, but after a while the army becomes your home and your family.'

Carbo nodded.

'And it's difficult when you leave your home and family, right?' asked Brocchus cautiously, his face sympathetic.

'It is,' said Carbo. 'Especially when you are with people who have never seen what you have seen, done what you have done. Experienced the… stuff.'

'Too right. Your slave…'

'Ex-slave…'

'Right, Marsia? She seemed worried about you.'

Carbo's first reaction was to shrug it off.

'I'm fine.'

'She said something about hard times.'

Carbo bristled at the thought of Marsia talking to a stranger about his personal problems. But he didn't doubt that she had his best interests at heart. And what was the harm in opening up to this man? Stranger he may be, but he was a fellow centurion, who had served in Germania at a similar time. He probably understood Carbo much better than even those he was closest to.

'Maybe. I went through some tough times in the legions. When I came home, it was hard to deal with the feelings.'

Brocchus' expression was open and understanding. Carbo hadn't come here for counselling, just to make contact with a potential ally. But now, once the words started to flow, it was hard to hold them back, like the flood from a breached dam.

'I get these feelings – like total panic. They can come from nowhere. Drinking helps, but not for long. Gambling takes my mind away from it. But that lost me my tavern and my slave. There was a woman, the first one I had become close to for many years. And she was taken from me. I had my revenge, but still… She should be by my side.'

He swallowed, aware that his voice was cracking and his eyes were misted. Brocchus put a hand on his shoulder.

'Carbo, I've heard of you. Your exploits in the legions are well known. You made pilus prior, leading a cohort, though you could have easily been made primus pilus of the entire legion.'

'I didn't want that responsibility,' said Carbo. 'Besides, the primus pilus doesn't get to fight so much. He is an administrator. You know, when you are fighting, being scared feels right. When you are sitting alone in a dark room with your heart racing and your skin soaked in sweat, that is when being scared makes no sense. I would rather feel scared because of a real threat than because of what happened in the past.'

'What happened? We all have bad experiences if we serve long enough, but I get the impression something worse happened to you.'

Carbo pursed his lips. 'I was captured. At the Varian disaster. Held and... tortured.'

'I'm sorry,' said Brocchus. 'I can't imagine what that would have been like.'

'No, you can't,' said Carbo. 'But. I escaped.'

'Well thank Fortuna for that. I met one chap a little while ago up in Germania. We were patrolling deep in barbarian territory and found this fellow who had been held captive for the gods know how many years. Terrible state he was. He didn't know if he was coming or going. Tried to help him, but you could tell he was badly messed up by the whole thing.'

Carbo's eyes widened as Brocchus spoke, and the breath caught in his throat.

'What was his name?' His voice was little more than a whisper.

Brocchus thought for a moment, looking up for inspiration, rubbing his fingers against his palm in concentration.

'Cicero,' he said finally. Carbo felt himself relax, until Brocchus said, 'No, that's not right, is it. It was like Cicero. Cicurinus! That's it.'

Carbo sat back and stared at Brocchus.

'Did I say something wrong?' asked Brocchus, confused at Carbo's flabbergasted expression.

Carbo took a moment to gather himself, then spoke quietly and earnestly.

'Have you heard about the murders that have been taking place in the Subura?'

'Not much. I overheard some people gossiping when I was in a tavern, but no more than that. I haven't been back in Rome long.'

Carbo explained about the killings, the type of people and the graffiti left behind.

'Terrible. But I don't see how…'

'It was Cicurinus. Same man.'

Brocchus whistled, shaking his head. 'I can't say it surprises me. There was something unhinged about him. He's been apprehended?'

'No, he is still at large.'

'Then how do you know it was him?'

'Because he tried to frame me for the murders. He looks a bit like me. And he seems to have something personal against me. I lured him to the baths, and we talked, then he attacked me. I was arrested, but he killed again while I was imprisoned, so at least some people now know I'm innocent.'

'Amazing.'

'Listen, this celebration at the tavern tonight. We have set the whole thing up as a trap for him. But I'd give it a miss if I was you. In some strange way, he was quite attached to the village you burnt down. When he came to Rome, he even brought the village's priestess with him, someone called Veleda. Presumably the same one that tortured him.'

'Veleda? You're sure that was the name? Did you meet her?'

'Yes I'm sure and no I haven't met her; he told me about her. She is behind his whole insane mission to purify the city, she is the one urging him on to commit his atrocities.'

'That can't be right.'

'Why not?'

'Because Veleda died in Germania. We caught her soon after we attacked the village. I watched my optio strangle her to death with my own eyes.'

Chapter Seventeen

Cicurinus paced up and down the small apartment room, the floorboards shaking under his heavy tread. His fists were balled, and he gnashed his dentures, the rough surfaces of the fake teeth grinding against each other.

'How dare they?' he hissed. 'How dare they? I will make them pay for this.'

'I know you will,' said Veleda. 'You will not let them show such disrespect to the gods and people of my country this way.'

Cicurinus had been keeping his head down since he had killed Camilla. Veleda hadn't shown herself, and he had been feeling adrift and uncertain of what to do next. Then he had seen the poster painted on a wall advertising the so-called festival. His jaw had dropped and a rage had built up inside him as he read about a tavern, Carbo's former tavern no less, honouring Roman victories over the Germans, mockery of the German gods and people, all celebrated by whoring and drinking and gambling.

The rage had barely faded, still bubbling away inside him like a pot left too long on the fire, but the memory of the words on that poster dripped constantly into his mind so the stewing anger would never boil dry.

'I'll kill them all,' he said. 'Every soldier that throws a dice. Every whore that lifts her tunic. Every customer that takes a sip of wine. They will all die by my hand.'

'Calm yourself, Sextus,' said Veleda.

'Don't call me that,' he said sharply.

'Calm yourself, Cicurinus,' she corrected herself. 'There is no need to kill everyone. Your mission is to teach the Romans, not to wipe them out. An example is sufficient.'

'Who?'

'The man who owns the tavern of course, who has organised this whole thing. Olorix.'

Cicurinus pictured the corpulent freedman, always dripping with the finest perfumes, dressed in the most expensive and gaudy jewellery. Strutting around the quarter with his bodyguards, displaying to all his wealth and power. All Cicurinus could see in him was decadence. With his appearance, his money, his business interests and his general behaviour, he was the epitome of all that Cicurinus considered was wrong with the Empire. What a mark it would make, to end Olorix. Especially publicly, in the middle of his offensive celebration.

'Yes. I will do it. I will go to this abominable festival this evening and I will show everyone the consequences of his life, his sacrilege.'

'You will do it before everyone? You won't pretend to be Carbo any more?'

Cicurinus hesitated. How long should he keep up that pretence? At least until Carbo was executed. He wondered how long that would be. Surely it would be soon. But it wasn't the sort of thing you could ask about in casual conversation on the street, and he didn't really know anyone in Rome, certainly not anyone with connections to the authorities that could find out more for him. As far as he knew, Carbo was still rotting in his cell, awaiting trial. If he killed Olorix, would that be taken as proof of Carbo's innocence?

But this opportunity could not be missed. Olorix could not be allowed to live.

'Maybe Carbo has outlived his usefulness to me.'

He looked at Veleda, who was regarding him steadily.

'You don't agree?'

Veleda shrugged. 'Consider what Carbo is to you.'

Cicurinus thought about that, really thought about it. What did that man mean to him? He couldn't honestly answer nothing. They were too connected. But was that enough?

'If Carbo isn't executed by the authorities, he will die by my hand, or I will give my own life.'

When he spoke the words out loud, they had a finality about them. A vow, made before his priestess. One way or another, one of them would die.

–

Carbo hesitated outside the IInd station of the vigiles. Sica had persuaded him to go and talk to Vespillo, before whatever would happen that evening came to pass. She had given him emotional and practical arguments.

The practical argument regarded having the vigiles onside, or at least not actively getting in the way. Carbo hadn't accepted this. He didn't need the vigiles, and he certainly didn't need Vespillo, after all the harm he had caused by not trusting Carbo.

The emotional argument involved making peace with his friend while he still had the chance, meaning – it was unspoken – that he might not survive the night. Carbo had grudgingly accepted this. In his time in the legions, he had made it a habit before a big battle to seek out and make amends with anyone he had quarrelled with, whether it was a fight over a dice game, or just a joke taken the wrong way.

So here he was, readying himself to walk into his old friend's office and talk to him man to man. Say his piece, ventilate the bad air, and return to how things were. Simple. So why was his heart racing, why were his hands trembling?

The watchman at the entrance to the headquarters looked at Carbo quizzically. 'Can I help you, sir?'

Carbo swallowed, committed himself. 'I'm here to see Vespillo.'

'Who shall I say is here?'

'Carbo.'

The watchman's eyes opened wide. Carbo hadn't seen him before – maybe he was new, or transferred from another station, or just hadn't been on duty when Carbo was imprisoned, or any of the times Carbo had worked with the vigiles or visited Vespillo in the past. But he clearly knew the name.

'I'll… right, I… Stay here. I'll fetch him.'

The watchman hurried inside, and Carbo took a deep breath, willing himself to be calm. He looked down the street, always alert for threats, because of both his training and his ever-present anxiety. Movement at the far end of the thoroughfare caught his attention. The sound of hob-nailed boots stomping in time on the cobblestones.

He narrowed his eyes and saw the crowds on the streets parting, hurrying to get out of the way. Down the centre, marched a dozen soldiers of the Urban Cohorts. And at their head, back straight, chest thrust out, marched Tribune Pavo.

Their eyes met at the same time, and Pavo recognised Carbo instantly.

'There he is,' yelled the Tribune. 'Apprehend that man!'

Shit. The Tribune obviously wasn't as convinced as Vespillo of Carbo's innocence.

Carbo looked in the other direction down the road, instantly assessing his escape options. Although there were no wheeled vehicles, there were plenty of people walking to and from places of work, homes, shops or their patrons' houses, as well as the occasional mule or donkey laden with baskets, and a litter carried by four hefty slaves, bearing some noble or dignitary. He was not a fast runner because of his injured leg, and the congestion on the street would slow him down further.

As the lead four soldiers of Pavo's men broke into a run, Carbo made a decision, and darted inside the vigiles headquarters.

A few watchmen milled around, one sweeping the floor, one sharpening his axe on a whetstone, two in conversation, lounging against the wall. All of them stopped and looked at him in surprise.

'Trouble outside,' he said. The watchmen were immediately alert. The two conversing vigiles reached for their nearby clubs and moved to the doorway. The one with the axe stepped up behind them. The one with the broom held it up uncertainly.

'Get Vespillo, now!' said Carbo. His tone was sharp with the authority of years of command, and the young man dropped his broom like it was on fire and hurried away.

'Get out of our way,' came a loud voice from the entrance to the station.

'State your business,' said the axe-wielding watchman.

'We are here on the business of the Urban Cohorts.'

'On whose authority?'

'The authority of Tribune Pavo. Now stand aside.'

Carbo looked around for a weapon, but unsurprisingly, there were none lying around. In desperation, he picked up the broom, snapped the head off over his knee, and stepped up behind the three watchmen who were barring the entrance to the station with their physical presence.

'Get out of here,' said the watchman with the axe. 'Leave this place.'

From behind the Urban Cohort legionaries came another voice, a commanding voice, albeit high and shrill.

'Force your way in! I will have that man!'

The Cohort legionaries pressed forwards, and the three watchmen braced themselves, leaning forwards, feet back. Carbo added his bulk to the shoving match, his shoulder against the back of one of the watchmen. The air was full of grunts and curses.

'Move aside, little bucket boys.'

'Bugger off, you pretend soldiers.'

The watchmen were outnumbered, but the entrance was narrow like the neck of an amphora, so at first they could hold the intruders back. The legionaries shoved, kicked, threw punches, but the watchmen held.

'Use your swords,' screamed Pavo from the back. 'Kill them if you have to.'

For a moment, the pressure against the defenders eased as the legionaries stepped back, but it was only to give them room to draw their gladii. Carbo stepped up beside the watchmen, two armed with clubs and one with an axe, and brandished the broken stump of the broom at them, feeling scared, furious and a little absurd at the same time.

One of the legionaries, clearly thinking a broom-armed civilian to be no threat, thrust towards Carbo, a blow with real intent that would maim or kill if it landed. Carbo swatted the blade aside with a flick of the broom handle, then brought the stick round hard across the side of the legionary's head. There was an audible crack and he crumpled to the floor like an ox felled by a priest at a sacrifice to Jupiter.

The other legionaries roared their anger and rushed forward as one. Carbo and the watchmen parried sword thrusts desperately with their weapons, inferior as they were in reach, agility and damage. One jab went under Carbo's armpit, lightly grazing the skin over the side of his ribs. Another sliced the side of one of the watchmen who bore a club, who grunted and swung his cudgel hard against his attacker's arm. There was a crack as bone broke. The legionary screamed and fell back, but another immediately took his place.

The watchmen next to Carbo took a step back, then the one on the other side, and he could tell their initial bravado and defiance was dissipating, and they were ready to break. Carbo readied himself for the collapse of the resistance.

'Stand down!'

Though a little breathless, this was a voice that held real command and authority, unlike the petulant whining of Pavo, and it was obeyed instantly, by watchmen and legionaries alike. Both sides took a step back, panting for breath, pressing hands to bruises and cuts and glaring across a narrow space at each other.

Carbo risked a glance behind him and saw Vespillo trotting up, fresh from wherever deep in the bowels of the headquarters he had been. With him was the watchman from the door, as well as Taura, Pinarius and the diminutive secretary Plancus. They had all stopped to pick up weapons, the usual assortment of dual purpose crime control and fire-fighting tools, though Vespillo carried a sword.

'What is the meaning of this lawlessness?' Vespillo demanded, his deep, booming voice carrying without the need to shout.

Pavo pushed his way to the front of his men.

'Tribune Vespillo, I heard that you had released that criminal.' Pavo jabbed a finger in Carbo's direction. 'I had come to demand you re-arrest him.'

'You have no right to demand anything from me, Pavo.'

'And I find him loitering outside your station,' continued Pavo as if Vespillo hadn't spoken, 'a free man, looking for all the world like he is guilty of nothing.'

'Guilty of nothing? That I doubt. Guilty of those murders? Definitely not.'

'It is not your decision to make.' Spittle was frothing from Pavo's mouth, and Vespillo made a show of wiping his eye.

'It is absolutely my decision. He was my prisoner, and I decide whether to keep him or let him go.'

'Well now you have let him go, I can arrest him instead. And this time he can stay in my cells, and I will personally make sure he is thrown to the beasts.'

Vespillo shook his head.

'Get away from my station, Pavo. And you can be sure your superior will be hearing from me about your thuggery.'

'It was my superior who ordered me here, you fool. Now hand him over.'

Vespillo stepped away and put an arm around Carbo. He put his mouth close to Carbo's ear. 'I don't know what you are doing here. We can sort things out between us another time. But you need to be gone. Pavo isn't going to take no for an answer and I can only hold him for so long.'

'Vespillo, there's something big happening tonight.'

'No time.'

'Vespillo!' came Pavo's whine. 'I'm going to count down from ten, then I'm coming in.'

'Fine,' said Carbo, 'but come to my old tavern later. Be discreet about it. I might need your help.'

'I'll see what I can do. Now go down the stairs, through the barracks, into the kitchen. There is a trapdoor for food supplies that leads back up onto the street. Go!'

Carbo clapped Vespillo on the shoulder then hurried away. From behind him, he heard Pavo count down to one, then urge his men forward. Vespillo in turn called to his men to hold firm. Carbo hoped they wouldn't resist too long, or they would get hurt, maybe killed. He rushed past the rows of beds, though the rudimentary kitchen with pots and pans hanging from the walls and a brazier glowing and smoking in the middle of the room. He spotted the trapdoor at the top of a short, steep wooden staircase, yanked the bolt and emerged out onto the street.

One or two people gave him a semi-curious glance, and damping down his anxiety, he gently closed the trap-door and walked slowly away, blending into the crowds.

—

The old tavern was packed to the rafters. Carbo sat at a table near the back, making small talk with the inebriated legionaries that sat with him. It was hard making yourself inconspicuous when you were Carbo's size, and so he hunched forward, keeping low over the table, and keeping his voice down.

He had mixed feelings about seeing the tavern so busy. While it meant that the publicity for the celebration had been successful, and that Cicurinus was therefore likely to be aware of it, he also reflected with melancholy what he could have done with the place if he had paid it the attention it deserved. He resolved to do better, if he ever got the place back, then almost laughed aloud as he reflected how many areas of his life and relationships he should improve, if he ever got the chance.

Olorix was making sure he was a centre of attention. He had arrived after Carbo, and hadn't spotted him in the throng of happy drinkers, nor was he showing any inclination to make the rounds of his customers. He sat on a raised dais, dressed like a centurion with a polished chest plate and a helmet with a transverse crest. He waved a gladius around dangerously, clearly having no idea how to use one, but having tremendous fun nevertheless. He had one bodyguard by his side, the bald Syrian who Carbo had fought before, and who was fending off overly friendly patrons wishing to thank Olorix for his largesse, while at the same time keeping an eye on the sword so he could duck some of the more perilous sweeps.

Since the tavern was so crowded, the hired dancers were pressed up against the customers, constricting their performances, and leaving them exposed, scantily clad as they were, to pinches and blatant gropes from uninhibited drinkers. The party had spilled out onto the street, and the prostitutes brought in for the night were mainly plying their trade in nearby alleys and up against the walls of the neighbouring houses and businesses. The dicing tables that had originally been set up inside the tavern had also been moved out onto the streets to make more room. The wine was flowing freely, and though it was priced cheaply, Carbo suspected that Olorix had brought it in even more cheaply, and between the whores, the gambling and the wine, he was making plenty of money. The broad smile on the fat bookmaker's face certainly suggested that was the case.

Marsia was rushed off her feet, though she took any opportunity she could to attend Carbo's table, reassure as best she could with a glance or a half-smile. She was dressed in a skimpy breast band and loin cloth with an iron collar around her neck, an outfit she wore with obvious bad grace. Sica, Carbo knew, was out in the street, keeping to herself, no doubt ably fending off amorous advances while she kept a lookout.

Vespillo was somewhere in the tavern, though Carbo couldn't see him at that moment. They had nodded to each other when Vespillo had arrived, but the Vigiles Tribune had seated himself far from Carbo, correctly presuming that Carbo would prefer him to be present but separate. They hadn't had the chance to speak since he had fled the vigiles station that lunchtime, so Vespillo had no idea what was going on, and on reflection, Carbo thought, that was probably for the best. While he would have no objections to the plan to trap Cicurinus, and would not mourn the killer if he died in the attempt to catch him, Carbo suspected he would not approve of using Olorix as expendable bait.

Carbo sipped a cup of water. He was too anxious to eat, and was only half paying attention to the conversation of the legionaries, who were babbling about what a great idea this whole thing was, how no one gave enough credit to the legions for keeping Rome safe, and how the barbarians were savages who deserved to be crucified and their families sold into slavery. Surely Cicurinus had seen the advertisements. Surely he would be infuriated. Surely he would come here, to make sure Olorix received his retribution.

Or he might realise it was a trap. Or he might not care enough. Or he might have left the city. So many what ifs. And Carbo knew that, after his narrow escape earlier that day, though Vespillo believed him innocent, more powerful people still wanted him executed for the murders. This had to work.

The sun fell, dusk turned to darkness. The party showed no sign of ebbing, but Cicurinus showed no sign of turning up. When Carbo caught sight of Vespillo through the crowd, the Vigiles Tribune shot him questioning looks, to which Carbo could only shrug in return.

Carbo half-listened to the legionaries chattering at his table, his attention fixed firmly on the tavern door. This was a gamble, he realised. He had bet on Cicurinus taking their bait. The odds weren't fixed this time, but he wasn't sure they were in his favour. And he was gambling his life.

Chapter Eighteen

Even at this late hour, Cicurinus had doubts. He hesitated at the end of the street that led to the tavern, turned around, almost walked away. He had lived in the shadows for so long. Both before and after his release from captivity. Much of his time as Veleda's prisoner – or was it protégé? – was spent in a dark hut, with only the visits of the priestess to keep him company. Though he had feared her and hated her at first, eventually he came to relish the time spent with her, whether she was treating him with kindness, or giving him the stern chastisement of a disappointed parent.

And since his return to Rome, commencing his sacred mission, he had stayed out of the sun, working in the dusk and the gloom, in the dark places of the city. Was he ready now to come out into the harsh glare of the daylight, where all could look at him and see him for who he was? That night was now falling did not alter the fact that if he killed Olorix now, in front of so many witnesses, he would be marked. There would be no hiding, ever again.

What would be his fate after that? Would he be seized, punished, executed? That would only make his message all the stronger. Or maybe the gathered legionaries who were debauching themselves would be shamed by his example. Maybe they would follow him, acclaim him...what? Imperator? King?

A glow built inside him. His path was set. There was no turning aside. What would happen would happen. There was just one thing about which he had no doubts whatsoever. He would make Veleda proud.

He straightened his back, pushed out his chest, stroked the handle of the knife he had concealed beneath his tunic and strode purposefully down the street.

–

Carbo didn't think he could stay still a moment longer. Every instinct in him was telling him to lash out, or to run. It was all he could do not to leap up, overturn the table, smash his drunken companions in the face, then run screaming out of the tavern. Clenched guts, dry mouth, a cool dampness on the back of his neck, beads of sweat on his forehead, heart thumping so he could feel the pulse in his throat. Bodily reactions to stress that were so familiar to him now, he had almost become inured to them. Almost.

He craved wine. That would blunt the sensations, loosen the tightness inside. But what would Marsia say? Would she even serve him? And what about Sica, after all the care she had taken of him?

And as he thought of the young Dacian freedwoman, she suddenly appeared in the tavern, scanning the crowd, looking for him. He raised a hand carefully, then tucked it back down again before anyone else noticed. Maybe it was an unnecessary precaution in the raucous disorder of the party, but if Olorix spotted him now, it could ruin everything.

Sica weaved her way through the packed bodies until she reached Carbo's table. One of the legionaries sitting with him reached out to pinch her backside, but she slapped his hand away impatiently. When the legionary looked affronted and prepared to make his displeasure clear, Carbo squeezed his arm, and once he had his attention, gave a single shake of his head. It was enough to make the legionary sit back and turn to his friend to grumble about killjoys.

Sica leaned into Carbo's ear.

'He's here.'

Carbo's head jerked up and he scanned the tavern.

'Where?'

'Coming down the road now. Looked like he might change his mind. He stopped. But he will be here any moment.'

As she finished the sentence, Carbo saw Cicurinus enter, and stand framed in the doorway. Carbo regarded him. Tall, dark, broad. Eyes flashing with anger. Cicurinus' gaze drifted across the drunken crowd towards Carbo.

Carbo grabbed Sica, his hand round the back of her neck, and pulled her face against his. Close-mouthed, he kissed her, keeping his eyes open, watching Cicurinus the whole time. Cicurinus' gaze drifted past Carbo without pausing, clearly not recognising the small part of Carbo's face that was visible from behind Sica's head. The killer turned to the raised dais on which Olorix sat like an oriental satrap, dispensing largesse to his subjects and enjoying the decadent fruits of his position.

Carbo released Sica, and she pulled back, face flushed, breathing quickly, looking searchingly into his eyes.

'Sorry,' muttered Carbo. 'I thought he was going to see me.'

Carbo wasn't sure if the look that passed fleetingly over her face was disappointment, but he had no time to consider it. Cicurinus was moving slowly through the throng towards Olorix.

But so was Vespillo.

The stocky Vigiles Tribune had seen Cicurinus enter, and while he may not have known who he was, he had an instinct for trouble born from years patrolling the violent night streets. He stood and moved forward, politely asking those in his way to stand aside, not yet suspicious enough to make a fuss, curious enough to want to find out if this newcomer was a threat.

Carbo cursed and got to his feet, started pushing his way through to intercept Vespillo.

Cicurinus' whole attention was now fixed on Olorix. He walked slowly forward, one ponderous step after another. Those who were too slow to move aside got shoved, and though some were tempted to push back, the look on the imposing man's face soon made them think better. A space began to open around Cicurinus as he got closer to the dais.

Olorix was stroking the bare leg of a young slave girl who was draped across his lap, and drinking from a jug of wine that another was pouring from a height into his mouth. The red liquid overflowed down his chin, and he coughed and spat some over the girl he was fondling, then laughed uproariously at the expression of disgust on her face.

As Cicurinus approached Olorix, the Syrian bodyguard stepped forward to block his path.

'Stand back. Boss is busy.'

The knife flashed almost too fast to follow with the eye. The Syrian looked puzzled for a moment, then held a hand up to his neck, where a red line had appeared. As he felt for it, blood trickled, then gushed, flowing in crimson rivulets down his front. He opened his mouth, and more blood flowed through his lips and down his chin in a fatal mirror of Olorix's wine. Still uncomprehending, he toppled to his knees and slumped forward, twitching.

The slave girl who had been pouring the wine dropped the jug and screamed. Her piercing cry and the smash of the clay vessel as it hit the floor cut through the noise of the revellers, and there was a moment's quiet.

Olorix stared at Cicurinus who faced him, bloody knife in hand, face suffused with anger. Cicurinus pointed at the fat bookmaker with a trembling finger.

'You,' he said, in a hoarse, shaking voice that was nevertheless audible to every person in the tavern. 'You are everything that is wrong with Rome. You sit there, dressed in your finery, drinking and whoring, making money from the poor, the hard working, the brave soldiers who fight to keep the Empire strong.'

The tavern was silent now, everyone staring in fascination, spellbound by the killer's words, by the exsanguinating corpse lying prone in the straw, by the terror on Olorix's face. Only Carbo and Vespillo moved, struggling towards Cicurinus.

'It is because of men like you,' continued Cicurinus, oblivious to anyone else present, 'that I had to embark on my mission in the first place. It is because of men like you that Rome needs to be purified. Cleansed. By blood.'

A murmur went around the crowd inside the tavern. The words were familiar. From the graffiti. Purified. Cleansed. This was the killer that had been terrorising them all these weeks. Now unease began to spread. Those nearest the exit decided that it was better to leave than watch the drama unfold, in case they became victims themselves. Who was to say that this madman didn't find the behaviour of every single one of them at the party objectionable, punishable by death? As legionaries, citizens, performers and slaves crowded for the exit, the doorway became jammed, and panic spread like a flame on kindling. The change from expectant stillness to frenzy happened in the blink of an eye, and everyone was shouting, yelling, pushing.

Carbo saw Vespillo buffeted by those fleeing, but the tribune braced himself and pushed forward, determined to reach Cicurinus. Carbo did the same, using his bulk, as well as his elbows and knees, to lever himself through the crowd. They were both within feet of Cicurinus and Olorix now, but the jam of bodies was becoming denser.

'Who are you?' asked Olorix, his voice high-pitched and strangled.

'I am justice. I am fate. I am the representative of the gods of Germania and the gods of Rome. And I will deliver their vengeance.'

He drew his arm back to strike. Olorix flinched.

Vespillo lunged forward, grasping for Cicurinus' knife arm.

Carbo grabbed Vespillo and threw him backwards. Vespillo landed on his back, the wind knocked out of him.

The knife thrust forward, burying itself in Olorix's belly. Cicurinus stepped forward, pushing harder, ensuring the blade penetrated the rolls of fat and lacerated the guts beneath. He sawed upwards, under the ribs, into the liver, into the chest. Olorix gaped in disbelief, grasping the hilt of the blade ineffectually. His legs gave way, and he slid off his chair, tumbled off his dais, rolled onto the floor and lay on his back, sightless eyes staring at the ceiling.

Cicurinus looked down at the body, his face expressionless, unreadable. Then he turned to face the crowd.

Those trapped in the tavern by the bottleneck at the door shrank back in terror. Cicurinus looked at them in bewilderment.

'I did this for you,' he said. 'For all of you. To make you strong. To give you honour.'

No one spoke. Most of the slave girls, and one or two of the freedmen, were crying. No one prostrated themselves on the floor before him. No one praised him, raised their hands to him, lifted him onto their shoulders and proclaimed him their leader.

He looked around, as if searching for someone.

'Veleda,' he said, his voice plaintive. 'Where are you? Why have you abandoned me?'

Vespillo sat up, tried to speak, but he was having trouble getting air into his chest. Carbo stepped forward.

'It's over,' said Carbo, and his voice, even to his own ears, was surprisingly gentle. 'Come with me.'

Cicurinus stared at him for a long moment, as if not recognising him. Then his face creased into a furious scowl.

'You. This is your fault. You were the start of all this.'

'Me?' Carbo was shocked, despite everything. Just because he had rejected him in a mood of hungover self-pity. That was what this madman blamed his killing spree on?

'Get away from me,' yelled Cicurinus, and shoved Carbo hard in the chest. Still processing the strangeness of Cicurinus' statement, the sudden assault took him by surprise and he staggered backwards, losing his balance and nearly tripping over the recumbent Vespillo.

Cicurinus bolted for the exit.

Those trying to force their way out saw him coming, and scurried out of his way. Those few to slow to remove themselves from his path were thrown bodily aside. Cicurinus disappeared out onto the street.

Carbo cursed and surged forward, inserting himself in the lacuna within the crowd that Cicurinus had created, squeezing through and out of the doorway. Behind him he heard the voices of Sica and Marsia, unified in anxiety, begging him not to give chase, not to endanger himself.

Maybe they had the right of it. Carbo was exonerated in the plain sight of all. Olorix was dead. Cicurinus was no longer his problem.

And yet, it felt like he was. From the very beginning, Carbo had been there, caught up in the whole mess. And Cicurinus himself blamed Carbo.

Carbo had to be the one to end it.

Carbo emerged onto the dark street, full of milling people, drunk, scared, confused, some of whom had witnessed the events that had just occurred in the tavern, many of whom hadn't and were pressing for an explanation of the commotion. He looked desperately up and down for sight of Cicurinus.

If Carbo had been shorter, or Cicurinus, then maybe he would have lost him. But they were both tall men, and a score of yards away, Carbo saw Cicurinus' dark head, bobbing up and down as he fled.

Carbo gave chase. He hated running. He had never been built for distance, with his bulky physique, and his fitness had suffered from the abuse he had inflicted on his body recently. What's more, his injured leg shot a jolt of pain through him every time it impacted the cobbled road.

But that didn't mean he couldn't run if he put his mind to it. Within him was still that core of strength, and of will, that had seen him survive so much. So now he used it, pounding along the road, gritting his teeth against the pain, breathing hard to keep the air hunger at bay.

The chaos at the tavern was quickly left behind, and Carbo followed Cicurinus as he zigged down an alley, zagged along a cut-through. There were still people out on the streets – Rome was never completely quiet at any time of day, and the night traffic had its own character. But these back streets were not crowded, and the pedestrians and wheeled vehicles were sparse enough to be no impediment to pursuer or pursued.

Cicurinus showed no sign of slowing down, and Carbo felt his heart pounding harder, leg muscles burning like acid. Where was he going? Was he just trying to lose Carbo, or did he have a destination in mind?

If it was the former, he would probably be successful. Carbo was lagging, and whatever the state of his willpower, if his flesh was unable to meet its demands, there was nothing more he could do. Cicurinus glanced behind him, and the smile of triumph as he saw his pursuer dropping back bit into Carbo. He redoubled his efforts, but he knew the race was as good as lost.

–

When Cicurinus saw Carbo dropping back, his initial emotions were of victory and relief. He was going to get away, and he was going to do it in the face of the great hero Carbo. If there was anything that would prove to Veleda his worth, surely the events of tonight would suffice.

Or would they?

Yes, he had killed the odious bookmaker who had denigrated the honour of the Germanic peoples. But then what had he done? When the people had failed to praise him, he had run, like a cheap criminal. He was not a criminal! He was a saviour!

He stopped and placed a hand against a wall, breathing accelerated but controlled. So how would the dawning of a new day find him? Not triumphant. Hiding. Nothing changed. Had he really thought Rome was going to change its ways because of him? He was just a man, for all the encouragement Veleda had given him. And now, even she had deserted him.

'Do you really believe that?'

He started at the gentle voice by his ear, turned to find himself looking into Veleda's deep, dark eyes.

'Priestess, where have you been?'

'Nearby, watching. As always. You did well tonight.'

'I did?' He looked down the street. Carbo had been pursuing him ever more slowly, clearly struggling to close the gap between them and had not yet appeared around the last corner he had turned.

'You made a mark, but it is not enough.'

Cicurinus bowed his head, chagrined. But she was only confirming his own thoughts.

'You are mortal, Cicurinus. To change worlds, you need the help of the gods.'

He nodded, listening, watching for the approach of Carbo.

'And the gods will not help you without sacrifice.'

'Who should I call upon? The Roman or German gods?'

'This is Rome, where the gods of Olympus are supreme. Woden will not aid you here. Who is the chief of all the Roman gods? Who has the mightiest temple?'

'Jupiter Optimus Maximus of course.'

'Then go there, go to the heights, and make your sacrifice.'

'Whose sacrifice?'

Veleda looked down the street, towards the sounds of the heavy, laborious tread of Carbo's boots. 'That is for you to decide.'

—

Carbo rounded the corner and found Cicurinus waiting for him, a mere half a dozen yards away. He came to an abrupt halt, breathing hard, suddenly acutely aware how fatigued he was if he had to fight.

'Wait, Cicurinus. Let's talk.'

Cicurinus let out a single, barking, humourless laugh.

'Oh, now you have time to talk. Well, better late than never.'

'What do you mean? Why did you say it was all my fault? Just because I didn't become your new best friend?'

Cicurinus shook his head.

'Come on old man, let's see if you can keep up.' He set off down the road, his long legs eating up the distance with a loping stride. Carbo groaned and forced himself into motion once more.

Now, Cicurinus seemed to be taunting him, the way he had heard wolves sometimes toyed with the hunt. Just out of reach, leading the chase, always in control. They left the Subura, heading west towards the Forum Romanum, and Cicurinus led him down the via Sacra, past the Temple of Vesta, the Temple of Castor and Pollux, into the forum itself beneath the rostra. Few paid them any attention. The two men looked like trouble, and whether one had robbed or assaulted the other, or been found in bed with the other's wife, was no concern of theirs.

When Carbo felt himself falling behind, Cicurinus slowed, and Carbo wondered where he was being led. Surely it was some sort of trap. Yet what was he to do? Abandon the chase? Instead, he reduced his speed further than he needed. This was clearly no longer a chase, and it was prudent to conserve at least a modicum of energy.

Just east of the rostra was the Carcer Tullianus, the small underground cell in which many famous prisoners had awaited their execution, like Vercingetorix, leader of the Gauls, and Jugurtha the Numidian king. Carbo wondered who was imprisoned in there at that moment, as they ran past. Sitting in the dark and the damp, waiting to die. He shuddered, acutely aware how close he had come to that fate himself.

They reached the Arch of Tiberius, built a mere decade earlier in celebration of regaining the lost Eagles from the Teutoberg disaster. It was a place of honour to Carbo. Cicurinus spat on it as they passed.

From here, Cicurinus led them on to the Clivus Capitolinius, the road leading up the Capitoline Hill, and Carbo groaned as he saw the steepness of the route he would have to take. His pace was barely more than a fast walk now, and even that was exhausting. But Cicurinus did not let him drop behind, calling out a mixture of insults and encouragement to him.

'Just tell me where you are taking me,' Carbo yelled, 'and we can walk there hand in hand.'

'Just a little further, old man. We're nearly there.'

At the top of the Capitoline Hill stood the Temple of Jupiter Optimus Maximus. Tradition had it that the first Temple to Jupiter on this site was completed by the last king of Rome, Lucius Tarquinius Superbus, but that edifice was burnt down during the civil wars of the dictator Sulla's reign. This 'new' building was now a century old, but it still looked magnificent, the marble columns of its portico white in the moonlight. On the gable at the top of the face was a statue of the obscure god of nocturnal thunder, Summanus, greatest of all the Manes. Carbo remembered pondering this deity when he had first returned from his service in Germania, wondering if he was somehow equivalent to the Germanic thunder god Donner, in the same way that the Greeks called Jupiter, Zeus.

But it was on the pitched, red-tiled roof of the temple that the real power in the pantheon was celebrated. A gold and ivory statue of Jupiter Optimus Maximus, the best and greatest, looked sternly down over the Eternal City. The chief of the gods was seated on a throne and dressed in a tunic covered with palm leaves and a gold and purple toga. In one hand he held a sceptre, and in the other he clutched a jagged thunderbolt, ready to hurl down on any mortal that caught his eye. He was flanked by the other two deities that comprised the Capitoline triad, Juno, queen of the gods, and Minerva, goddess of wisdom.

The temple was a sight that never failed to awe, whether viewed by a newcomer to the city, or a cynical old resident who had lived their entire life within the Servian Walls. And it was to this iconic monument that Cicurinus was leading Carbo.

Cicurinus mounted the steps of the portico, and turned at the top, smiling broadly, watching Carbo struggle up to the top of the hill and approach the temple. When Carbo was a dozen feet away, he stopped and put his hands on his knees, bent double as he sucked in lungfuls of air.

'So we're here,' he said, gasping out the words. 'Now what?'

'Our journey's not quite ended yet.' Cicurinus leapt onto the dais of one of the numerous statues that encircled the base of the temple, donated over the centuries by victorious generals in honour of their triumphs. Putting a foot on a protruding spear, using the open mouth of a decapitated barbarian for a handhold, Cicurinus quickly climbed to the top.

Carbo groaned. The way his body was protesting at the exertion, he felt he would rather fight and die right there, than have to follow Cicurinus any further, even if it was to eventual victory. But already, Cicurinus was scaling the wall at the side of the temple, skilfully using cracks in the stucco, the uneven brickwork and the reliefs of religious and military scenes, to haul his way up.

A young priest, toga tied back with the Gabine cinch, one fold pulled up over his head like a shawl, hurried out of the temple and gaped up at Cicurinus.

'What's he doing? Get down here, or I'll call the vigiles!'

Cicurinus looked down and waved.

Carbo took a breath, then said, 'I don't suppose there are any stairs to the roof?'

The priest looked at him in surprise. 'Of course not. No one goes up there. If repairs are needed, they put up scaffolding.'

'I thought you were going say that. Oh well. I'd better go and get him.'

The priest gaped as Carbo followed Cicurinus' lead, climbing as high as he could on the statue, snapping off the tip of a spear as he reached for the wall. Slowly, laboriously, he clambered after Cicurinus.

The wall was over a hundred feet high and by the time Carbo was halfway, he was beginning to think he had made a huge mistake. If he had found the running tiring, pulling his big frame vertically up the side of an enormous monument was completely exhausting. Soon it was no longer about willpower, but the burning in his arms, the hammering in his chest. Rapidly, he felt his strength failing, as he pushed his body's endurance beyond its physical limitations.

Three-quarters of the way to the top, the strength in his grip gave out. His hand slipped off the smooth marble head of an embossed deity, and his upper torso swung out, away from the wall. He looked down, saw a small crowd had gathered to watch. They already appeared tiny, and his head spun as he was gripped by a sudden terror.

Desperately, he threw himself back at the wall, and his hand found purchase on the extended wing of a Pegasus. He held on tightly, regaining his composure, letting the blood flow back to his weakened limbs.

'Hurry up, Carbo. It's cold up here.'

Carbo looked up to see Cicurinus peering down at him over the side of the pitched roof. He gritted his teeth and began to climb again.

Every foot of height now was hard won, and he tried not to think about what would happen when he got to the top. He had precious little strength left to fight, and that was if Cicurinus even gave him the opportunity of getting onto the roof in the first place. A stamp on fingers or a boot in the face would easily send him spiralling down to a quick end on the flagstones below.

Abruptly, his exploring hand encountered only air, and he looked up to see he had reached the top. All he had to do was drag himself over the lip of the roof, that protruded outwards about a foot.

But that simple last obstacle seemed insurmountable. He would have to suspend his full weight from his hands, lift himself up and over while his feet dangled free.

He couldn't do it.

And yet, what was the alternative? Even if he wanted to descend again, he didn't think he could do it before his strength failed completely and he plummeted to his death.

He took a deep breath and reached out to grasp the edge of the roof. His feet left their footholds, and his legs swung out into fresh air. His arms took his full weight, as his fingers gripped the tiles.

He tried to pull himself up, but the strength just wasn't there – he could get the top of his head level with the roof edge, but no further. He eased himself back down so his arms were at full stretch once more, and tried to fight down the rising panic.

He swung his body from side to side, trying to get enough lateral momentum to latch a foot onto the edge of the roof. He nearly succeeded, but as his heel swung down, it cracked the tile. His foot slipped off, his legs tumbled downwards, and his forearms screamed under the strain. He tried to pull himself up once more, but he knew that if he had failed once, fatigue would make the chances of a second attempt succeeding virtually impossible. Though he strained his muscles with every ounce of his being, he barely elevated himself at all.

His fingers began to slide, to loosen. Despair warred with terror. He kicked his legs helplessly.

A strong hand gripped his wrist. Pulled.

Carbo used the last of his reserves of energy to help the man dragging him up onto the roof. Once his upper body was over the lip, he crawled forward and rolled onto his back, gasping for air like a landed fish.

Cicurinus' face appeared over his own. Then disappeared again.

Carbo rolled over onto his front, got to his hands and knees, then slowly stood, swallowing and squeezing his eyes shut against the sudden wave of dizziness that accompanied a strong feeling that he might faint.

When he opened them again, Cicurinus was sitting in Jupiter's lap, his arm around him. Despite Cicurinus' size, the statue dwarfed him so he looked like a child seated on his father.

Carbo approached him cautiously. He had no idea what was going on in the killer's mind, but the beatific expression on his face suggested rationality was no longer present.

'Alone together at last,' said Cicurinus.

'You wanted me here.' It was a statement. 'Why?'

'Because you are the beginning of all this. And you are the end.'

'You keep saying this is my fault, that I started this. Are you really blaming me for the deaths of all those people? People you killed? Just because I turned you away?'

'Carbo.' Cicurinus' tone was disappointed, melancholy. 'I know it's been a long time, and I've picked up the odd scar. But have I really changed that much?'

Carbo looked into the man's eyes. Though Cicurinus appeared younger than Carbo, his eyes were old, tired. But there was something about them. And the hair, and the nose. He shook his head, attempting to deny it, even as it hit him like a bucket of cold water had been dumped on him. But it was no use. It was undeniable.

'Sextus.'

'When you left Rome, what, some twenty-five years ago, mother was distraught. And you never came home. You wrote, you sent money, but you never came back. In all that time, did you never get the chance? To volunteer for an escort mission? Take some leave?'

'You don't know what happened to me out there,' said Carbo defensively. 'I was captured and tortured after Teutoberg. The army became my family, my security. I couldn't come home and face the people I knew and loved. I thought it would break me. You don't know what that's like.'

Cicurinus – Sextus – laughed sourly. 'I don't know? I was held captive for years. But unlike you, I came to relish my captivity. It turned me into who I am.'

'You say that like it's a good thing.'

'And you would prefer I had become like you? The drunkard, the gambler, the wreck? There were so many times I wanted to be you, you know. When the stories came back about your exploits, when we heard of your promotions, all everyone could talk about was Carbo the hero. It's why I joined up as well. So I could be like my older brother, though it broke mother's heart.'

'No,' said Carbo, his voice not much more than a whisper. 'You shouldn't have done that. I'm no hero.'

'I know that now.' Sextus cocked his head on one side, as if something had just occurred to him. 'Why did you never try to find me?'

'Mother wrote to me, and told me you had died.'

'And did you mourn me?'

'Of course I did,' snapped Carbo. 'I know we weren't close. Different fathers, a big age gap. But you were family. You are family.'

'So, now you see why this all began with you.'

'And how does it end?'

Sextus hopped off the statue and walked to the edge of the roof. The collection of onlookers staring up at them had grown to a small crowd, despite the priests trying to move them on as if there was nothing untoward occurring.

'All I wanted was what was best for Rome,' said Sextus. 'But I can't undo the years of decline and degeneration on my own. The people of Rome must rise up, embrace the old ways. The historians write about a better time, when the men held duty and morality first, served their city, fought as true warriors when they were needed, farmed the land when they weren't. Like Cincinnatus. But no one does anything about it. Because nobody has an example. A beacon to guide them.'

He turned and looked at Carbo. 'This ends in sacrifice. So there can be a new beginning.'

Carbo tensed, wondering if the moment had finally come that they must fight. His strength was returning, at least in part. But he no longer had any desire to kill this man, his enemy, his brother.

'Why do you believe these things? What if you are wrong? What if Rome is strong enough, moral enough? That it is the barbarians who are savage and immoral and cruel?'

'I know that is not true. I have seen them for myself. And besides, she tells me it is so, and she does not lie.'

'Who is she?'

Sextus frowned. 'Veleda, the priestess.'

'You mentioned her before. But Sextus…'

Sextus held up his hand, tilted his head slightly, like he was listening.

'Yes,' he said. 'You're right. Too much talking.'

'I didn't say…'

'Quiet, Carbo. Do not interrupt her.'

'She… she is here now?'

Sextus looked to his left, then back to Carbo in genuine puzzlement. 'I know it's dark and you are getting old, but I didn't think you were yet that blind.'

'Sextus,' said Carbo, and his voice was gentle but cautious, the tone you used to get a child to put down something sharp before they hurt themselves. 'Veleda is dead.'

Sextus turned to his side once more, then looked back at Carbo. 'Have you lost your wits?'

'She died in Germania. Shortly after your rescue.'

Sextus' eyes shifted from side to side, as if he was suddenly searching for escape. 'No,' he said. 'She is right here.'

'I met the centurion, Brocchus. They massacred that village you were held captive in, as a reprisal. The priestess escaped, but she came back. She tried to rescue you. They caught her, and they killed her, there and then. They didn't tell you, they thought you had been through enough and didn't know how you would react.'

'You're lying to me. You are just trying to… to…' He glanced to his side, then turned round rapidly in a full circle. 'Veleda? Veleda! Where have you gone?' His voice held tones of panic.

'Sextus. She was never here. She never came to Rome. She is dead.'

Sextus stared at Carbo and his eyes held absolute despair. Tears welled in the corners, trickled down both cheeks.

'She can't be. She guided me. I… loved her.'

'I'm sorry, Sextus. Come back down with me. We can talk. You can help me understand.'

Sextus took a step back, then another, closer to the edge. Carbo put out a hand in warning. 'Be careful!'

'It doesn't matter. If she wasn't with me in body, she was here in spirit. And I did what she wanted. I made her proud of me.'

Carbo reached out towards him. 'Come, Sextus. Let's return to the ground. You can teach me her words.'

'No.' A firmness had returned to his tone. 'I said it ends here. There will be sacrifice. So that Rome will see her truth.' He took another step backwards.

'Sextus, stop!'

His heels were on the edge of the roof now. He looked Carbo straight in the eyes.

'Please, brother.'

Sextus folded his hands over his chest, and leaned backwards. Carbo darted forward, lunged for him. He caught a piece of his tunic in his fist.

The fabric ripped, leaving him clutching a small handful of wool. Silently, Sextus tumbled through the air. Carbo watched him all the way down, until the moment of impact, the sound of the wet thud dulled by distance. Tears fell from Carbo's eyes, dropped like rain onto his brother's body.

The onlookers looked down in curiosity at the dead man. Two slaves emerged from the temple, and at the direction of the priest, they took him by the feet and dragged him away. The priest shooed the crowd, and the excitement over, they shrugged and dispersed.

Soon, there was no sign that anything had happened, except for a dark stain on the flagstones.

Chapter Nineteen

Vespillo looked up as Carbo entered his office.

'I would say you look like shit, but I've seen you looking worse.'

'Thanks.' Carbo had spent the night at Sica's, nervous exhaustion and profound fatigue uniting to render him unconscious until the sun was high in the sky. He had woken to a new world. Not the sort of new world that Cicurinus had envisaged. Just new for him. No longer wanted for murder. No longer subject to Olorix's myriad mockeries and humiliations. And, he hoped, no longer a slave to gambling and drinking. The last was more tentative, but Sica had shown him he could do it, and she had assured him she was going to support him as long as he needed it.

Could the same be said for Vespillo? After what had passed between them over the last few weeks?

Vespillo narrowed his eyes.

'Are we good?'

Carbo considered then gave a short, sharp nod. Vespillo looked at him carefully, and then gave him a half-smile.

'And how much trouble are you in with Pavo and the Urban Prefect?'

Vespillo waved the concern away, but Carbo saw an uncertain look in his eyes, and wondered how much his friend had sacrificed in standing up for him. Then another look came into Vespillo's eyes. He looked down and scratched the back of his thumb.

'Fabilla wants to see you,' he said cautiously.

Carbo swallowed, and for a moment he found it hard to form words.

'I think… I think I would like that too,' he said.

Vespillo's smile broadened.

'Anyway, thanks for coming over so promptly. I know you must still be tired, and you have other things to do, but this is important.'

Carbo felt a familiar unease growing inside him that had started when he was disturbed by Pinarius, coming to Sica's to inform him Vespillo requested the pleasure of his company as soon as it was convenient.

'So, it seems Olorix died intestate,' said Vespillo. 'It doesn't surprise me. Men like that always think they will live forever.'

'I see,' said Carbo, not really seeing at all.

'Furthermore, since he died, we have had a number of people coming forward, testifying to his activities. Lots of claims of criminal activity. Fixing races. Extortion. Bribery. It's likely that most of the riches he has accumulated will be confiscated by the state. People who feel they have been taken advantage of by him can of course apply for restitution in the courts.'

Carbo raised an eyebrow. 'You're saying I should sue his estate?'

Vespillo shook his head. 'That would take a long time. And be very expensive. And once the state has their hands on money and property, they are very reluctant to ever let it go.'

Carbo nodded. He didn't feel disappointed. For all Olorix's trickery, and Camilla's duplicity, he really couldn't blame anyone else for his losses. He was alive, and free. That was enough. He could take on bodyguard work. Or help Sica in her fullers. It didn't matter.

Vespillo tossed a couple of scrolls across his desk to Carbo.

Carbo picked them up curiously. 'What are these?'

'Plancus found them amongst Olorix's private documents when he was searching his house. He thought I might prefer to keep them out of the hands of the authorities. Restore them directly to their rightful owner, without the need for protracted litigation.'

Carbo squinted at the scrawled writing, reading slowly and carefully. His eyes opened wide as he realised what he held.

'These are the deeds for my farm and tavern!'

Vespillo smiled.

'You know what? I know it's early, but I feel like a drink. Do you know anywhere decent?'

Carbo grinned broadly. 'I think I might.'

'Oh, and you might want to bring this with us.'

He passed Carbo a felt cap. Carbo turned it over in his hands, puzzled. Then understanding dawned, and he looked at Vespillo gratefully. 'Thank you. Friend.'

They grasped hands, exchanged a wordless moment, then set off for Carbo's newly recovered tavern.

When they entered, Myia was first to react, jumping off Vatius' lap and barking excitedly at Carbo's feet. He bent down to tousle the little dog's head.

Marsia emerged from the backroom to see what the noise was about. When she saw Carbo, she pressed both hands to her mouth. Then she ran to him, and held him tight.

He hugged her back, and they were both crying, wetting each other's shoulders with tears of relief and joy.

Eventually Carbo disentangled himself from the hug. He put his hands on Marsia's shoulders, then dried her eyes with his tunic sleeve.

'I'm sorry,' he said. 'So sorry, for what I did, how I behaved.'

Marsia opened her mouth to speak, but Carbo put a finger to her lips. 'But most of all, I'm sorry that I didn't do this a long time ago.'

He took the felt cap from beneath his tunic, and gently, almost reverentially, placed it on her head. She reached up to touch it with her fingertips, stroking it in disbelief.

'Is it really... you're giving me the pileus?'

'No one deserves it more. I was selfish, not giving it to you sooner. I suppose... I didn't want to lose you.'

'Carbo, you must know I'm not going anywhere, with or without this.'

Carbo nodded, swallowing hard, not trusting himself to speak.

'Of course,' said Vespillo, 'your manumission is not official until you have gone before the Praetor, and had your head shaved, and so forth. But we'll sort the formalities out in short order.'

Marsia didn't seem to be looking. She leaned forward, and kissed her former master's cheek gently. Then once more, tentatively, as if it might have disappeared already, she touched the pileus, the felt cap, the symbol of emancipation. For the first time since she had been taken from her family by the Romans, all those years ago, she was free.

Author's note

I hope you have enjoyed spending time with Carbo again after a long hiatus caused by other writing commitments (namely four novels in the Imperial Assassin series!). It was five years from planning and starting to write the first few chapters of this book to finishing it, yet hanging out with Carbo again was like meeting up with one of those old friends you haven't seen for yonks, and the conversation picks straight up like you last saw them the day before.

There isn't a lot to discuss about the contemporaneous history of this novel, since the story doesn't touch too much on the real events of the time. Tiberius was in self-imposed exile in Capri, and Sejanus the Praetorian Prefect was the de facto ruler of Rome. While this may have been a concern to those of senatorial and equestrian rank, who feared his ambition and power, it would have likely had very little impact on the inhabitants of the Subura, who continued to work, struggle, fight, love, laugh, be born and die, without interference from the state. There really was a plague of cold sores in Rome around this time, and public kissing was outlawed. And Julius Caesar really did write a play about Oedipus, and the fact that it is lost to time suggests it may not have been as well received as his autobiographical histories.

Serial killers in Ancient Rome are not well-documented. One murderer who is commonly thought of as one of the first serial killers was Locusta, a poisoner who worked for Agrippina the Younger and Nero. But she appears to have been more of a paid assassin or executioner than the sort of person we associate with serial killers in modern times, with the usual presumption of some form of mental instability associated with their behaviour. Did Jack the Ripper style serial killers exist in Ancient Rome? We will likely never know, but basic human psychology and behaviour has not evolved significantly since those times, even if culture has changed. So it would seem likely there were individuals who for self-gratification, or because of mental delusions, felt the urge to kill. If this is the case, why didn't we hear about them? Because, as explored in this book, no one "important" in Rome cared about the poor, provided they weren't rioting. If Jack the Ripper had been active in the Subura in the first century, it is likely that the authorities would not have batted an eyelid, and it wouldn't have even made a passing mention in the histories. Of course, the locals would have been scared, and there would have been some attempt at mob justice, and likely some innocent scapegoat would have been accused and beaten to death if they couldn't find the real culprit. But the poor didn't write the history books.

This novel is just fiction. Could it have happened for real? You can decide.

Alex Gough 2021

Acknowledgements

Thanks to Michael Bhaskar and Kit Nevile from Canelo for their advice and help, to Laurel Sills for a great copy-edit, and to Naomi and Abigail for all their support. And of course to my readers – without you this whole exercise would be pointless!